GIRLS' NIGHT OUT DOWN UNDER

I sit at the bar watching everyone else drink their cocktails as I wait for Sarah. It's a tradition that we don't start drinking until we're both present and accounted for, but as I sit I begin to think it's not much of a tradition, because it's always Sarah who's late. Don't get me wrong, there's nothing bad about being late, I do it myself all the time. But there *is* a limit. Late for work, late for the dentist, late for 8 AM lectures I can understand, but late for cocktails . . . never!

Anyway, she's late. I tell myself I'll give her another five minutes before I start ordering. After all, there's late and then there's *late.*

So, I guess while I'm waiting I should really fill you in on the whole "cocktails thang" (note: twangy American accent). Sarah and I have been doing cocktails on Fridays for about three years now. It all started when I had a real job. You know the type, one of those sit down office-type jobs where they pay you every two weeks. You might even have one yourself. I lasted all of six months at that job. I simply couldn't bear it. Let's just say I don't work well with others.

Anyway, for all my bitching and complaining there was at least *one* thing I loved about that job. I think I already mentioned it. Yeah, that's right, I got paid.

Office job or no office job, Sarah and I have still kept up with cocktails. The only difference is now I can't afford them.

Ha! Not that that's ever stopped me . . . **MAIN**

Friday Night Cocktails

Allison Rushby

KENSINGTON BOOKS
www.kensingtonbooks.com

KENSINGTON BOOKS are published by

Kensington Publishing Corp.
850 Third Avenue
New York, NY 10022

All Kensington titles, imprints and distributed lines are available at special
quantity discounts for bulk purchases for sales promotion, premiums, fund-
raising, educational or institutional use.

Special book excerpts or customized printings can also be created to fit specific
needs. For details, write or phone the office of the Kensington Special Sales
Manager: Kensington Publishing Corp., 850 Third Avenue, New York, NY
10022. Attn. Special Sales Department. Phone: 1-800-221-2647.

ISBN: 0-7582-0825-1

First Kensington Trade Paperback Printing: December 2004
10 9 8 7 6 5 4 3 2 1

Printed in the United States of America

RUS

AEU-9351

Acknowledgments

Firstly, I'd like to say a big thanks to all the girly Web sites on the Net for giving me the idea behind allmenarebastards.com. :-D to http://www.ekran.no/html/revenge for the (sometimes worrying) tips on how to get back at your ex and ;-)to

http://www.wankers.com for the creative wanking terms :-) to

http://www.2211.com/pop.htm,

http://www.WinkingJesus.com, and

http://www.yoni.com/bitchf/bitchboard.shtml for Gemma and Sarah's Net adventures.

An extra large dish of chocolate-coated pellets for my ever-loyal female guinea pigs: Nat, Heidi, Tiff, Sam, Tash, Nilly, and Nanna (who didn't "get it," but was polite enough to say she liked it anyway).

Yay for Mum and Dad who supported me all the way.

Cheers to Annabel for getting the manuscript and running with it.

Hooray for Nick who stepped in at the last minute, but contributed enormously.

And the biggest round of applause to David, not only for the handy "eight character" rule, but for never thinking I was wasting my time.

Men.

Some of them just shouldn't be allowed the privilege of being able to pee standing up!

Don't get me wrong, I'm not about to launch into one of those boring "all men are bastards" speeches. I might have a couple of months ago, but not today.

You see, I used to believe what TV told me I should think about men. I used to read man-hating bumper stickers and honk accordingly. In fact, I used to think our united sisterhood hatredship of men was empowering.

Yeah, a few months ago I believed in all those things. But not anymore . . .

The bastard list gets an airing

I get the call from Sarah at 4:30 Friday morning. Yes, that's right, 4:30 *AM*.

When the phone rings, I do that thing where you just work the noise right into your dream. In my dream, I am quite happily swimming around in a giant margarita. The tequila is nice and warm and I've just paddled to the side and am sitting with my back to the edge of the glass, arms hooked up on the salt-encrusted rim, when I hear the phone ring. Shit, I think, now I'm going to have to get out of the margarita and answer the bloody phone. And that's when I wake up, sit bolt upright in bed, and then lunge for the phone, which is somewhere on the floor, covered with a week's worth of clothes.

"Someone better be dead," I say, eyeing the bright red numbers of my bedside clock.

"Sorry, Gem, I know it's early but I had to talk to someone, I just couldn't sleep."

It's Sarah.

I roll over onto my back. "What's up?"

"It's Darren, we broke up."

I groan inwardly, wishing she *had* left it until our weekly Friday night cocktail binge to spill the story. Because frankly, even for me, the best friend, it's a little too early in the morning to deal with the fallout of a breakup. I try to pull myself together and sound supportive anyway. "What happened?"

"Well, he went out Wednesday night with a couple of old friends, he asked me if I wanted to go, but I said no—I mean, it wasn't like I knew them or anything. So I tried to call him

Thursday morning to see how it all went, but he hadn't come home yet. He hadn't come home at all."

"And then what?"

"He rang eventually, Thursday night."

Oh yeah, I could just imagine the reception the poor guy had gotten when he called. I knew Sarah, and she would have spent the whole day at work sitting at her desk worrying herself into a frenzy and imagining Darren in various orgies across the city, each one worse than the last. "And what was the story?" I push on.

"Get this, he told me he'd better tell me in person and that he was coming over."

"Really?" I look around my bedroom floor casually to see if I can find any matchsticks to hold my eyes open with. "So he came over and . . ."

"And you'll never *believe* what he said."

I suddenly wish Sarah was here so I could torture her to make her finish the story quickly and let me sleep. Something involving hot oil, salty water, and the rack might well do the trick. I decide to try the direct approach. "Sarah, darling, don't make me get my whip out, what did he say?"

"He said he'd met an old girlfriend from college and they got drunk."

"And they slept together, right?" I try to finish off the story quickly and painlessly.

"Wrong, worse."

Worse? My brain ticks over and I begin to wake up a little. What could Darren have done that was worse? "What do you mean?"

"He went back to her place and they slept in the same bed, but they *didn't* have sex."

I groan for real this time. Ever since I can remember (and believe me, this is a long time—I met the girl in preschool) Sarah has always had her own kind of logic. To give you an example, she only goes out with guys who match up with this specific questionnaire she carries around in her handbag. A questionnaire from a 1989 edition of *Cosmo* (over the years she's grown quite adept at making most guys pass in one way or another). Usually Sarah-logic is quite endearing, but at 4:30, no, 4:45 in the morning, she's pushing her luck.

"Sarah, I know I shouldn't ask this, but how is Darren not having sex with her worse?"

"How is it worse? You should have seen him, Gem! He came over with a bunch of flowers and spilled his story all Sensitive New Age Guy-like and then expected me to *congratulate* him for his efforts. It was like he'd made this big effort not to sleep with her to please me—as if this made him a great guy or something, a real find."

"So what did you do?"

"I just laughed, it was all I could do. But now I'm not so sure . . ."

"Sarah," I butt in. "He was drunk. He probably *couldn't* get it up, I doubt it was for a lack of trying."

There is a long pause before Sarah speaks again. Then . . .

"Oh," she says thoughtfully, "I didn't think about it like that."

There's a pause as Sarah thinks about it a bit more. "I didn't think about it like that *at all*. OK, thanks, Gem, see you at cocktails, and don't forget to bring the list." She hangs up and I'm left holding the phone in one hand.

Now, you might think this is all a little abrupt, but Sarah getting over this whole thing so quickly is completely normal—all she wanted was an explanation of Darren's motives, she wasn't really looking for sympathy. You see, Sarah only ever goes out with guys for two to three weeks before she finds a decent enough excuse to get rid of them. Most of the time I don't think she even enjoys the company of half the guys she goes out with. It's just that she doesn't like to be without a boyfriend to take places—you know, to weddings and parties and corporate stuff.

7

As I hang up my end of the phone, I curse the day she met Darren. I can remember it clearly. After all, it was only two weeks ago and it had been me, fool that I am, who introduced them in the first place. If I'd known it would all come down to being woken up at 4:30 in the morning, I never would have introduced them at all.

I roll over, trying to get comfortable again and tell myself that we'll discuss the whole dastardly deed that night at cocktails.

I sit at the bar watching everyone else drink their cocktails as I wait for Sarah. It's a tradition that we don't start drinking until we're both present and accounted for, but as I sit I begin to think it's not much of a tradition, because it's always Sarah who's late. Don't get me wrong, there's nothing bad about being late, I do it myself all the time. But there *is* a limit. Late for work, late for the dentist, late for eight AM lectures I can understand, but late for cocktails . . . never!

Anyway, she's late. I tell myself I'll give her another five minutes before I start ordering. After all, there's late and then there's *late*.

So, I guess while I'm waiting I should really fill you in on the whole "cocktails thang" (note: twangy American accent).

Sarah and I have been doing cocktails on Fridays for about three years now. It all started when I had a real job. You know the type, one of those sit down office-type jobs where they pay you fortnightly. You might even have one yourself. I lasted all of six months at that job. I simply couldn't bear it. Let's just say I don't work well with others—something Ms. Danko, my teacher in grade two, wrote on my report card after I stuck a half-chewed Mintie in Lisa Mullins's long, blond hair during group work and it had to be cut out. And frankly, I don't think anybody else has ever hit it on the head quite so well again. I really *don't* work well with others. With my office-type job, I think it had something to do with the never-ending of-

8

fice politics. Let's just say I'll never forget the time I used the wrong mug, and the other time I got caught stealing a spoonful of sugar for my coffee.

Sarah was the one who got me the job in the first place (gee, thanks Sar). She already worked casually at Star Graphics as a graphic designer and when another graphic designer got fired (probably used someone else's coffee) she hauled my arse in quick smart for an interview. And, seeing as they were pretty much desperate to get a big job finished at the time, I started immediately.

Anyway, for all my bitching and complaining there was at least *one* thing I loved about that job. I think I already mentioned it. Yeah, that's right, I got paid fortnightly (not much, mind you). I kind of miss getting paid fortnightly now that I'm freelancing. If you have one of those office-type jobs you should try working from home for a while to see how the other half lives. When the social highlight of your day is a quick jog to meet the postman for a chat, or to pat him down in case he's stealing your checks and hiding them somewhere on his person (if you freelance, rampant check paranoia is compulsory), you really know your life has reached new heights.

Office job or no office job, Sarah and I have still kept up with cocktails. The only difference is now I can't afford them.

Ha! Not that that's ever stopped me.

I'm already onto my third margarita (hey, first of all I couldn't wait and, secondly, it's happy hour, OK? I'm *saving* myself money) when Sarah plonks herself down on the stool beside me. "Sorry I'm late, gorgeous," she winks. "Long time no drink."

"How was work, honey?" I ask, ignoring her tardiness—something I've come to expect.

"Oh just fine, darling, if you like spending weeks on tampon ads it's a dream job. Soon they'll be calling me tampon girl."

"Any freebies?"

Sarah opens up her bulging bag to show me the contents and runs her hand over the top *Wheel of Fortune* style. "Madam, we have a wide range of feminine protection products for your pleasure this evening. Light, medium, or can I tempt you with my personal favorite—a cheeky little super?"

My eyes widen in amazement. That bag is like the tampon bank. Sarah must have about a year's supply of tampons in there at least, the little scammer. Oh how I love her. Sometimes I do miss that job. But it's never for very long.

"Not bad hey?" Sarah laughs, zipping her bag back up and dumping it on the floor. She motions to Pete, the bartender, that she'll have what I'm having, then exhales loudly. "So, did you bring the list?" She eyes my bag hopefully.

"How could I forget?" I search for the pink plastic folder I'd so gingerly placed the list in that afternoon. I pull it out and place it on the bar.

"Careful!" Sarah says. "There's a wet spot." She wipes the bar down with the sleeve of her best Donna Karan suit and places the folder on the clean surface with a slight smile. "There," she says. "That's better."

I guess you're thinking we're a bit strange right about now. What with all this talk of a "list" and how careful we are with it, even when it's covered in garishly colored plastic. Well, let me explain . . .

The list began when Sarah and I were studying at graphic design college. At the time, we were living in a share-house with three other girls from the college. As you can imagine, where there are five twenty-something not-so-bad-looking girls, there's usually also a swarm of guys. And where there are a host of twenty-something guys and gals, there's also a lot of yearning, bed-swapping, dumping, and weeping. This yearning, bed-swapping, dumping, and weeping is basically why the list started up.

To make a long story short, the girls of the house started

the list one night when three of us had been dumped in quick succession.

One, two, three.

Huddled around the kitchen table with five teaspoons and a family-sized tin of Milo for sustenance, we wrote each of the guys' names on a piece of paper, exactly what it was that they had done to us, and then our reasons why the other girls should avoid him as any kind of love interest. When we were done, we stickytaped the pieces together and stuck the completed list on the fridge.

We began to call it the bastard list.

Slowly, it grew.

And all in all, the bastard list was a bit of a giggle. Most of the guys on it hadn't done anything *really* bad and about 97 percent of the entries ran along the lines of: *Mr. X asked me out for dinner and then when it came time to pay, he didn't have enough money. I had to pay for the entire bill and he never gave me any money back, even though he said he was going to. Girls! Don't go out with what you can't afford. Or at least wait till you win the Lotto.*

So, as you can see, the guys on the list weren't exactly criminals. Though I do remember one, Sean I think his name was, who *did* turn out to be a criminal, because he managed to nick off with our stereo right before he fled town.

The bastard.

Anyway, every time we came across a new bastard in our lives, we'd sit around together and add him onto the list. As the years passed, the other girls fell by the wayside, and Sarah and I were the only two left of the hard core, but I'd managed to nab the list when we moved (it was conveniently lost) and it now took pride of place on my fridge.

I open up the pink plastic folder and Sarah and I gaze at it with awe. The list, which was once pristine and an innocent shade of white, is now yellowed and torn, the stickytape gummed and useless, its pages hanging off here and there. It even comes complete with suspicious red and brown stains

11

(the red stains I know are spaghetti bolognaise, the brown ones I'm not so sure about. Milo? Who knows?).

It is twenty pages long.

I place the list on top of the plastic folder, being careful not to damage it any further.

Look, I'm still not sure if you understand. This list, the bastard list—it's like a bible to us. There's a definite pattern to its usage. Either one of us can "call a bastard." All we have to do is to tell each other we're calling a bastard to add to the list and then we have to meet as quickly as possible. You can't change your mind, either—this was one of the rules we made up back in our share-house days. We decided that the list wasn't going to be about silly squabbles. Once the bastard was put on the list, he was on the list for good and there was no taking him off. We also decided that any guy would be eligible. For example, the next door neighbor's cat from the share-house has a hilarious entry (he liked to piss on my bedspread and, yes, he was male, we checked). My father has an entry too, but, unlike the cat's one, it's not one I like to read very often.

So now there are all kinds of bastards on the list—big bastards and small bastards, fat bastards and thin bastards, white and black and pink and purple bastards.

Over the years we haven't been picky. If he does the crime, he does the time.

However, the most important rule of the bastard list is the "no chicks" rule. However much of a bitch someone has been, there are to be no chicks on the list.

Ever.

It's bastards with a capital B only.

I see Sarah look hesitantly from the list to the pen waiting beside it. "Are you sure?" I ask her. There have been guys who've seen their entry on the list after it's been written in and they haven't been too pleased. If Sarah wanted maybe to patch things up and keep seeing Darren, it wasn't such a hot idea to put him on the list. Usually the list was used cathartically, to cleanse the system of the bastard and to put him behind you, all that new age shit.

So you have to be sure.

I pop a few peanuts in my mouth, wondering about the way in which Sarah's latest and greatest handled things. It's all a bit strange really.

Time to dissect Darren.

We gabble on about him for a bit, trying to work out his motives, before I decide I need a guy's opinion on this. So I turn to the guy sitting on the stool next to me. I know he's been listening to us—I'd seen him tune in as soon as Sarah sat down.

Men tend to do that when Sarah's around.

"What I don't get," I say to him, getting straight down to business, "is that he told her he was cheating when he didn't even do anything." I pause to collect my thoughts. "I mean, it's just not a guy thing. If you're a guy and you're cheating you don't tell, you just wait until you're found out, right?"

The guy, who looks a bit shocked that I'm asking his opinion, nods and then looks across me at Sarah. "She's right, you know."

Sarah meets his gaze. "But it was like he wanted me to *congratulate* him for not sleeping with her, like he'd done me some kind of weird-ass favor."

The guy puts his drink down and toys with it for a minute as he thinks. "Let me explain it to you," he finally says. "You see, this guy . . ." he looks to me for a name.

I look up. I've been engrossed in the bowl of peanuts, trying to forget that study I'd read about in the paper that showed there were traces of nine different people's urine in the average bowl of bar nuts. "Darren," I say, choking on a mouthful of uriney bar nuts.

"Darren," the guy repeats after me. "Darren's attracted to this girl and, believe me, he probably wants to sleep with her, but he doesn't want to cheat on *you*. By telling you that nothing happened between them he's trying to demonstrate to you that you're more important to him than she is." He picks up his drink again.

"I'm more important, eh? Well he's got a funny way of showing it," Sarah says, starting on another margarita. And as I watch her down it quickly, I wonder if it's her second or third. For her size, Sarah is a bit of a lightweight, a Cadbury kid (a glass and a half), or however you like to put it. If she keeps up at this rate I realize I'll have to strap her to the bar stool to keep her upright.

"Well, what happened after that?" I ask when she's done.

"He asked if we could work it out."

"And what did you say?"

"I think my exact words were 'Not bloody likely, Darren.' "

"Eloquent and concise at the same time," I nod in approval and give her arm a well-deserved pat.

"Thank you," Sarah makes a small bow. Then she turns and leans forward on the bar so she can see the guy sitting next to me. "Men really bite," she spits at him, her eyes narrowing.

Obviously it *had* been her third margarita.

"Not all men," he shakes his head a little sadly.

"Yes, all men," Sarah says. She turns to me and cocks her head thoughtfully for a moment before she speaks. "Gemma, back me up here."

I look at the guy and shrug. "I'm afraid she'd know. She's dated most of them."

Sarah leans forward again. "And, as a man, I think you should buy us a drink to make up for all the bastards in the world."

"Well, OK," the guy motions for another round of drinks. "If it's for the brotherhood."

Sarah digs me in the ribs with her elbow, raising and lowering her eyebrows like some bad Groucho Marx imitation before she turns back to him. "You're all right, but your evil brother Darren must be made to pay, he's going to be officially put on the list." She picks up the pen and turns to the last page of the yellowed, torn paper. "So," Sarah looks up at me, pen poised. "I guess this is it."

"I guess so." I watch as she prints Darren's full name and description onto the last page of the list, which means she now can't go back on adding him in.

Then, care of the guy on the stool next to me whose name we don't even know, we proceed to get very, very drunk.

After proceeding to
get very, very drunk,
I wake up with a hangover

When I wake up I only vaguely remember the night before. I have a foggy recollection of too many real—not dream—margaritas and some guy whose name I can't remember. There're also bits and pieces of peanut in my mouth that will probably do for breakfast at a push.

I do, however, have one not-so-vague souvenir of last night's cocktails evening, and it is now causing me pain, throbbing endlessly away in my head. Trying to ignore it, I swing my legs out of bed and groan. Then I sit for a bit and groan again. Then I sit for a bit more. Then I realize how pathetic I'm being and go and groan in the shower instead.

When I'm done and am feeling 10 1/2 percent better, I stagger into the kitchen for a cup of coffee, pulling on my daggiest jeans and jumper as I go.

I open the door to the kitchen cautiously and stick my head around to see if Imogen is in the kitchen and, if she is, how she's feeling this morning.

Now, before we go any further, let me explain two simple things to you:

1. Imogen is my cat; and
2. I am shit-scared of my cat.

You see, Imogen has a few problems—the vet says she has the pussycat version of schizophrenia. This means that one minute Imogen will jump on your lap and want a cuddle and the next minute she will try to gouge out your eyes with her claws. Kind of a feline version of Jekyll and Hyde. When she's not gouging, she likes to spend her time crouched on various objects around the house (preferably at human head height) hissing at people. The vet says I should put her down, but I can't do it, so every morning I have to shove ten bucks' worth of medication down her throat. This gives her yet another reason to hate me (well, that and the fact that I have to keep rolled up newspapers around the house to beat her with when she has her "bad days"—please, don't tell the RSPCA).

Anyway, I can't see Imogen, so I open the door fully and proceed with caution to the kitchen bench.

Where I discover there is no coffee left.

I look up at my shopping list, written on a blackboard hanging next to the fridge. "Coffee" is written in large, and rather urgent, letters. There are also three exclamation marks to remind me that coffee is very, very important.

Naturally, I have forgotten to buy any.

I push myself to go the distance to the fridge where I pour myself a glass of old, pulpy orange juice, well past its expiration date, but as there's no mold yet and it doesn't smell too bad, I'm satisfied. Then I walk back to the lounge to plonk myself on the couch for my weekly dose of tacky teenage video clips.

Except, just before I sit down, I realize Sarah is asleep on the couch. Snoring. This is the last straw on a hangover morning. My inner two-year-old rears its stinky diaper and begins to throw a tantrum. I need coffee. I need tacky teenage video clips. I need my couch.

Now.

I'd settle for just the coffee though. And maybe the paper, too.

Quickly, so my throbbing head can't change my mind, I finish my o.j., grab my house keys off the hall table, shove twenty bucks in my pocket, look at my shoes (but decide it would be unwise to bend over and put them on), and throw myself out of the house. Then I let myself back in the house, find a bucket in the bathroom, and place it right beside Sarah's head before I let myself out again. As well as being a light-weight, Sarah is also a notorious thrower-upper. Once, she deliberately spewed down the inside of her shirt to avoid the $75 fee that the cabbie would demand if she dirtied his car. She thought he wouldn't notice if she did it quietly.

He noticed. We ended up bargaining him down to $50.

I stop, take a big gulp of air, and try not to think about alcohol, Sarah and her shirt, buckets, and upchucking in general.

Call me a sympathetic spewer.

It's warm outside and bright, and I stagger around a bit until I put my sunglasses on. I spot Imogen soon enough. She's terrorizing one of the kids who live two doors down from me. A group of them are riding up and down the footpath on their training-wheeled, pink for girls and blue for boys bikes. And I take it this particular kid was quite happy doing the same thing until Imogen decided she'd latch onto his jeans leg. Now he's trying to kick her off by wildly flailing his leg around. It's not working, so I run over to give him a hand.

"Keep still," I say, as I pry her claws off one by one and hold each leg back so she can't reattach (do I look like I'm used to this, or what?). When I'm done, I run over and stick her in the front yard, hoping she'll stay there, but doubting very much that she will. I know from experience it's kind of like the shark thing, once she smells blood, the killer instinct is switched to "on."

As I start down the footpath again, the kid stares at me. He doesn't look very grateful. "Don't mess with the cat, kiddo," I give him a word of advice as I pass. He doesn't say anything and I figure he's either completely dumbfounded by my bravery, or is simply too polite to swear at me.

Down the street, the people who don't have cats attached

to their legs are doing normal everyday things, driving their cars, weeding their gardens, playing cricket with their kids. This surprises me for some reason. And I don't know why I think everyone should have a hangover on a Saturday morning, I just do. I guess it's the years of Friday night cocktails that's hardened me to the inevitable Saturday morning hangover. Thankfully, after a couple of good, strong coffees, a mound of greasy food, and a packet of Panadol, it usually subsides and is gone by lunchtime (note: lunchtime is around five PM on weekends).

At the shops I pick up some hazelnut-flavored coffee, six chocolate chip bagels, and some vanilla cream cheese. I also pick up the paper, the other third of my Saturday morning ritual. It's bagels, coffee, and Heidi Killman every Saturday morning. Heidi Killman's my favorite columnist—a scream in 800 words or so. She never fails to have a go at men and she's spot on, let me tell you. Her column's always worth reading and I never miss it, no matter how hungover I am.

When I've got everything, I turn and head for home.

Back there, Sarah is still asleep on the couch. I stand in the doorway and watch her for a minute or two.

Now, to jump or not to jump? Should I be a pal and make the coffee first before I wake her up, or be a pain in the arse and do it now?

Now seems both fun and *so* much more my style. Let's just say subtlety isn't one of my stronger points.

I put the goodies on the floor and bend down near Sarah's ear. Now for some fun.

"Oh, Sarah," I moan sexily, trying not to giggle.

She groans and rolls over.

I try again. "Oh, *Sarah,* that's good, yes, yes," I wait for a reaction.

A flicker of a smile crosses her face.

Time for my pièce de résistance. "Oh, Sarah, baby, do it to me, yes, yes, *yes!*" I yell.

Sarah's eyes jolt open and she looks over at me. "What are you doing, you idiot?" She rolls over and takes a swipe at me.

I grin. "Just fucking with your mind," I say, trying to pull away the blanket, hoping that she'll get up, but she snatches it back instead.

"Go away."

"No. You can't stay in bed today," I pull the blanket again.

"Why not?"

"Um, I don't know. Because I say so?"

Sarah wrenches the blanket back out of my grasp. "Piss *off!*"

"Come on, come into the kitchen and I'll make us some coffee." I dangle the goodies from the shop enticingly above her head. "Mmmm, look, *hazelnut* coffee and *chockie chip* bagels and special *vanilla* cream cheese."

Sarah opens one eye to check if I'm lying. "Is there really vanilla cream cheese?"

"Yup," I nod my head. Sarah was a full-time model for a year or so after she finished college, but she gave it up two years ago so she could have periods and food. Not necessarily in that order. Naturally (as only best friends can), she's only gained eleven pounds even though she eats whatever she wants, so she still models a bit on the side. I'd had ulterior motives in buying the vanilla cream cheese. For a start, I knew it'd get her off my couch. It's her favorite.

Sarah groans, echoing my earlier soundings, and hauls herself off the couch. In one fluid movement she trips over the bucket, curses, snatches up the still-warm blanket off the couch, and pulls it around her. Suddenly I envy her all those years of modeling. Sarah always looks graceful, whatever she's doing—even tripping over buckets. Often I'll catch a glimpse of us in mirrored windows in shopping centers and the like. She's the tall, upright one, carefree and breezy free, just like the tampon ads that she models and works on (that's what she meant by the "tampon girl" comment). As for me, I'm the other reflection. The Neanderthal, Quasimodo-type, my hands dragging along the ground as I walk beside her.

That's right—the one with the great personality.

Ha ha.

Even now, after a big night out, with mussy hair and big black panda eyes, she still looks good.

Life—it just isn't fair, is it?

I scoot down the hall behind Sarah, avoiding the mirror. In the kitchen, she pulls out a chair at the gingham-checked kitchen table. "Berocca? Panadol? Aspirin?" she begs, her hands shaped in prayer.

I pull the medicine bucket down from out of the cupboard and we both help ourselves, hoping the drugs will work their magic. Then, when we're all drugged up and the coffee's ready, we sit down to eat. The bagels are great, still warm, soft and chewy, just how I like them. I watch as Sarah slaps great mounds of vanilla cream cheese onto hers. "Want some bagel with your cream cheese?" I ask her.

"Very funny," she says, stuffing half a bagel into her mouth at once.

I watch her finish the piece she's eating and move straight onto the next half. And it's nice to see Sarah eating like a normal person again (well, normal for us anyway). Not like before, when she lost all that weight.

"Mmmff mmf mmmf mmf mmfff," she says as I keep on watching her.

"What?"

She finishes what she's chewing. "It's really yummy, how do you afford all this stuff anyway?" she gestures at the goodies. "I thought you were poor now."

"Some things are important, Sarah." I still have a bit of the money I'd put aside when I was working full-time. And the freelance business isn't that bad.

Yet.

Sarah reaches over and grabs the coffee, hiccupping as she

pours it into the two mugs and adds the sugar. "Milk?" She hiccups again.

I pass it to her. Sarah opens it up, hesitates, and then takes a quick swig from the carton.

"Sar-*ah!*"

"Sorry, hiccups."

"Can you at least wipe the cream cheese off your chin?"

She wipes the cream cheese off her chin with the back of her hand and licks it off as Imogen pads into the room. Sarah eyes her as she jumps onto the kitchen bench. If it had been anybody else in the room I'd be worried, but Imogen's more scared of Sarah than anybody else—even the vet. This is because Sarah isn't scared to give Imogen a good, swift kick if she deserves it.

Sarah passes me my coffee and as I pull the mug toward me, I spill a little on the table.

"Careful!" Sarah yells, as the list soaks it up.

I have a nasty feeling of déjà vu. Didn't this happen last night?

"Sorry," I say and pass her the list for safekeeping.

"Let's just take another look at our friend Darren's listing," Sarah says, putting down her coffee and flicking slowly and carefully through the pages. Halfway through the list, she looks up. "You know," Sarah says, "I'd say about a third of the guys on this list are yours."

"I don't think so."

Sarah tries to pass the list to me. "I'm not joking. You used to date like it was going out of style or something. Here, look."

I cross my arms and refuse to take the list. I've seen it enough times to know what's on there and there is no way as many as a third of the guys on it can be claimed as mine.

Sarah pulls the list back toward her and keeps on flicking slowly through it. A smile crosses her face every so often as she remembers bits and pieces of our bastard list history. But then, as I keep watching her, the smile leaves her face and she eyeballs me directly. "How long is it since you've been out with anyone, Gemma Barton?"

Gee, I wonder. As if she doesn't know the answer to that one. Everyone knows the answer to that one, they just don't dare say it in front of me.

"1865," I answer belligerently.

"You should get out more," Sarah says.

"Yes, Mummy."

Sarah puts the list down on the table so she can harass me properly. "No, I mean it. And I notice *he*'s still missing from the list."

I glare at her, as if daring her to say *his* name. As it was, she was getting dangerously close to pissing-me-off territory.

Sarah meets my glare. "Gemma, there're plenty more fish in the sea than Brett. You should put him on the list and get over him."

I pretend to ignore everything she's said now that the big "B" word's been spoken. And for God's sake, she really *did* sound like my mother now, spouting all that "fish in the sea" crap.

"Yeah, he was probably flake. That's why he *flaked* off," I pun, trying to steer her away from the man I now only refer to in two ways—as "that bastard who left me," or, like I said before, the big "B."

"Oh very funny," Sarah says, rolling her eyes before she continues. "There's someone out there for you, Gemma, you just have to get over Brett and move on. I'm sure there's a piece of barramundi swimming around out there with your name on it."

"I'll just pop down to the fish shop, shall I?" I try to humor her, hoping she'll shut up. I hate it when people remind me of Him. It makes my stomach hurt.

Sarah pokes her tongue out at my fish shop comment and picks the list back up, turning to the last page. I watch as she reads the entry from last night. But as her eyes flick down the page, a frown starts to cross her face.

"What's the matter?" I ask.

"Did I write this?" Sarah asks, passing me the list.

I take a look at the entry. It goes something like, *Darren bastard A class, hate him, can't remember why, just bastard, hate him. Bastard!*

"It's definitely your handwriting," I pass it back to her, trying not to smirk. "Your I'm-on-my-third-margarita-and-counting handwriting."

"Maybe I should write Darren in again," she says, now eating vanilla cream cheese straight off her knife.

"Now?"

"Nah, can't be bothered. Eating. Pin it back up on the fridge." She passes the list back to me again.

I stand up and grab the large magnet that usually holds the list in place and put the whole mess of paper and stickytape back in its usual spot. But it doesn't stay. It slides down the fridge and lands on the floor. I pick it up and try again. Once more, it slides down, down onto the battered old linoleum.

"What's the matter?" Sarah asks.

"Must be too heavy with the extra pages I tacked on."

"Why don't you put it somewhere else then? It's getting all yellow from where the sun hits the fridge anyway."

"Where should I put it?"

We both look around the kitchen for a minute before I put the tattered list back in the pink plastic folder and leave it on the kitchen table where we both know is probably its new home.

"Want to watch some video clips?" I ask.

We take our coffees out to the living room where we turn on the TV and huddle up on the couch, only occasionally squabbling over who has more blanket and who gets which section of the paper first.

Eventually we settle down and I find Heidi Killman's column, fluff up the pillow I'm leaning on, and get ready for my usual Saturday morning chuckle. Today she's writing about her son, Buster, and how he's turning into a miniature version of her ex, who she likes to call the "lower invertebrate." I practically wet myself all the way through the column before I notice Sarah staring at me like I'm crazy.

"Listen to this," I say to her, and I realize I'm getting asthma from laughing so much.

So how do they learn? Well, I reckon there's a "How to Be a Bastard in Ten Easy Lessons" book they give them at birth. You know how they pop out and then the doctor whisks them away? Well, that's not for medical purposes, believe you me. It's so they can give them the book and fill them in on all the other male stuff, like how they should wince and fall down on the ground in agony every time someone hits them in their nether regions, how to act like they're dying when they've got the flu, the best way to get lipstick out of a collar. I don't know about you, but I never really believe them when they get hit in the balls—it's always that bit too far-fetched for me to believe.

I laugh and fill her in on what the rest of the column was about. "I never believe that balls thing either, it always looks so fake. How about you?" I ask Sarah who, by the way, isn't laughing.

She ruffles the section of paper she's hiding behind. "I hate Heidi Killman and her nasty little column. If she's not bitching about her ex, she's bitching about her son. I can't stand her."

"Come on, you've got to admit it's funny."

Sarah snorts, pulls the paper down, and rolls her eyes at me before she goes back to reading again. In defense of my favorite columnist, I shrug and tell myself Sarah's got no sense of humor.

After a few minutes we're on speaking terms again. "So, what're you up to this weekend?" Sarah asks.

I make a face. "I have to update my home page. I've been putting it off for months."

"Oohh, can I stay?"

If there's one thing Sarah loves, it's playing on the Internet. Now that I'm freelancing and don't have as much money, I've cut back the time I spend on the Net by half. Poor Sarah is having withdrawal symptoms.

"Michael wrote down a couple of great sites for me, and even one for you," she bats her eyelashes.

"Whatever." Suddenly I don't see myself getting much work done. I secretly thank Michael, old friend, Internet Service Provider (ISP), and all-round Internet guru, for telling her about the sites because I don't really want to do any work anyway.

Sarah bounds over to the computer (stealing the entire blanket, mind you), double clicks on all the appropriate icons and connects us up.

Imogen must have heard the modem, because she waddles on into the room and settles herself right down on top of it. I'm not surprised—the modem's her favorite spot in the whole house because when it's turned on, it tends to be nice and warm. Rather like a cat-sized electric blanket.

Sarah gives Imogen an "I'm watching you, cat" evil-type glare as she pulls over an extra chair for me. "Come on," she says, patting the spare seat, and I know she can't wait to get started.

We surf the Net

I lug myself over to the seat Sarah has put out for me, mumbling about blanket-stealing best friends, and whump down in it gracelessly. Sarah ignores me, grabs her wallet, and searches around in it until finally she pulls out a crumpled piece of paper and waves it around.

"What's that?"

"The sites Michael suggested," she says, sitting down and typing the first address in.

http://www.2211.com/pop.htm

I look on as the screen loads up with hundreds of tiny dots. "What the hell is that supposed to be?"

Sarah reaches for the mouse and turns the speakers up, a big smile on her face. "Watch this," she says, clicking on the dots.

Pop. Pop, pop. Pop. Pop, pop, pop.

I look at the speakers and then at Sarah, confused.

"It's virtual Bubble Wrap!" she says, laughing and popping away some more. "Here, you have a go," she says, passing me the mouse.

I grab it and start clicking.

Pop, pop, pop. Pop, pop. Pop. Pop.

Funnily enough, we only manage to pop for a few more minutes. If you ever try it, you'll find you tire of popping virtual Bubble Wrap rather quickly. Probably just as quickly as you tire of popping *real* Bubble Wrap.

"What's this one?" I point at the next address on the list and start to type it in.

http://www.WinkingJesus.com

I read the first paragraph on the page out loud to Sarah.

On April 23, 1996, this picture of Jesus Christ miraculously winked at me. This experience has changed my life. Over three hundred thousand people have come to witness this miracle. Many people have had a lot to say about their experience. If you are fortunate enough to witness this image of Jesus Christ wink, please tell your friends and family about this miracle! Rev. Jonathon C. Chance.

Sarah and I both turn and stare fixedly at the little picture. Then . . .

"Hey! It winked!" we yell together and laugh.

"So, is that it?" Sarah says when we calm down.

I check out the page. Winking seems to be all he does. Not much of a repertoire after all that water and wine jazz. Then I spot the box below that says "Jesus winked at me." "Hang on, we're supposed to click on this," I say, clicking on the box and quickly scanning the page that comes up. "You're supposed to write a reflection about your winking experience." I look over at Sarah. "What do you want to say?"

"I don't know. What's everyone else said?"

"Well, there's a 'best of reflections' page, let's go there." I click on the link and we start reading all the things people have written in. One of them makes me laugh out loud. I read it out loud for Sarah.

blessed winking Jesus
with his winky little eye
why is he winking at me
I don't know why
blessed winking Jesus
winking like a frog
when his eye is closed
he looks like my neighbor's one-eyed dog
her name is Biscuit
Thank you TMWJ!

After reading a few more, we decide that we can't top what everyone else has already written and that it's time to move on. I grab the piece of paper and check out the last address.

"Michael told me that this one's specially for you," Sarah says as I type the address in.

http://www.yoni.com/bitchf/bitchboard.shtml

I hate it when Michael's right. We end up spending two hours at the site reading entries from women all over the world and their stories of the bitches and bastards who've done them wrong. Simply put, it's fascinating and addictive. It's real. We read, and read, unable to get enough.

Eventually, Sarah draws herself away from the screen. "I'm starving."

Surprise, surprise.

"Yeah, me too," even I have to admit that our stomachs have been grumbling in unison for the past fifteen minutes.

"Want me to do a Maccas run?" Sarah asks. "I need something greasy."

"Sounds great." I fish the change from the twenty out of my pocket, my eyes not leaving the computer screen.

Sarah shakes her head as she gets up. "You got breakfast—this one's on me. What do you want?"

I think about it for a minute while she searches for her car keys. "Um, how about two cheeseburgers, a large fries, and a gigantic Coke?"

"No worries."

"And a chocolate sundae," I manage to stop reading for a second and yell at Sarah as the door closes behind her. Then, not being able to resist the bitchboard, I turn back to the screen and keep reading. I just can't help myself. I've always been a nosy person and the bitchboard is like butting into a whole bunch of people's lives at once.

What better way to spend a Saturday afternoon?

Two entries in particular make me laugh.

if one more oblivious and/or sexist cashier hands my boyfriend the change when I have just purchased the product, taken the money out of my pocket, put my hand in theirs in exchange for some rented video or fast food meal, things will get pretty ugly. Desaray—USA.

I am sick and tired of society telling me I have to shave my legs. I want to be hairy, to be natural, to be released from razor enslavement, to be free to walk down the street in shorts, or lay out by a pool without nasty comments and disgusted looks from both men and women and whispers or "eeewwww grooooosss" from little kids. I am a woman. I am not a child. My leg hair grows wild and free, born of the goddess. I am angry that the world forces us to be dainty, smooth, shiny little girls, grrrr. Peace and power to hairy women! ! ! Amy—USA.

I'm so absorbed in the site I don't notice Sarah has come back until she's standing right beside me. She dumps the Maccas fodder down on the desk unceremoniously and starts to gabble furiously as only Sarah can.

"Guess what, Gem, I've just had the best idea."

I tear myself away from the screen, "What?"

Sarah stuffs the remnant of a cheeseburger in her mouth. "Mmmf mmf mmf mmf mfff mmff."

"Will you stop doing that? I can't understand a word you're saying."

She swallows and tries again. "I *said,* I've just had the best idea."

"Yeah, I heard that, what is it?" I am a bit wary because Sarah has had some interesting "best ideas" in the past. These days they're usually harmless, run-of-the-mill Sizzler or all-you-can-eat-till-you-throw-up Pizza Hut fantasies. But I know that it's best to tread carefully because she's had some doozies. One of them had involved Sarah piercing my ears with her school badge when I was eleven (I wasn't allowed to get them done until I was thirteen, and I think my mother had something more sterile in mind). Another had been to skip half a day of school where only *I* had gotten caught.

Sarah sees me touch my ears protectively and she obviously knows what I'm thinking about because she shakes her hands vehemently. "No, no, it's nothing like that, no body piercing involved."

"Good," I lower my hands.

"I was just thinking that you should put the list onto your home page. It's just going to get wrecked sitting around the kitchen, and at least this way we'd always have a copy."

I fish a cheeseburger out of the Maccas bag and munch on it thoughtfully. "That's not such a bad idea."

Sarah keeps going, "And then I thought maybe you should

make it like the bitchboard, you know, let other people add their own bastards to the list."

I stop eating for a moment. "You mean add a submission form or something?"

"I don't know how you'd do it, but it can't be that hard. The bitchboard wasn't that fancy or anything, was it?"

It had been a pretty straightforward site. "It was reasonably simple. Anyway, forms are easy, I've already got one on my site for feedback."

"Well then, let's do it!"

I pick up some chips and nibble on them as I think. All we'd have to do is type the list in and that wouldn't take too long. And Sarah was right, at least we'd always have a copy if anything happened to the real list. Anyway, it'd be fun. A lark.

Why not?

"OK," I turn to Sarah. "How about if we put our list in first, with a bit of info on how it started, and then let other people write their own bastards in on a separate page?"

"Great." Sarah runs out of the room with half a hamburger in her mouth and comes back a minute later sans hamburger, but with the tatty-looking bastard list in her hand. "Let's get going."

We spend the next couple of hours typing in the entries. We have a good giggle about a few of them. Who could forget Trent, the bastard who asked Ella (one of the share-house girls) if those "dimples" on her thighs were chicken pox scars. Or Paul, who used to come over and pick out what Vanessa (another share-house girl) would be wearing each time he invited her out for dinner (he figured if he was paying, she should wear what he wanted—she drew the line at no undies). I make Sarah type in the entry for Charlie-boy. He's the guy who conveniently "forgot" about child maintenance payments, school fees, college fees, and who his wife was (even now he likes to sleep around and remarry on a regular basis). Charlie just happens to be my Bahama-dwelling, tax-evading, *la vida loca*-living father.

After we're done with our own list, we start on the form so the world can carry on our tradition.

We're about halfway through when I stop dead. "Whoa!" I say and quit typing mid-sentence.

"What? What is it?" Sarah turns in her chair to face me, eyes wide.

"Um, we'd better be a bit careful here."

"Why?"

"Well, we don't want to get sued for defamation or anything. We need some rules if our site is basically going to be based on libel."

"Oh, right," Sarah says matter-of-factly, as if she's some high-flying defamation lawyer who deals with libel on a daily basis. "Well, how about if we make it first names only or something?"

I start typing the rules in. "OK, first names only."

We pause and think about it a bit more. "Hang on," I say, "we'd better make sure they don't put down the guys' addresses or anything."

"First name and city only?" Sarah suggests.

I nod and type this in too.

"Can you think of anything else?" Sarah asks.

I keep typing. "Well, no chicks, I suppose, like our rule."

"Hey, what about one of those disclaimer thingies?" Sarah asks.

"OK, apparently they don't mean much, but it can't hurt, can it?"

We make up a quick disclaimer saying that we aren't responsible for the accuracy of information supplied or any information submitted whatsoever. So there. Then we put in the few Latin words we can remember to make it sound legal. Ipso facto and all that jazz.

We type and retype and add and subtract from the list until the early hours of the morning. I think Sarah leaves at 2:00 AM. At 3:00 AM the bastard list is up and running. At 3:05 AM I crawl into bed and zonk out.

Wheep beep beeep!
Ding dong ding dong
ding dong!

I must be needing to catch up on a bit of sleep, because when I wake up again it's 1:30 Sunday afternoon. Even so, when I crawl into the bathroom and take a look in the mirror, I realize I still need some beauty sleep.

Big time.

My face is splotchy, my eyes are red, and I've got another headache from staring at the computer screen for too long. My mornings are becoming a bit repetitious for my liking. I get into the shower, sit down on the floor under the warm water, and prepare myself to stay there until the hot water runs out.

It doesn't take long.

Out of the shower, into my daggiest tracksuit, and then the crawl to the kitchen.

As you can tell, I'm not a morning person, even at 1:30 in the afternoon.

A bowl of cereal, a splash of milk (not a big enough splash because I forgot to buy some more), and out to the computer again.

I want to check my home page in the off chance that someone has actually spotted the bastard list and decided to write in an entry. The chance that someone actually *has* seen the list is slim to none, considering how many hits I've had on my home page in the two years it's been up and running (about 550, and they were mostly me). But I submitted the search words "bastard," "men," and "list" to most of the main search engines last night, so if anyone searched for the words, or a combination of them, the link to my page should have come up. I even went around to any newsgroups I could find on men and put a link up there, too.

Imogen's on the couch this morning and as I skirt around her, cereal bowl in hand, she eyes me warily and slowly gets to her feet. I know what's coming if I don't play my cards right. I stop where I am and stare right back at her. "Vet," I say, and as she starts to reach her paw out, she hesitates. "Vet," I say a little louder and then with an expression that looks like I'm really not joking, "Needle." The paw goes back in and she sits down again.

The psycho cat from hell taken care of, I sit down at the computer, flick on the modem, and dial away.

I love the noise the modem makes.

Wheep beep beeep! Ding dong ding dong ding dong!

It always makes me happy when I hear it because I know I'll soon be skimming across the world on the magic carpet that is my keyboard.

I wait eagerly for my home page to flick onto the screen, with the feeling that maybe someone *has* seen the bastard list. I hope so, for Sarah's sake at least. She'd been so taken with the whole idea of the bastard list on the Web that I'd practically had to pry her fingers from the keyboard and force her to go home earlier this morning, even though her eyes kept closing and her head kept hitting her chest then trouncing back up again.

I click all the right buttons to get onto the bastard list and then close my eyes, hoping that there is at least one entry on the page. After a few seconds I flick them open again, not being able to handle the suspense.

Shit!

Two, four, six, eight, ten, twelve, fourteen.

Fourteen entries!

I lunge for the cordless phone that I've left sitting on the couch. Doing so, I push my cereal out of the way and onto the wooden floor where the bowl cracks and milk and cereal go everywhere.

Shit, fourteen entries!

I have to tell Sarah.

I put the phone back down, remembering I'm on the Net, and flap my hands around a bit trying to think what I should do next. I can't call Sarah while I'm on the Net.

Print, print!

I press the print button and print the two pages of text out, reading bits and pieces as the printer spits the pages out. The first thing I notice is the difference in the length of the entries. Some are short, some are long, some are in-between. The second thing is that the entries are from all over the world. Australia. The United States. England. Sweden. Brazil.

I hang up the connection as quickly as I can and dial Sarah's number, clutching the two pieces of paper in my hand.

"Hello."

"Hi, Sar, guess what . . ."

"This is Sarah, sorry I'm not home right now . . ."

Bugger, the answering machine.

"Leave a message after the beep," Sarah's voice continues.

Beep!

"Hi, Sar, it's me. You've got to call me back right away, there're *fourteen* entries on the bastard list. Call me back as soon as you get in." I hang up the phone and look around me, unsure what I should do next. I spy the cereal spilled Pro Hart style all over the floor and then remember the papers clutched in my hand. I look from the floor to the papers. From the papers to the floor, then rush over to the couch to read the entries myself.

The cereal can wait.

Dean (Portland, Oregon, USA) Because he was born that way and couldn't claw himself out of the ditch to be a real man.

Brian (Bristol, England) We saw each other for a year before he told me he loved me and then three weeks after he said the magic words he slept with not one, but two of my friends.

Chris (Cairns, Queensland, Australia) There's nothing worse than a spineless bastard, and Chris was certainly a spineless bastard. We went out for several months and I even did the whole "meet the parents thing." We were seeing each other most nights, when suddenly he just stopped calling. After a few days I called him and he was full of lines like "maybe we can get together this weekend" and "I'm really busy at the moment, but we'll see each other soon." This went on for two to three weeks, during which he never called me, I only called him, but he kept on pretending that everything was OK. I started to think he might be one of those "six-monther" kind of guys who freaks out at any relationship that goes over six months. So I finally called him up and confronted him about it, asking him if he wanted to see me anymore or not. Only then did he admit to not wanting to see me, saying he was trying to "let me down gently," like he was doing me a favor or something. What bullshit.

Paul (Boston, Massachusetts) Because he tries to play mind games with everyone and thinks he's really good at it. The truth is, he's a complete dumbass and everyone can see right through him. Hope you're reading this, Paulie baby.

Tyson (San Antonio, Texas, USA) When I met Tyson I was 14 and he was 20. After a couple of weeks I thought I was in love and he convinced me to have sex with him. So after he basically raped me, I asked him if it was good and he said no. He went on to tell me that this was because my tits weren't good enough for him and that I needed to save up for implants because he "liked big bouncy ones." He suggested that I ask my parents for them for my sixteenth b-day. Oh, and that they should throw a nose job into the bargain as well. Can you believe it? Anyway, if you're reading this, Tyson, you piece of shit, screw you. You never deserved me or my tits. Oh yeah, and guess what, dickhead? THEY GREW.

The phone starts ringing as I'm halfway through reading the entry, but I can't stop to pick it up. On the tenth ring, I lunge for it, bashing my elbow on the TV cabinet as I go.

"Ohshitohshitohshitohshit," I answer the phone.

"Charmed, I'm sure," the voice says.

"Michael!"

"Gemma!"

"Darling!"

"Gorgeous!" We run through one of our many over-the-top greetings. If he were here in person a kiss on each cheek would have followed. Michael loves nothing more than playing at being gay. I mean, he is gay, but he likes to play around with the stereotype, if you get my drift. For example, when we go out together he likes to call me his fag hag. God knows why, but he really gets his kicks out of it, so I'm usually happy to oblige.

"Hey, I haven't heard from you in ages," I complain. "What've you been up to?"

"Work, work, and more work. Business is booming."

As I said before, Michael is my ISP and all-around Internet guru. I remember his tip sheet from yesterday. "Hey, thanks for the bitchboard address, it was pretty funny."

"I thought it was your kind of thing."

"What's that supposed to mean?" I pretend to be offended, but the papers in my hand distract me. "I've got something to tell you," I say in a sing-songy voice.

"And just what is that?"

"You know the bastard list?"

"How could I forget?" Michael says and I remember he's actually got an entry in the list himself—some guy he went out with for a couple of months who two-timed him.

"Well, it's gone online. I put it on my home page."

"That's nice."

"No, no, that's not the best bit," I say. "I put in a form as well, so other people can write their own bastards in."

"That's nice."

I save the best bit for last, knowing full well what will impress Michael—hits. "And I've had fourteen entries in twelve hours, that must be at least fifty hits!"

"Really?" Michael's listening now I've started talking hits. "Let me have a look," he says and I hear a clunk as he puts the phone down on his table.

Ha! I knew it, forget his stomach—hits are the way to Michael's heart.

As he picks up the phone again, I'm thankful for his full-time cable connection—this way he can talk me through what's going on. I hear him type something on his keyboard. "Jesus, Gemma, you've had over one hundred hits in the past twelve hours and they haven't all been *you* for a change."

"Hey!" Now I am offended.

"Yeah, yeah, anyway, what did you do to get so many hits?"

I tell him about the search engines and newsgroups. And while I'm talking, Michael must have loaded up my home page because now he laughs and says, "I like the last one. Short and not so sweet."

I scan the list down to the last entry.

Kevin (Seattle, Washington, USA) Kevin: ugly, short, cheap, idiotic.

"Kevin sounds like a real find," I laugh.

Beep beep, beep beep.

"I've got a call coming through, want to hold?" I ask Michael.

"Fine. Leave me. See if I care," he says.

"Hold or not?"

"Nah, I only called for a chat . . ."

"Bye, Michael, call you later," I say, already pushing the buttons to pick up the other call—if I wait any longer they'll hang up. "Hello?"

"Gem?" It's Sarah. "What's going on?"

I fill her in on what's happened and she's speechless for a moment, only managing to make a few bird-like cheeping sounds. Then, "What are they like? What did they say? What? I'm coming over . . ."

"Well, they're," I start, then stop, realizing Sarah has hung up and is on her way over.

As I put the phone down my eyes swivel across to the computer and rest there for a moment (guiltily). I know this feeling all too well. When I'd gotten my first e-mail address I'd checked my e-mail approximately every twenty minutes hoping there'd be something new there. Now I had that "it's only a local phone call" feeling all over again (conveniently forgetting how quickly those "it's only a local phone calls" had added up last time to equal a $350 phone bill that my mother had had to chip in for). Trying not to think about it too hard, I press the dial-up button for the second time this morning.

Wheep beep beeep! Ding dong ding dong ding dong!

As I wait for my home page to load, I bounce my knee up and down in anticipation. Waiting, hoping, that there's another entry.

There is. In fact, there are sixteen new entries and the hit counter has climbed dramatically. I work out that my home page has had more hits in twelve hours than it had all of last year.

When Sarah comes in, I'm still staring at the computer screen. Not reading, just staring in sheer amazement. She grabs a chair and plonks it down in front of the computer next to me.

"So, show me!" Sarah tugs on my sleeve. "Hey, Gem," she tugs a bit harder before I realize she's there at all.

"Huh?" I'm still dazed.

"Show me the entries," Sarah tries again.

I shake my head, trying to clear my thoughts. "There're more."

"More? Since when?"

I tell her about the sixteen new entries.

"Sixteen more!" Sarah yells. "No way."

"Yes way."

Sarah grabs the mouse and starts to scroll down the list. And I'm dying to read the new entries, but I'll just have to wait until she gets to them.

Kris (Frankfurt, Germany) Kris and I had been seeing each other for about a year and a half when things started going not so well. Our choice was to have an open relationship, which is something we decided on together. We had some rules for the open relationship. Number one, we decided that we must wear a condom if we slept with anyone else and number two, we would not tell each other about any other relationships we were having. Let me just say, I think Kris was very excited about having an open relationship and it was also mostly his idea (I think he probably had someone in mind). Everything went fine for four weeks and then Kris's friend told him that I had slept with two other guys in this time. Then Kris comes over to my house and slaps me in the face and calls me a slut because I slept with these people. He wants to know why I did not tell him that I slept with them. So I tell him that I did not tell him because that was our rule and he says no, I did not tell him because I don't want him to think I am such a slut! After this he left but he rang me up later to tell me he was sorry etc. so I did not break up with him. For the next month I did not see anyone else because he had been so angry, but then I found out something that made me break up with him. For the whole time, even before he had suggested this open relationship, he had been sleeping with a 16-year-old girl. When I confronted him about this, he just admitted it, as if there was no problem. And when I asked him if he used a condom every time, he said, "No, because she is sixteen and she is very clean." This time I really dumped him. So this is why Kris is a bastard and deserves to be on this bastard list.

Barry (Tulsa, Oklahoma, USA) Barry, I have no idea why I went out with you and your car for a whole year. I must have been insane. It obviously wasn't for your money, though, you cheap bastard! Did you know I used to tell this joke about you at parties? I'd tell people that you were so cheap, that instead of personalizing your number plate you'd decided to change your name to match the plates because it was less expensive. Guess what, Mr KD5AFD, some people actually believed me!

"Shit," I say to Sarah. "Did you read the one about the cheap guy?" I point out Barry's entry.

Sarah nods. "Some of these guys are awful. Look at this one," she points out one I haven't read yet.

John (Melbourne, Victoria, Australia) We met over the Internet in January last year. For about a month we chatted daily over the Net and then John started calling me on the phone. We spoke every night on the phone for about two months, sometimes for four hours at a time. We even exchanged photos. John wasn't all that gorgeous, but I told myself it didn't matter because he was so sweet and such a nice guy. And he was sweet, he sent me flowers every week, told me he loved me and that he couldn't wait for his holidays so he could come and see me. Eventually his holidays came around (by this time we had known each other for about four to five months). John drove for six hours to come and see me and we arranged to meet in a café. When he arrived at the café, I'd been waiting 15 minutes and was already sitting down. John came and sat down at the table and we chatted for a bit before we ordered. I thought it was a bit strange that he didn't kiss me or anything, but I figured maybe he was just shy as we hadn't met before. When I went to order, he kept shaking his head at me. When I asked him what was wrong, he said that I shouldn't be eating things like that (a low-fat muffin and coffee) because they had too much fat and sugar in them. Then he went on to say that I was a lot bigger than in the photograph I had sent him (I'd gained about fifteen pounds since that photo, but was only 121 pounds in the photo I'd sent). John then said that he needed to think about his "image" and that it wouldn't look good in his line of work (real estate?!) if he went out with a fat person. Then he got up and left. What a bastard!

I shake my head in wonder. "These guys really *are* bastards, I mean, our bastards are nothing when you look at what's happened to these poor girls. Our bastards are just . . . well, wankers, I guess."

Sarah checks her watch. "Can you print these out for me? I've got to run."

"And just where are you off to, Missy?"

Sarah looks at me sheepishly. "To the movies."

"With?"

"Um, you remember that guy sitting beside you at the bar the other night?" Sarah toys with her watch, avoiding my eyes.

"The one who bought us the drinks?"

Sarah nods. "That's the one."

"You're dating the guy from the bar?" I hadn't even seen her talk to him apart from the "men really bite" comment.

Sarah nods again.

"You're incredible," I say, shaking my head wearily. I don't know why I'm surprised. Sarah dates like waves roll into the beach. One after another. And I realize that, just as I'd thought would happen, Darren's been long forgotten, even though she only broke up with him a few days ago.

I print out a copy of the new bastard list and hand it to Sarah who's waiting near the front door. "Here you go."

"Thanks," she says, starting down the steps.

"And Sarah."

"What?" She looks back up the stairs at me.

"Watch out for Imogen." I've just spotted her crouched in one of her favorite visitor-pouncing spots in the shady bit under the last step.

"Thanks."

"And Sarah."

"What?"

"Be good."

"I will," she smiles and waves before jumping over the last step and running out to her car.

I sigh. Being good was a big ask for Sarah. I just hope the guy from the bar knows what he's in for.

Trouble brews on
yonder computer

There's something in the air on Monday morning. As soon as my eyes flick open I know that the day will bring trouble. I can almost smell it wafting around the house and I guess that it's emanating from the computer.

But I can't help myself.

I hop out of bed like a spring lamb and run to the computer to check how many entries people have made on the bastard list overnight.

Wheep beep beeep! Ding dong ding dong ding dong!

I can feel my heart beating in my chest as I wait in anticipation.

How many will there be? Fifty? Sixty? Seventy?

There're 234 entries.

Two hundred and four more than last night.

I look at the figures again, thinking they must be wrong. But the counter isn't wrong.

Two hundred and four more entries.

Oh my God.

My computer's become *The Blob*.

I pick up the phone, knowing it will kick me off the Net, but not caring, and dial Michael's number.

"Hello?" a voice answers groggily.

"Michael, I need help," I'm getting a bit worried that thousands of entries will be flooding in as we speak.

"What time is it?"

I look at the clock on the computer. "It's 7:30, but it doesn't matter. Michael, there're two hundred and four new entries on the bastard list this morning."

"Two hundred and four?" I can hear Michael waking up now and scrambling out of bed. Soon enough there's a *blip!* as his computer screen turns on.

"Shit," he says in a low voice.

I get down to business. "Am I going to run out of space on my home page, or what?"

Michael pauses. "Well, at this rate you'll run out of space in a couple days."

I start breathing again. I thought I'd be running out of space in the next few minutes. "So what should I do?"

"That depends on what you *want* to do."

I don't have either the time or the patience this morning. "Michael," I snap, "I don't know what I can do. You have to spell out the options for me. You're my ISP, remember?"

"Testy, testy."

"*Michael,* I'm running out of space as we speak."

"For God's sake, Gemma, calm down, it's not the end of the world. I guess you've got a couple options . . ."

And for the next half hour, Michael tells me just this. My options. I've got a few. But in the end, it really comes down to one option and one option only.

A whole new site.

With a new URL. A new name. And I can call it practically whatever I want.

And even though it's really the only option I have, something tells me to wait and see if the entries keep coming in so fast. Who knows? They might die off altogether, the whole thing might just be a fad. "I think I might see how it goes," I tell Michael, a bit calmer now, "And I'll get back to you."

"Oh, you'll get back to me, will you?"

"Yeah, I'll pencil you in for lunch sometime. Ta ta." I hang up the phone.

The rest of the day is spent in front of the computer until five PM, finishing off some work for a client. Oh, don't think I'm good and sit there working the whole time. Of course I don't. Between snack and coffee and toilet breaks there are my "must do the dishes" breaks, "oohh, *Ricki Lake* is on" breaks, "*Judge Judy* is on after *Ricki Lake*" breaks and my all-time favorite, "I deserve to make caramel popcorn because I've worked hard today" break.

But I'm reasonably good, because not once do I get on the Net.

Not once!

And I resist the temptation until eight PM, when I've had dinner and a shower, there's nothing on the TV, and the modem starts calling to me. "Gemma," it sings, "Gemma, you know you want me . . ."

And, once again, I just can't help myself.

Within minutes I'm sitting at the computer, dodging Imogen who's on the modem, and, well, you know the drill . . .

Wheep beep beeep! Ding dong ding dong ding dong!

Then I wait, playing with the frayed edge of my pajamas top, to see how many new entries have made it onto the bastard list.

There are only twelve new entries.

"Only twelve!" I shout at the computer, then realize I'm shouting at a computer.

I'm so disappointed. I know that just a few days ago twelve entries had been the greatest thing since sliced bread, but now things were different. I'd been expecting another fifty at least. And then I remind myself that I shouldn't be disappointed because that's why I'd held off this morning—it's what I'd thought would happen all along. The entries were a twenty-four-hour thing. An Internet flu, if you like.

So much for my new site.

Depressed, I switch off the computer, not even bothering

to read the new entries. Then I go to bed to curl up and read a book, even though it's only 8:15.

The next morning, I can't be bothered to check for any new entries. What's the point? I figure that, at the most, there'll be twenty new entries if I'm lucky. Hardly even worth connecting up for.

So when I check my home page that night I almost die of shock.

In total, there are 1,765 entries. One thousand five hundred and nineteen more than last night.

I press three on the speed dial and wait.

"Hello?"

"Michael," I say, "let's do it."

The list takes off

On Friday there's a knock on my front door at six PM on the dot, just as I'm getting ready to leave for cocktails.

It's Sarah. "Hey, what're you doing here?"

"Idea. Big idea . . ." she gasps and I figure she must have run all the way from the bus stop, the way she's carrying on. I grab her arm, drag her inside, and sit her down on the couch in the living room.

"Now, take a deep breath and tell me what's going on," I say, watching her carefully.

Eventually, she catches her breath.

"OK. I had this great idea for the site name. It came out of nowhere and I just got up and ran for the bus. I hadn't even finished what I was working on and then the lift wouldn't come for ages and . . ."

"Sarah! What is it?"

"What's what?"

"The name for the site!" I want to slap my hand against my head. Or hers, for that matter.

"Oh! Right. How about this," Sarah makes a majestic hand movement, "allmenarebastards.com!"

Silence.

"Gem?"

I sit down on the couch beside her. "Sarah, I think that's just about the best idea you've ever had," I pat her on the knee.

She shakes her head. "No way. Remember when we went down the coast with all those people and they went bungee jumping and dared us to as well and I thought we should go shopping instead and just tell them we went bungee jumping and we did and you got that great skirt on sale for $17.95? That was a *way* better idea."

I nod. "Too true. Too true. But this one's close. Damn close."

She nods. "Oh, and Michael rang my cell on the bus to see what we're doing tonight and I told him I had an idea, but I had to run it by you first, and he said that if you liked it we should come over tonight and he'd register it and everything!"

"You'll run out of breath again," I warn Sarah. "What about cocktails?"

"We can skip. Just this once. I told him we'd bring some dinner over."

And that's just what we do. We pick up some Chinese at our local and treat ourselves to the *second* cheapest bottle of champagne at the bottle shop next door (not the cheapest like we usually do).

When we pull up at Michael's, he's already sitting out in a low-slung deck chair in the front yard, halfway through a jug of his favorite alcoholic lemonade. I'm surprised to see that he's not inside participating in his usual Friday night ritual—sticking a piece of paper over the subtitles on SBS and making up his own dialogue. But then I check the time and realize why he's not—it's too early, the movie won't start for at least an hour and a half yet. Plenty of time to eat, register the site name, and leave him to it (like Sarah and my addiction to cocktails, he can't bear to miss his weekly subtitle substitution fix).

"Hey, darlings," Michael waves. "Want a drink?"

I hold up the bottle of champers. "We brought our own."

Next to me, Sarah holds up the Chinese food. "And your favorite honey prawns."

"You truly are goddesses," Michael says, getting up and

dragging an extra two chairs over so we can sit and look at the stars as well.

I hand around the plastic knives and forks and pop open the champagne (narrowly missing some passers-by on the footpath in the process). I wave sorry, then take a swig from the bottle before I pass it to Michael who's sitting next to me.

"Gemma, baby," he says, "you're all class."

Michael takes a swig too and then passes the bottle on to Sarah who doesn't look too impressed as she takes it in her hand. I know from the look on her face and the way she's paused that she's considering wiping the top, but is struggling not to for manners' sake. I try and hide my smirk. Sarah has always been a bit funny about "germs." She takes a small sip from the bottle anyway before passing it back to me.

Michael opens his container of honey prawns and carefully selects a morsel. "So? What's the name to be?" he asks with his mouth full.

Michael knew we were going to discuss the name of the site at cocktails. I'd asked him along, but he'd said he didn't want to break with tradition (guys weren't usually allowed at cocktails).

"Allmenarebastards.com," I say confidently, pretending to be engrossed in my Mongolian lamb, but really sneaking a glance at Michael's expression because I know what's coming.

He looks at me. "What happened to thebastardlist.com?"

Sarah takes the bait. "Well, I had this idea . . ."

Michael nods and looks over at me as Sarah trails off.

"Michael, it's just a phrase people will remember and then they'll go to the site and there'll be more *hits*." I try to make him see the positive side, really laying some emphasis on the hits part. Hits are Michael's favorite thing in the world, right after his brand new computer—Big Bertha.

Michael shrugs and pushes his honey prawns around in their plastic container. "You know how I feel about that phrase, Gemma Louise Barton."

I try not to groan because boy did I know how he felt about that phrase.

I'd had the "all men are *not* bastards" speech one too many times already this year. Michael hates man-bashers. Being a man and simply adoring men, he has every right to I suppose, even more than most. But it's the way he goes *on* and *on* about it that gets up my nose. Let's just say it gets a little tiresome after you've heard the speech for the zillionth time. Only a few weeks ago I'd been in the shops with him and he'd pulled over a woman who was wearing a T-shirt emblazoned with the slogan "so many men, so little intelligence" to give her a piece of his mind. The whole incident had been excruciatingly embarrassing and I'm wincing now, just recalling it. "Think of the *hits*, Michael," I try again.

And this time I must have got the emphasis right, because his face brightens a little. "I guess it *would* stick in people's minds," he says.

"That's right," I encourage him and pass him the bottle of champers.

We spend a few minutes in silence (apart from intermittent munching and champagne guzzling). Eventually I look at Michael who has speared another hapless honeyed prawn on his fork and is examining it intently, like it's off or something.

"What's wrong?" I ask him.

"Nothing. I was just wondering if you'd thought about a bit of PR?"

"PR?"

"Yeah, you know, we could send around a press release, try to get a couple of reviews."

I hadn't thought about PR at all. "Do you think we need to? The site's way out of control *now*. What'd happen if we sent a press release around?"

"Well, you might get some advertising for starters," Michael says, taking a swig out of the champagne bottle.

"Advertising?" Sarah and I say at the same time.

"Yes, advertising. You do understand the concept? I hear they've got it on TV, radio, and even the papers now." Michael looks at us as if we're from another planet.

I sit, my Mongolian lamb forgotten on my lap. Advertising? I'd never considered making money off the site. I thought I'd just be paying money *out*. I was down $500 already and it seemed I'd also be shelling out for a full-time connection to the Net soon enough.

"You mean I could make money out of this thing?" I turn to Michael. The plastic food container falls off my lap, but I don't care.

"Sure."

Thank you, baby Jesus, I send up the silent prayer I learned in kindergarten.

"Now that you've chosen a site name, we should arrange to get some T-shirts and stickers and stuff done too," Michael says.

"To give away?" I ask.

Michael laughs. "Get real, Gemma! To sell, of course."

Now I know he's crazy. "Like anyone would buy them."

"You'd be surprised," he says, getting up and collecting the empty Chinese containers. "Anyway, it's something to think about. You guys want some ice cream?"

Sarah and I nod in unison, never ones to say no to ice cream.

When Michael is out of earshot I turn to Sarah. "You really think I could make money out of this thing, or is he nuts?"

Sarah looks at me blankly and shrugs. "I dunno. I guess people do."

And with these few words of Sarah-type wisdom, I realize she's right. People *do* make money out of their own small sites. I remember Michael showing me some article in a magazine about a couple who made pots of money by taking digital photos of the woman posing naked in front of various American landmarks. They put the pictures onto their site

67

and charged people $5 to see each one. They also did a sideline in worn undies for $20 (you could even ask for a particular color or brand!) and satin sheets that they had slept on for an exorbitant price I don't remember.

I laugh, thinking how no one would ever want my worn cotton undies or sensible flannelette sheets.

"What's so funny?" Sarah demands.

"I just don't believe I could actually make money out of the bastard list, that's all."

"Me either," Sarah says as Michael appears with a tub of super-deluxe chocolate chocolate chocolate wicked ice cream and three spoons.

And you can see the adoration on Sarah and my faces. Michael. He's just our kind of guy.

"So how long will it take to get the site up and running?" I ask him as he gives me my spoon. "A month or so?"

"Gimme one week," he says with that I've-got-contacts-in-the-IT-industry glint in his eye.

Together, we polish off the tub of ice cream, the alcoholic lemonade, and the rest of the champers. Then we head inside, fluff up some beanbags, and watch Michael do a bit of subtitle substitution before the movie and the food kick in and Sarah and I both fall asleep. At eleven PM, Michael wakes us up, coffees us up, and ships us home.

And when I get there, my home page has already filled up. Two thousand and thirty-five entries, fifty-five countries.

Jayden and Keith (Sydney, New South Wales, Australia) These two arseholes were my two best friends' boyfriends. As if I didn't hate them enough already, one day I was invited over to one of the guys' houses (all four of them were there). When I got there, the two guys decided they wanted to go smoke some pot with this friend of theirs who lived up the street (only about 100 feet or so). Instead of walking, they drove. They thought this would be really funny. Especially with all the little kids in the area playing cricket on the street. Also, apart from this, they owed my friends a whole lot of money, cheated on them whenever they thought they could get away with it, and didn't even have the balls to come up with decent excuses later. I won't even go into all the other stupid, pathetic things they did as it'd fill up this whole site.

Karl (Long Island, New York, USA) Because he asked me if we could have a threesome with my best friend.

Damien (Brisbane, Queensland, Australia) Damien and I had been going out for about six months when we made plans one Friday night. It was definitely a plan, he was going to pick me up at my place at 7:30—that's a plan, right? Well, I thought so anyway. So 7:30 rolls around and I'm ready to go, but no Damien. All my flatmates are getting ready to go out too, and at 8:00, when they're waiting for their taxi, they ask if I want to come with them. But I tell them no, thinking Damien's just been held up and that he'll either be here, or call, soon. 8:30, no Damien. 9:00, no Damien. 9:30, 10:00, no Damien. By this time I'm getting frantic, thinking he's had an accident or something. I've called his cell, which isn't answering, but the weird thing is his home phone is just ringing out and he *always* leaves the answering machine on—never forgets. Eventually I go to bed, but I keep waking up during the night having this dream that Damien's in bed with some blonde. This dream is so annoying that at three AM I get in the car and drive over to his house and let myself in with the key he gave me. To give Damien his dues, I was wrong about the dream. She was a brunette.

The two dickheads who sat near us at the opera last night (New York, New York, USA) I have no idea what these two dickheads' names were and I don't really care. However, they must have been stupid to start with, because they couldn't even manage to book seats sitting beside each other for the opera. Instead, my boyfriend and I were sandwiched between them and their two partners (both blond bimbos). Before the opera started, these two idiots got out their cell phones and called each other. The blond bimbos thought this was hilarious and couldn't stop giggling, tossing their hair around and batting the guys' arms playfully. I'm sure they had names like Bambi and Candy or something. As if this wasn't bad enough, the two guys didn't even stop when the overture started and the house lights dimmed. My boyfriend actually had to ask the guy sitting next to him to put his phone away and for this he got a big look and a really loud "What's your problem, buddy?" Eventually an usher had to come over and ask them to turn their cell phones off.

allmenarebastards.com is born

"Michael, what the hell is going on?" I blurt out as he picks up the phone.

"Well, I've got some people over tonight . . ."

"I didn't ring to ask about your social life, I meant the Web site."

"Oh, right. What's wrong with it?"

What's wrong with it? I didn't even know how to begin answering that question. It wasn't that there was anything wrong with it as such, it was just that it had gone crazy. That is, the women of the Net had gone crazy—they were flocking like lemmings to the site in a frenzy to write about the bastards who had done them wrong. From Neil in New York to Fred in Finland, the entries had just kept right on rolling in.

Rolling in too quickly for me to read them all.

When Sarah and I had first put the bastard list on my home page I'd added a feedback form so people could comment on the site. I'd promised to answer each and every (sensible) e-mail that came in. And so far I'd got some really good comments on how to make the site better and more accessible. But now, with all the feedback I was getting, along with the numerous inquiries about advertising, I just couldn't cope with having to read and reply to all my e-mail. Square eyes glazed and head spinning, I was living on coffee, peanut butter out of the jar, and month-old digestive biscuits. My skin had turned into a zitty, oily mess, and most nights I ended up on the couch, too tired to crawl to my bed down the hall.

Every day was a new experience; every week set a new record.

On Monday the site got 5,543 hits.

The next Monday it got 6,975 hits.

The Monday after that, 7,246 hits.

And on the following Friday, I got knocked sideways. There were 14,487 hits, 876 new entries, 243 feedback e-mails and 7 hate e-mails (I was well used to the hate e-mail by now).

And that was why I had rung Michael. To see what the hell was going on . . .

"Gemma?" Michael says, "I asked you a question. What's wrong with it?"

"There's nothing *wrong* with it, it's just gone berserk. I haven't got time to read all the entries or even to reply to the feedback I'm getting. It's out of control."

"Oh, that'll be the press release," Michael says casually.

"What press release?" I hadn't sent out any press release.

"Um, the one I sent out."

"*Michael!*" What did he think he was doing sending out press releases and not even telling me? I wished he were here so I could put my hands around his lily-white neck and throttle him.

"Well, I thought it might help you get a few more hits. I gave people your cell number so you wouldn't be disturbed at home or anything."

"Gee thanks," I wrestle around in my bag to find my cell, which I know has been switched off all day. "And may I ask what I said in this press release?"

"Just a bit about the start up of the site and how many hits you'd been having. All that kind of stuff."

I find my cell and switch it on. I have three messages. "Hold on a second," I tell Michael, "there're messages on my voicemail."

I put down the phone and push the buttons to get to my voicemail. The first message is from my mother, the second is from *The Australian,* and the third is from *Wired,* some magazine that I vaguely remember hearing about somewhere or other.

I pick up the phone again as I turn my cell off. "Well, it looks like *The Australian* and *Wired* are interested."

There's silence for a moment before Michael speaks. "Bullshit," he says quietly.

"The chick from *The Australian* said she'd call later, but the guy from *Wired* left a number. Should I call him back now? What time is it there?"

"Bullshit, Gemma. You never got a message from *Wired*."

I begin to think Michael's making an awful lot of fuss about one little message. "Well?" I say, getting impatient. "Is it worth calling them back, or not?"

"Gemma," he says. "Don't you know what *Wired* is?"

"Isn't it some site for computer geeks or something?"

"Gemma!"

"What?"

"Wired is just about the biggest, funkiest, coolest Net mag out there. If you don't call them back right now . . ." Michael was obviously lost for words, "I'll . . . I'll come over and disconnect you forever. You don't deserve to be on the Net if you don't know what *Wired* is. "

I look from my computer to my cell and back to the computer again, becoming a little disillusioned about the whole Web site thing. What was once my nice, regular home page with photos of my friends and family now reminded me of something akin to Pac-Man. In my eyes it was working its way around the Net, chomping up space in some frenzied kind of race. I actually think I was beginning to get scared of it. Some nights I worried that if I went to sleep, in the morning it would have taken over the house, as if the Net itself couldn't contain it. But Michael didn't seem perturbed at all. It was as if he had some kind of *vision* for the site. I wished I had it too. He was so excited about *Wired* calling, whoever or whatever they were, and I just wasn't. Frankly, I felt like a fish out of cyberspace.

When I tune back in to Michael, he's still ranting.

"Call them, Gemma," he says. "Call them *now!*"

"But I don't know what to say—to them or to *The Australian* either. Can't you do it?"

"It's your site, Gem, not mine."

"I'll give you twenty bucks!" I plead.

"Gemma, I very much doubt you *have* twenty bucks."

"Hey!" I say, but I grab my wallet off the couch anyway to check if he's right.

He's right.

I flop down on the couch in desperation. "But I don't know what I'm doing. And I'm so *tired.*"

And Michael must sense how close to the edge I am. "How about if I come over later and we work some kind of mini-business plan? With over one thousand hits a day you should really start arranging some advertising and make some money out of this baby."

"But what about *Wired*?"

"Well," and I can hear the pain in Michael's voice as he says it, "they'll just have to wait till Monday."

"Thanks, Mikey-Wikey."

In the end Michael comes over, we work it all out, and are both happy. Michael will deal with the advertising and take a 15 percent cut in any advertising revenue we get. I will deal with the editorial side of the site and keep it updated, replying to the e-mail, referring advertising requests on to Michael, and dealing with orders for merchandise when we get it up and running.

He still makes me do the interview with *Wired,* though, and the one with *The Australian*. I get an interview with the local paper too. And, all in all, it isn't too bad, this PR stuff. Before the *Wired* interview I'm under the impression that they'll try and nail me for being a man-hater, but they don't. They're more interested in Michael-type things like hits and stats and why the whole thing seems to be working so well. In fact, they don't seem to be very interested in the *content* of the site at all.

And just when everything's starting to come together smoothly, advertisers are expressing interest on a daily basis, I realize I'm making far more money than I ever expected, and I'm feeling a whole lot better about the site in general, my cell rings and I get my first call from a lawyer.

I get a scary call from a suit

"Is this Ms. Gemma Barton?"

"Yes."

"This is Clayton Warner of Warner, Rankin, and Post Lawyers of Boston, Massachusetts."

"Yes," I say again, but more carefully this time, wondering what on earth he wants with *me*. I hope that it's something along the lines of a rich great-aunt that I've never met has died and left me her fortune.

"I'm calling on behalf of my client, Dr. David Turner."

That doesn't sound like the name of a rich great-aunt.

"Who's David Turner?"

"Dr. Turner is apparently listed on your Web site called," he coughs, "allmenarebastards.com."

Uh-oh. I could hit myself, because instantly I know what this is going to be about. I'd thought that I'd be safe just using the guys' first names and the city and country they lived in. And even if I hadn't read all the entries, I'd made sure that this was all that was listed about each guy because I really, really didn't want to get sued. I dig my nails into my palm and wish I'd spoken to a lawyer myself.

"And how can I help you, Mr. Warner?" I try the suck-up approach.

"My client feels that the information given in the entry concerning him on your site is defamatory. He would like it taken off."

I wonder just what "Dr. David Turner" has actually done, because it must have been pretty bad if he's gone to the trouble of hiring a lawyer. Juggling the cell into my other hand and holding it on with my shoulder, I go over to the computer and start the search for his name.

"Mr. Warner, I'm very careful that only the person's first name and their city and country of residence are published on my site. There must be thousands of Davids in Boston and probably quite a handful of David Turners."

"Nevertheless, Dr. Turner would like the entry taken off the site."

"Why? Didn't he do it?" I don't see why "Dr. David Turner" should have his entry taken off unless it's false.

"Whether or not Dr. Turner 'did it,' as you say, is beside the point. He feels the information is defamatory and he would like it removed."

"Well, I'll have to speak to my solicitor about that, Mr. Warner, and I won't be deleting anything until I hear what she has to say about it. Good-bye." I press the red button to hang up with difficulty because my hands are shaking. As it turns out there is only one David listed for Boston and he's just one of the many bastards on the site who've decided to cheat with another woman. The only difference is that this one's a surgeon—one of the wealthier species of bastard. Wealthy enough to afford to put a lawyer onto me, anyway.

I get up and go over to the couch to sit for a minute and take a few deep breaths. There's so much that I've got to do. For a start, I've got to call my solicitor. No, actually, I've got to *get* a solicitor because I lied about that bit. Then I've got to phone Michael and tell him what's happened. And on top of this I've got hundreds and hundreds of e-mails to reply to and thousands of entries to read. I've got to . . .

I've got to make a cup of tea.

I drag my body into the kitchen and go through the motions of making some. Teabag in cup, sugar in cup, water in cup, stir, stir. But it's like I've left my brain back in the living room. I think this is what they call shock and I remember something to do with frozen peas, so I go over to the freezer and wrench it open. There're no frozen peas. I knew there wouldn't be—since when have I ever bought frozen peas? Then I realize that frozen peas are for bruising, and it's sugar and sitting down that are for shock, so I add a couple more teaspoons of sugar to my tea and sit down at the kitchen table.

I take a sip and realize it tastes disgusting, but I make myself drink it anyway while I try and figure out what I'm going to do about the phone call. At first I go way overboard and panic, thinking maybe I should take the whole site down. When I've told myself this is silly, I then consider listing just the first names of the bastards and taking out where they live. It's only when I've totally calmed down that I start to see this whole thing for what it really is. Dr. David Turner (bastard MD) is just trying to scare me. He thinks by hiring a lawyer for a couple of hundred bucks he can quickly and easily get rid of his little Internet "problem." After all, there's not much he can do beyond scaring me. He couldn't really get me to take his listing down, because the listing doesn't name *him*, which means it's not defamatory . . . I think. After all, it could be any David in Boston. I take a deep breath and then exhale slowly. Later, I'll ring a solicitor just to make sure, but right now what I need is distraction.

On the chair next to me I spy an old magazine, so I pick it up and start flipping through, skipping carefully through the fashion and beauty pages (I already feel inadequate enough for one day). Finally, I stop at the quiz. I don't usually do the quiz, but this one's grabbed my attention and is now calling out to have its little boxes ticked. I find a crusty old pen underneath the table.

The quiz is entitled "Are You the Kind of Girl Who Needs a Life Coach?"

Ha! As if I don't already know the answer to that question,

but I decide it might be fun anyway. I take a slurp out of my cup of tea, burn my tongue, make a face at the high sugar content (again), and start on the first question.

1. Do you do your washing:

(a) every morning?
(b) on the weekend?
(c) when you remember?
(d) only when you've got nothing left to wear?

Not a good start considering I have a hard time separating the washed from the unwashed clothes that are usually having incestuous relations on the floor of my room.

I circle *(d) only when you've got nothing left to wear,* and move on to question two.

2. How much television do you watch each week?

(a) five hours or less
(b) five to ten hours
(c) ten to fifteen hours
(d) fifteen hours or more

I feel quite good about myself when I circle *(c) ten to fifteen hours.* At least I don't watch *(d) fifteen hours or more.* That would be piggy. I try to forget about the time I had cable. That was different. You need to get your money's worth with cable.

3. How much alcohol do you drink each week?

(a) one to two standard drinks
(b) three to five standard drinks
(c) five to ten standard drinks
(d) more than ten standard drinks

Uh-oh. Even I know that *(d) more than ten standard drinks* is bad. Life coach here I come.

4. What is your work desk like?

(a) neat and tidy with papers filed away daily
(b) neat and tidy, but a few papers here and there that I've been working on in the past week or so
(c) pretty messy, but I can still find everything
(d) I have a desk?

Hmmm. Have to circle *(d) I have a desk?* This can't be good. I skim question five: *How much exercise have you done in the past week?* Question six: *How many of your New Year's resolutions have you broken this year already?* Question seven: *How many bills have you received notices for this year?* And question eight: *How long do your relationships generally last?* until I can't take anymore questions. Duh! Of course I need a life coach! Who bloody doesn't? But the whole thing sounds a little too close to nagging for my liking. Who'd pay someone $150 a week to nag them about crap they didn't want to do for a reason? Not me, that's for sure—my mother calls me up and does it for nothing. And anyway, even if you *did* hire a life coach and he/she made you do all those nasty-nasty things like do the washing every day and clean up your desk, after you'd done it they wouldn't let you have a drink to celebrate anyway! I sit back in my chair and this vision of my day with a life coach comes to me. *Clean up your room, Gemma! Have you made your bed, Gemma? How long since you de-molded the bathroom, Gemma?* Oh yeah, I need a life coach like I need all my wisdom teeth pulled out at once without anesthetic.

I push the magazine across the table in disgust. I don't need a life coach—what I need is some kind of a mafia-type to go and rough up the people who don't pay me on time.

That's what I really need. Well, either that or a personal assistant.

This thought stops me in my tracks.

Oohhh, I think, taking a sip of my now cold tea. A *personal assistant.*

I dream about getting a PA

I'm practically drooling into my tea now. You see, I've always wanted a PA.

And not one of those corporate PA-types who just do typing and answer phones and stuff. I mean a *real* PA. Like on the sit-coms. One that picks up the dry cleaning, and when you forget to buy fresh basil for the pasta sauce you make them go out and get it for you. Yeah, one of *those* PAs.

I lean back on my chair *(Don't swing on your chair, Gemma,* the life coach says). Ignoring his protests, I lean back even further and sigh out loud, dreaming of all the things I could make my PA do. For a start, he/she could answer all those nasty calls from the defamation lawyers. If I'd got one call, I could be sure I'd be getting more, right?

What else could my PA do? Well, help me to reply to all that feedback e-mail, for a start. There was no way I was going to be able to do it all. They could deal with the PR from the site. *And* with my parents. Even I had to admit my excuses were getting a little lame—last week I'd found myself saying "Gemma doesn't live here anymore," when I'd picked up the phone and realized it was my mother calling.

There's no doubt about it, Gemma, I tell myself.

You're one chick who needs a PA.

Needs a PA? Hell, *deserves* a PA is more like it.

And then I stop dreaming because while I know I *need* a PA and I know I *deserve* a PA, I'm not quite so sure whether I can *afford* a PA.

I get a PA (ha!)

Holding this thought, I run into the living room, disconnect from the Internet, and dial Michael's number.

"Can I afford a PA?" I blurt out as soon as I hear the receiver pick up.

"Um, who's this?" a guy's voice replies.

"Michael?"

"Hang on, I'll just get him," the guy says.

Shit. Who was that?

"Hello?"

It's definitely him this time. "How much money am I going to make off this thing?" I decide to get straight to the point.

"Why?" Michael asks and I can hear the caution in his voice. "You haven't gone out and put a deposit on a Lear jet or anything, have you?"

"No," I laugh, "not yet, anyway." (Although I catch a glimpse of myself whizzing about town in a stylish pink Lear jet, rather like Lady Penelope and her pink Rolls Royce from *Thunderbirds,* and I like what I see—Thunderbirds are go!)

Michael pauses for a moment. "Well, I guess it depends on how much advertising we can swing."

"Can you give me a ballpark figure?" I am *so* desperate for that PA. I could be cool if I had a PA.

"Well, I'm not making any promises, but with the advertisers we've already got, the hits the site's getting, and the interview coming up in *Wired,* it could work out to be over $50,000 a year."

I pull the chair out from my desk and sit down. Fifty thousand dollars? "You're joking, right?" I say. Maybe Michael is just pulling my leg.

"You've already made $35,000 for the next year with the advertising contracts you've got. Excluding my cut, of course."

"Of course," I assure him. "I wouldn't forget your cut, Michael."

"Just checking," he says, and I can hear the smile in his voice.

I get up and do a little dance around the room as we talk, realizing I don't have to worry about money anymore. No more freelancing for people I don't like. No more freelancing at all if I don't want to. Well, for as long as the site stays successful, anyway (a sobering thought). "So you think it could be even more?"

"Could be," he says. "It's hard to tell so early on."

"Michael," I say in my best whiny voice, "do you think I could afford a PA?"

"It's your money, Gemma. You have to do what you want with it."

This isn't what I want to hear. What I'm looking for is *permission* to get a PA. I want someone to tell me it's a good idea, that I'm not being extravagant or self-indulgent. "But do you think I should?" I try asking the question a different way.

"Well, you probably couldn't afford to get one full time."

"Oh, no. I was thinking maybe fifteen hours a week or so."

"What do you want one for?" Michael asks.

I decide it's not the right time to fill him in on my dry cleaning/fresh basil sitcom-type fantasy. "Oh, you know, to deal with some of the PR and the feedback e-mail and stuff. I've hardly got time to breathe at the moment and . . ."

"Hey!" Michael butts in.

"Hey what?"

"I've got the perfect person for you. Chris is here."

"Chris?" I have to think for a moment, being bad with faces *and* names.

"You know, Chris Patterson. Chris used to be a PA!"

Chris Patterson rings a bell. I vaguely remember a Christine with long, dark hair from Michael's uni days. "Oh, right."

"Well, Chris is looking for some work. This would be perfect. And you guys have got *so* much in common. Hang on," Michael says and then I hear a muffled, "Hey, Chris, come here."

"Michael," I say when he gets back on the phone, "this was just a thought. I'm not sure if I can afford a PA yet."

"Well, Chris is cheap," he says and I hear a whump. "Ouch," Michael says. "Chris is also mean."

"Always a good trait in a PA."

"Look, Chris was just about to leave anyway, and you're just round the corner—why don't you two meet up and see how you get on? How about now?"

"Michael, I don't know."

"Come on, Gemma, it's just a meeting, half an hour will do."

"Oh, all right." I give in, thinking nothing will come of it.

"Great! See ya," Michael hangs up and I'm left holding the phone in my hand. I look down at what I'm wearing. Daggy shorts, jumper, and no bra. Not the look of a hard-core professional. I sprint into my room and drag out something a little more businesslike. Well, home businesslike, anyway. And seeing as my home business wear generally consists of pajamas in some shape or form until at least midday, I consider the long-sleeved linen shirt and linen shorts I don (which I'll call *fashionably crushed* so I won't have to iron them) quite reasonable. I even put on a pair of leather mules for the occasion and slap on a bit of makeup. I don't want my maybe future PA to think I'm a frump. If I hire her, she'll find that out for herself soon enough.

Just as I'm applying the last bit of lipgloss, the doorbell rings. I grab a tissue automatically and blot and then realize

I'm wearing lipgloss, not lipstick, and have probably wiped it all off. I throw up my hands in despair (I mean, what would my life coach say?) and head for the door.

When I open it, it isn't my PA. It's some guy.

"Yes?" I say.

"Hi, I'm Chris," he says, extending his hand.

I stand there and look at him, putting out my hand just as he drops his. He puts his out again just as I drop mine.

"But . . . but," I stammer.

"But what?" he says, confused. "You are Gemma, aren't you? Is this the right house?"

"But, you're a guy."

He nods. "Last time I looked, and I guess it does account for the facial hair."

I stare at him, stunned. "But when Michael said Chris, and that you used to be a PA, I just . . . oh." And with this I realize I've just made the politically incorrect blunder of the century.

"Ah, so you thought I was a *female* Chris. Welcome to the new millennium, Gemma," he says, smiling. "Anyway, remember you spoke to me before on the phone?"

I look at him blankly, not remembering speaking to him at all.

"You said something along the lines of 'Can I afford a PA?' if I remember correctly."

I cringe. "Oh, right. Sorry about that."

"No worries," he says obligingly. "Happens all the time."

I realize the poor guy is still standing in the doorway. "Come in, come in," I say, holding the door open. I give him the sly once-over as he walks past me and I think to myself that if I have to have a male PA, this one wouldn't be too bad.

Not too bad at all.

Don't get me wrong, Chris isn't anything outstanding, my eyes aren't boggling out and my tongue's not on the floor. But he's nice-looking. Pleasant.

A boy you could take home to your mum.

Not that I'm looking for anything like that, of course.

It's just that he's got the kind of brown eyes I've always fancied having myself. You know those cow-brown colored eyes that make you trust people who have them? Well, Chris has eyes like that.

And I'm still busy doing the once-over when the most amazing thing happens.

Imogen walks right up to Chris and starts doing figure eights around his legs—just like she's a normal cat or something. "Hey," Chris says, bending down and picking her up. "What's your name, gorgeous?"

"Imogen," I say, and I start to think I should warn him. "Um, I wouldn't do that if I were you."

"Why not?" He's cradling her like a baby now and tickling her under the chin. "Who's a pretty girl? Who's a pretty pussycat, eh?" he gushes.

I stand there hardly being able to look because I know exactly what's going to happen next. She's going to turn, she's going to turn on him and rip both his eyes out. The poor guy will never PA again.

Wait for it . . .

Wait for it . . .

But nothing happens.

And I've never seen her like this before. She's playing this whole I'm-a-sweet-pussycat-don't-you-love-me game and purring, purring, purring at Chris like she's in love.

Eventually I want to try it too.

(Holding Imogen, that is, not purring at Chris like I'm in love.)

"Can you give her to me?" I ask, holding my arms out.

"Sure," Chris passes her over.

And that's when she does it. As soon as she's in my arms, she turns, flicks one of the claws out, and runs it straight down my arm to slow her down a margin as she jumps to freedom.

The little traitor.

We both watch her stalk down the hallway. "God I hate that cat," I say.

Chris looks at me as if this is my fault, as if I've done something to the cat.

"She's schizophrenic," I say by way of explanation.

We look at each other a while longer before my brain kicks in and I remember my manners. He's not looking at me like that because he thinks I'm a cat molester, he's waiting to be invited in past the hallway. Shit. "Sorry, come in, come in. Um, would you like some coffee or tea or something?"

"No thanks, I just had some at Michael's. But, you might need a tissue," he says, looking at my arm.

I follow his glance to my arm and realize I'm bleeding. My arm's bleeding and to make matters worse it's dripping onto the floor. I grab a tissue from the hallstand and mop it up, then bend down and do the floor before I stand up again.

Chris is still standing there looking at me.

As I shove the bloody tissue in my pocket I know I have to do something to end this disaster. I have to get us out of the hallway. "Let's take a seat," I say, leading the way into the lounge.

I sit down on one of the easy chairs and face Chris who's taken a seat on the couch. "So you were a PA?"

"Yeah," he nods, "for a financial adviser. He worked from home too." Chris looks around my flat as he says this.

"A bit fancier than this, huh?"

He shrugs. "It was OK. I liked the job."

"How long did you work for him?"

"Two years. He moved overseas, though," Chris says, answering my next question.

My cell phone rings and we both turn and look at it. I sigh out loud, not really meaning to, and Chris catches on.

"Is that your work phone?" he asks. "Just for the site?"

I nod.

He picks the phone up off the table and answers it. "Allmenarebastards.com, Chris speaking, how can I help you?" And in five minutes flat he's worked out another $750 worth of advertising for the coming year along with a bit of free PR.

When he hangs up, my jaw is still sitting on the floor. "How did you do that?" I ask. Everything Chris had said had come out so easily. He'd even cajoled an extra $150 on top of the advertising fee I'd usually ask for. Normally, I'd stammer and ummm and ahhh, because I hated asking for more money, but Chris, he came right out and asked for it. Bang, just like that.

Chris simply looks at me with the tiniest of smiles and shrugs that shrug of his again. "Michael told me how much the advertising costs and the rest, well, it's my job."

"Too right it's your job, you're hired, mate," is all I can say back. The way he scammed money, Chris would pay for himself. "I can only afford twenty dollars an hour though," I qualify. "And how about we start at fifteen hours a week and see how we go?"

"Great!" Chris stands up and I can see that he's genuinely happy.

"Great," I repeat after him.

Chris hands me back the cell. "I'm so relieved. I've been here for four weeks and hadn't found a job yet. I was beginning to think I'd never get one."

"Oh," I say. "I thought you were from around here. Where'd you move from?"

"The most boring place on Earth, actually. You really don't want to hear about it. So, when do you want me to start?"

I look over at the computer and think about all the e-mail that hasn't been answered yet. I'm desperate, but I can probably cope for one more day on my own. "How about Monday?"

We agree to start at 9:00 Monday morning. But it isn't until Chris is walking down the footpath toward his car that I remember what Michael said about us having a lot in common. And as I watch his car disappear down the street, I wonder what it is.

http://www.allmenarebastards.com

Aaron (Melbourne, Victoria, Australia) When I told Aaron I didn't want to see him anymore, it didn't go down too well. He did this really disgusting begging thing, pleading with me not to leave him, and when this didn't work, he tried to turn the situation around, saying that *I* wasn't breaking up with *him, he* was breaking up with *me.* I just didn't want to see him anymore, so I said "fine, tell people what you like, I don't really care." And I didn't care, so long as Aaron was out of the picture. But then, a few weeks later, I met up with some of his friends at a club. They kept asking me all of these weird questions, like "are you feeling better?" and "is it good to be back home again?" I had absolutely no idea what they were talking about. Eventually it came out that Aaron had told everyone he'd broken up with me because I was mentally ill and that I'd been institutionalized for "probably a very long time." But I got my own back by telling them the "real" reason we broke up, which was because Aaron was crap in bed. I told them not to tell him this though, because it wasn't his fault he only had a three-inch dick.

Joel (formerly of San Francisco, California, USA) He's in jail for murder, what more can I say?

Zach (Bristol, England, UK) Zach and I met at college, became an item, and eventually moved out together to share expenses in our final year. After graduation,

Zach landed a great job at a computer firm. But while Zach was doing really well for himself, things hadn't gone so great for me. I hadn't found any work in the area I wanted and still had my casual job from college waitressing at a café. But I was happy for Zach, because I figured if I kept going to interviews and being positive about things, something would eventually turn up like it did for him. As the months went by, Zach seemed to spend more and more time at the office. However everything *really* went weird when he got his second pay-rise in six months. This seemed to go to his head and he went around bragging to everyone about how he was now on $63,000 a year and making more than his parents were, let alone his friends. I tried to talk to him about it, but he told me I was just jealous and that from now on I'd have to pay my own way, that he wasn't going to carry my "dead weight" anymore (remember this is coming from my boyfriend of two years, the guy who's making $63,000, while I'm making about $14,000 a year). So I scraped by for a while until Zach insisted on moving into a new apartment, an expensive one to go with his "new lifestyle." I told him I couldn't afford it, that I was moving back home to my parents and that I didn't want to see him anymore if he was going to act like a complete fool. The beautiful thing about it, though, was that six months later I got my dream job and he lost his. Sucked in Zach!

Dale (Auckland, New Zealand) Because I was stupid enough to get a tattoo with him just before I found out he was sleeping with someone else. It cost me over a grand to get his name taken off my sweet pink behind.

I call up Sarah to brag

Naturally, I have to call up Sarah and brag. Now that I've got a PA I'm so high up the evolutionary career scale that it's starting to make me dizzy. How can I explain it? It's like I'm suddenly so successful and important that somebody else has to be employed to do my job for me!

I know Sarah's still away on a shoot, so I try and call her cell. She hasn't rung to say how everything's going, which means that I haven't heard from her in over a week. I'm a bit worried that I haven't heard anything, because she usually calls every night when she's doing tampon-type commercials. Let me explain. These tampon commercials usually involve her and a few other models running around a beach with skimpy bikinis on in the middle of winter. While they do this, inevitably the local hooligans stand just out of camera shot and admire the models' nipples. The funny thing is, while most people think models are party animals, Sarah usually spends each night of these kind of shoots defrosting in the bath of her motel room so she doesn't get pneumonia. So, you see, that's why I get a bit worried.

It's ringing (the phone that is).

"Hello?" a guy answers.

Immediately I wonder if I've got the right number. "Hi, this is Gemma, is, um, is Sarah there?"

"Oh God, not you. Look, Sarah's busy right now."

The voice sounds familiar. Too familiar. And he obviously knows who I am. "Who's there?"

"Sarah's busy, all right? She'll be home Sunday morning, call her then," he says then hangs up rudely.

And then I realize who it is.

It's Barry.

Bastard Barry. Barry who used to be Sarah's modeling agent. Barry who used to tell her she was fat. Barry who used to tell her she was ugly. Barry whose fault it was that Sarah ended up in the hospital, way too underweight for her own good.

I put the phone down, stunned. Barry hasn't been around for years, not since Sarah quit modeling full time after the hospital stint.

And then I put two and two together.

Sarah did about four or five jobs last year in total when she was working full time. This year she's only been working casually at Star Graphics and she's managed to do twice the amount of modeling jobs she did last year and it's only April. It can only mean one thing.

Barry's back.

Barry's back as her agent and it's Barry who's been getting her the jobs.

Barry the Bastard.

I can't believe she'd be so stupid.

And I can't believe that she hasn't told me, her best friend. Oh, it's not that I don't understand *why* she hasn't told me—she knew that I'd go psycho. She knows me that well, at least. And why shouldn't I? This guy, Barry, first of all he drags Sarah's self-esteem so low it's practically invisible, and then he almost kills her by making her lose twenty-two pounds. Twenty-two pounds my very tall and very skinny best friend could ill afford.

I pace around the room looking for something of reasonable size and shape that I could beat Sarah over the head with. But it's a pointless exercise because a) I don't have anything big and heavy enough, and b) she's not here.

I fling myself onto the couch in disgust. How long did she think she could go before I found out? She must have known I'd catch on sooner or later.

Preferably later, I'm sure.

I hang around fuming about this for an hour or two, thinking of all the things I'm going to say and do to Sarah when I get a hold of her. "She'll be home Sunday morning," Barry said. Sunday morning. That's tomorrow morning. I decide I'll leave it till Sunday night to call her, so I can work out what I'm going to say.

But, in the end, I don't call her, because she calls me first.

At 7:00 I come to realize I can't be bothered cooking dinner (again) and head out to the local Thai for some take-out. When I get home, the red light is flickering on the answering machine. Instinctively, I know it's Sarah.

I push the button.

"Hi, Gem, it's me. I'm coming home tomorrow, but I've got some work to catch up on, so how about dinner tomorrow night? I was thinking about that pasta place, you know, the one we went to a couple of weeks ago. If you don't call me back, I'll see you there at 7:30, OK? Byeee!"

I'm glad I wasn't here to pick up the phone because I'm sure I couldn't have held myself back from quizzing her about Barry. I take my plastic bag out to the kitchen and while I eat my take-out, I debate the dinner thing. And I decide to go. Apart from the fact that it means I won't have to cook dinner again, it'll give me a whole twenty-four hours to cool off and gather my wits for the confrontation. The confrontation that Sarah has no idea is about to hit her with all the force of Cyclone Tracy.

I eye off the answering machine as if it's Sarah herself. Seven-thirty, hey? I can hardly wait.

Dinner

The following night, I coach myself in the fine art of friend intervention. I coach myself in the shower, I coach myself as I dry my hair, I coach myself on the way to "that pasta place we went to a couple of weeks ago." Keep calm, Gemma, I say to myself. Don't attack. Just act like everything's fine and see what Sarah has to say. Maybe there's a good reason Barry picked up the phone.

As if.

Because I can't see why there'd be *any* good reason for Barry to pick up the phone. Why would he? I wonder what kind of excuse Sarah is going to come up with (in case you don't know, Sarah is the lamest on-the-spot excuse maker on the planet). Maybe she'll tell me he just happened to be at Bondi one wintry Sunday and they bumped into each other. Or, by some freak coincidence he was seated beside her on the plane and, oops, they switched cells by mistake? Or perhaps it wasn't him, it was simply a passing alien who *sounded* like Barry?

When I walk into the restaurant Sarah is already seated at a table near the back.

Everything's normal, everything's normal, I repeat to myself as I make my way over.

That's right, everything's normal.

"Hey," Sarah says as I sit down. "It feels like I haven't seen you for ages."

I can't meet her gaze and suddenly, placing my napkin

square on my lap becomes the most important task in the world.

"Have you been avoiding me?" Sarah says, jokingly. "Your answering machine and your voicemail were on all day—I couldn't get through to you. I wasn't even sure you'd turn up tonight."

"Ha, ha," I laugh. But it's a laugh that doesn't sound quite real.

"So, what's new?"

The only thing that's new is my PA. But while I'd been bursting to tell my best friend all about it yesterday, I didn't feel like it now because of the Barry thing. I feel like she doesn't deserve to hear my good news. I try to think of what we'd talk about if everything were normal, if I didn't know about Barry.

That's easy—bitching—what else?

And I'd heard from my mother earlier that day, so I have *plenty* of material to work with. I get down to business. "Well, the man who calls himself my father has remarried again and then has failed miserably in some real estate venture, managing to rip off both his business partner and hundreds of poor people in the process," I offer, then fill Sarah in on the rest of the story. Except that, while I'm mid-bitch, Sarah laughs.

"What's so funny?"

"Your dad, he's such a character. He could con his way in and out of anything."

I look at her. "He's not a character. He's an MPB. A manipulative, philandering bastard. What's so funny about that? The fact is, sometimes I'm . . ." I pause. "Sometimes I'm ashamed I'm even related to him."

"Oh come on, Gemma, stop carrying on. You've got to see the funny side of it. He just can't help himself, he's sketchy to the core. But funny sketchy, like that Fagin guy, you know, out of that movie we saw on TV."

I roll my eyes in exasperation. She's talking about Fagin from *Oliver* and I realize she has no idea that it was once a book in any shape or form, let alone a book by Charles Dickens. But by the time I'm ready to correct her, she's moved on to talking about my parents.

"And your mum and dad as a couple, they're such a scream. Even though he's remarried again, you know they'll be back together within a couple of months. You have to laugh about it."

But I'm not laughing.

And I'm not laughing because it's simply not funny. This is my *father* we're talking about. He's supposed to be a bit above all this. He's supposed to be reliable and dependable, a pipe-smoking, retired university professor with two labradors, or a golf-loving, buggy-driving Rotarian like other people's dads—not some swinging cocktail on legs. Dependable. The word jumps out at me. For a moment it's hard to believe I just used this word in a sentence pertaining to my father. And while I hate it that I can't depend on him for anything, by now, it's something I'm well used to.

"There's nothing funny about it," I say. "He's been ripping people off again, his specialty. And if I know him, they're probably pensioners."

Sarah laughs, "Oh, come on, Gemma. You know he's not like that. Anyway, there're two sides to every story. You should call him, talk to him—he'd be happy to hear from you."

I snort. "No thanks."

"Whatever," Sarah shrugs. "I just think it might be different if you heard it from him. Maybe he's got his reasons."

Oh, I'm sure he's got his reasons. As for the new wife—younger, blonder, tighter bikini, better plastic surgeon. And the ripping people off thing—as far as my father's concerned money's money, right? I start to wonder whose side Sarah's on here, because I don't think it's mine. Thankfully the waiter gives us a reprieve (read: stops me from leaning over and throttling Sarah) by coming over to take our drink orders. I order a glass of chardonnay and hope it comes quickly, because I'm beginning to think I'm going to need it. Any kind of anesthetic is useful when I have to think about my father.

"So have you heard about Brett?"

Big mistake.

"No."

"Well, he's been seeing this girl for ages and rumor has it that . . ."

"Let's just stop there, shall we?" I wave my hand and butt in, because I think I know where she's going with this. And I'm really angry now, because Sarah knows I don't like to hear about "that bastard who left me" and what "that bastard who left me" has been doing and who "that bastard who left me" has been seeing and anything about "that bastard who left me" in general.

"What?" Sarah raises an eyebrow.

I don't answer her because she knows very well *what*.

The waiter brings our wine over and I swear the guy can feel the tension in the air, because he practically throws it at us and runs. I take a sip and a thought comes to me. "If 'that bastard who left me' ever does get married," I say, "If there's any girl stupid enough in the world to walk down the aisle with him, I could do that thing in the wedding ceremony, you know, at that bit where they ask if there's any reason they can't be married. I should stand up and say he's got herpes or something, that I'm from the STD clinic."

Sarah narrows her eyes as she looks at me. "Don't be stupid, Gemma."

And even I can tell that the usually patient Sarah is cracking under her foundation. I decide to push it to the limit, to see just how far I can go before little Miss Makeup will react.

"Since when have you been on his side? He was the one who left *me*, remember?"

"How could I forget?" she mutters into her drink.

"What's that supposed to mean?" I put my glass down.

Sarah puts hers down too, loudly. "So Brett left *you*, we all know that. God, how we all know that. But you'll have to get over it sometime and be able to speak to him civilly, won't you?"

I cross my arms and sit back in my chair. If that's how she wants to play it, fine by me. Two can play at this game and I've got the trump card.

Time to pull it out.

"So how was your trip. How was *Barry*?" I ask her.

Sarah picks up her glass and takes a sip of wine. "What?"

"I said, how was Barry?"

She eyes me warily. "What do you mean?"

"Oh, come on, Sarah. I spoke to him. He answered your cell. Anything you'd like to tell me about your little trip?"

She looks away. "So that's what you're so angry about. He's been getting me some work, that's all."

"So why Barry? Why not someone else?"

"He's the best," she shrugs.

I can't believe this. Has she forgotten everything that happened? How he made her lose all that weight and she ended up in the hospital. And now she's going back for seconds. I look at her and wonder—is she sane?

"What?" Sarah asks as I keep staring at her. "What?"

I shake my head. "This is just so, so stupid."

"What's so stupid?" Sarah butts in. "I know he's a bastard, but he's the best. He can get me the work and this time I'll just look after myself better, I'm a little older and a little wiser now. I'll be all right."

I take a good look at her. With the baggy jacket and jeans I can't really tell, but I take a stab in the dark anyway. "And how much weight have you lost so far?"

She looks me straight in the eye. "Eight pounds."

"I don't believe this."

115

"Oh, come on. I had to lose a bit if I wanted to start back up again. I was fat after all those bagels and cream cheese you fed me—I practically turned into bloated Elvis! I'm not going to lose any more than eleven pounds though, if you really must know."

Now I know she *is* insane, calling herself fat. Fat. Sarah's never been fat in her life. She doesn't know the meaning of the word. She puts eleven pounds onto her bony, skeletal-looking frame and she thinks she's fat. What did she think I was—the resident heifer? I look at her and shake my head. This stinks of Barry and there's no way I'm going to see her go through that again. I reach out across the table and grab Sarah's wrist.

"Get rid of him, Sarah."

She wrenches her arm free. "Stop overreacting, I told you I'm fine."

"That's what you said last time. You weren't."

"This isn't anything like last time. Listen to yourself, you sound like I'm working full time again or something. I'm only going to be doing a job a month or less and I'm still working at Star Graphics. It's just pocket money. I need to save a bit and it's better money than if I was working full time."

I snort. "You didn't save much last time, did you? And that was when you were working full time as a model." And I know she'll go ballistic as the words come out of my mouth because I've alluded to the unmentionable—the drugs thing that went along with the modeling. The thing that she hinted about, but never came right out and said. The reason she went away for a "rest" at a "special health resort" after she got out of the hospital.

Sarah narrows her eyes. "Fuck you."

I stand up. "Fine. If you can't see how stupid this all is, then that's your problem. How did you expect me to take it? It's like me walking up to you and saying everything's back on

116

with the big 'B,' he's left his fiancée for me and we're getting married. Want to be a bridesmaid?"

"Typical," Sarah spits, and stands up as well. "It's typical that this all has to come back to you and Brett. Poor Gemma, Brett left her. Well the whole Brett thing's getting a little sorry and old now, so why don't you just get the fuck over it? And while you're at it, try using his name instead of saying 'that bastard who left me' or 'the big "B," ' because it's driving us all insane. Anyway, maybe if you'd listened to him he wouldn't have left—maybe you'd have been able to work things out. But you didn't, did you? You just acted like there was nothing the matter, as if you could ignore it and it'd just go away. God, the number of times that poor guy called me . . . And I've tried to be there for you, really I have, but the way you twist the story, it's just not true. Brett leaving was just as much your fault as it was his and I'm sick to death of hearing your sick little version of the tale. And as for your father, I'm tired of hearing about that, too. Not everything's about you, you know. Take five minutes and get over yourself, Gemma."

I stand and listen to the entire rant. It's pretty funny actually, especially the way she runs out of breath about three times and has to keep stopping so she doesn't turn blue. Everyone in the restaurant is watching us, the evening's entertainment. But I do listen to what she has to say, if only to give her the bored expression that I know she hates so much. And when she's done I push my chair in and go to leave, stopping on the way past her.

"Enjoy your dinner," I say. "The toilets are at the back if you want to throw it all up later."

Touché.

I find out the
downside to having a
PA
(read: Chris makes
me work)

I push the whole Sarah incident to the back of my mind—I don't want to and can't talk to her while she's being so stupid. On one hand, I hope she's right, I hope Barry *can* get her work without affecting her mentally, but on the other hand, I don't quite believe this can be true. So, for a while, I decide I'll avoid her (which isn't hard because she's obviously decided to avoid me, too).

Meanwhile, there's plenty to keep me busy on the work front. My PA and I (*my PA and I,* oh how I love saying that) spend our first week together chained to our respective computers. On his first day at work, I drag out and dust off ye olde laptop (and I do mean ye olde) and from then on Chris works on that, the traitor cat Imogen lying at his feet. It may not be quite up to the standard of his former job (I find out the financial adviser he'd worked for had lived in a five-bedroom penthouse on the twenty-sixth floor of a luxury apartment building), but hey, it's a job and Chris seems to like it in his own way. As a bonus, I tell him he can have free "International Roast" coffee, stinky, expired milk from the fridge, and as much toilet paper and stationery as he can conceal on his person. So, all in all, it's pretty much like a real job.

And we get on fine, most of the time. At first, I think Chris is a little quiet, but I just put it down to him being the strong and silent type, which, incidentally, is my favorite.

Not that I am looking for anything like that, of course.

Because after the whole big "B" episode, I don't think it's likely I'll be seeing anyone for a long, long time.

By week two, I still haven't found out what Michael thinks we have in common. And by the end of week three I know I probably won't find out what it is from Chris himself, because I've learned that if there's one thing Chris guards jealously, it's his private life. He isn't just the quiet type, he's the mute type.

At first I don't notice what's going on. If I ask Chris a personal question, he'll distract me by turning the question around and asking me something instead, or by moving on to another topic. But as time passes, I start to realize that Chris knows a lot about me and I don't know much about him at all.

So with a lack of any real information to go on, in week four I start to make up my own. On Monday I decide Chris is running from the law (the one-armed man did him some terrible wrong). On Wednesday, he's an Austrian prince, but is searching the world for a good woman to marry (a peasant-type like me) who isn't after his money. On Friday, he's the love child of Elvis and Marilyn Monroe.

And I have quite a lot of time to think about these things, because Chris is very efficient, too efficient really, because he's not leaving me a lot of work to do. But he tells me things will get busier and I'll have heaps more to do once we get the T-shirts, stickers, and other merchandise for sale up on the site. Then I'll be filling orders, running back and forth to the post office, and organizing the paperwork for the credit card orders.

I can hardly wait.

Another thing Chris does all too well is organize my time. I'll get up and say something along the lines of, "I'm just going to the shops for an hour or so," and in under a minute Chris will have me sitting back down, working again.

I really don't know how he does it.

So, by 6:30 Friday night, we've done all of the work there is to do. We've replied to all the e-mail, fended off another defamation lawyer, scored $2,000 in advertising, opened up a special bank account, and deposited the first advertising check.

But what's even more impressive is that we'd cleaned up the mess on my desk and made Chris a whole little workspace of his own.

I have to face it. Chris is a breath of fresh air, a thing of beauty, the PA of my dreams (by now I seem to have forgotten about the dry cleaning and the fresh basil). In a kind of freaky way he reminds me of Radar from *M*A*S*H*. Remember him? Well, like Radar, Chris seems to sense what I want before *I* even know I want it. If I'm about to get up to look for a certain piece of paper, Chris will hand it to me. If I want a cup of coffee, one will suddenly appear beside me. When the poor guy brings me some advertising contracts to sign I manage to confuse him totally. "Hey, I didn't just sign for another distiller for the swamp did I, Radar?" I ask Chris, who just looks at me as if I'm from another planet (probably Venus).

I don't think he got it.

But, as I said, Chris really is *too* efficient, because on Friday he finds some new work for me to do over the weekend.

Homework!

And it's a definite shock to the system because I haven't had any since high school.

Chris wants me to work out a few T-shirt and sticker designs. But by the time he leaves at 7:00 Friday night, I'm so exhausted I can barely be bothered to move from my chair at the computer. It's cocktails night and I know I should be sitting at the bar with Sarah, but with us not talking, that's hardly going to happen, is it? I feel a bit sad really, because this is the first time in years that we've missed cocktails without actually agreeing to skip it. Even if we can't go on the Friday night, we'll usually arrange it so that we go for happy hour on the Wednesday or Thursday instead (we decided early on that it was a touch desperate for a nice girl to go to a bar on a Monday or Tuesday). In fact, I've only ever missed one week of cocktails before, and that was when I'd had the flu. I'd still tried desperately to get to the bar. It was when I'd thrown up for the third time (and hadn't even reached my bedroom door) that I'd decided I probably shouldn't go and had crawled back into bed.

So even though it's a Friday night, I stay home. I have a long hot bath, don my jammies, and plonk myself on the couch in front of the TV. I even grab a notebook and pencil in case "design inspiration" comes from above (or even from down below, I'm neither religious nor fussy).

But it obviously doesn't, because I wake up Saturday morning on the couch, TV still on, and nothing written in the notebook at all (oh, yes, and we'll overlook the drool patch on the arm of the couch, shall we?).

I try to figure out
Chris

The weekend passes and, as it tends to do, the work week starts back up again.

Today, Monday, we are deluged with e-mails and are working so hard we don't notice time passing at all. Chris arrives at 9 AM. Then, when I next look up at the clock, it's 2:30 PM and we still haven't had morning tea, lunch, or numerous smoke/water cooler breaks (neither of us smoke and we don't have a water cooler, but as workers of the world I feel we're entitled to the slacking off time).

I look over at Chris who is typing furiously, Imogen draped nonchalantly around his neck like some old fox fur, which can't be comfortable for either of them. "How about if we go out for lunch?" I say. "My treat."

Chris keeps typing as if his life depends on it. "Great, I'll just finish off this e-mail and we're ready."

I'm glad Chris has agreed (for a moment there I had visions of him stapling me to the computer and insisting I keep on working). But I have to admit that I have ulterior motives for our little working lunch. The whole Austrian prince/one-armed man/Elvis and Marilyn thing is getting a little tired by now and I want to get to know Chris a little better. He *is* my PA—aren't we supposed to do girly-type things like shoe shopping and foundation buying? Aren't we supposed to share secrets about the awful guys we slept with on the weekend? (The truth is, if Chris really *is* into things like shoe shopping and men, I don't want to know about it. However, if he's looking for a foundation I think I'd steer him toward an ivory beige.)

Well, I guess I knew from the start that things would be a little different with a male PA. Different to my sitcom fantasy, anyway.

However, what I do know for certain is that after working together for three weeks, Chris and I might be getting along like a house on fire, but I still don't know very much about him. Sure, he works like a trooper, but who *is* he? What is his life story? What does he think about the big issues like abortion and euthanasia? And, more importantly, as my PA, will he eat the black jelly beans and the pink marshmallows that I don't like?

Since I'd cottoned on to Chris's distraction tactics over the past few weeks, I'd tried to be a little bit more tricky with my line of questioning. I'd even tried the open-ended question thing. But still, he'd slipped past and evaded my questions like a greasy pig (now there's a disgusting thought). While this hadn't bothered me a week or so ago, now it was starting to piss me off a little. He knew plenty about *me*, too much actually, and now it was time to share and share alike, *Playschool* style.

Anyway, that was my little reason for our "social" outing. I thought that if I took him out for lunch he might loosen up a little and swing from the chandeliers.

I go and grab my purse and wait by the door while Chris extricates himself from Imogen's grasp. Then he makes a quick trip to the toilet. Now I know you'll think I'm a bitch when I tell you this, but when he leaves I spy his jacket still sitting on his chair and I do a quick once-through of his pockets.

Oh, come on, as if you wouldn't do the same thing! His jacket was just sitting there. Anyway, there wasn't anything in the pockets. Just an old hanky . . . Well, I was desperate, all right? I just couldn't help myself. I've never been very good with curiosity and resisting the temptation to read people's diaries and things like that.

We leave the house and as we set off down the road for the bagel shop I begin the interrogation. "So you used to live in the most boring place on Earth, hey?"

Chris nods. "Yeah, I grew up there—I've lived there all my life. My parents are still there, but my brother and my sisters moved overseas a couple of years ago."

I nod. So far so good, though I notice he still hasn't told me where the most boring place on Earth actually *is*. Personally, I'm guessing Canberra. So, I count that as one "personal question" point to Gemma (not that I'm keeping score or anything). I get a bit excited at my small victory and have to tell myself to wait for a minute or two before I ask the next question—I don't want to seem *too* obvious. I get to about twenty seconds before I cave. "So how come you moved?"

He shrugs. "For a change, I guess. It was just about as far away as I could get without leaving the country."

"Oh, right." (That's two "personal question" points to Gemma.) I spend the rest of the short trip to the bagel shop planning my next move.

Chris orders a chicken pastrami and salad on a sundried tomato bagel and I get my usual plain chocolate chip. When we sit down I quickly stuff a largish-sized piece in my mouth to stop me asking the "big question"—the question I *really* want to ask. We eat in silence for a while before Chris speaks up. "So is that a photo of Brett on your mantelpiece?"

I think I just lost all of my "personal question" points.

I choke and reach for my drink and wish I'd had the guts to take the stupid photo down months ago. Instead, I've just left it there to gather dust, pretending I don't see it, that it doesn't bother me, when I really know that it does. I open my mouth and am about to say a good few words about "that bastard who left me" when I close it again, because Sarah's words from our fight at the restaurant are ringing in my ears. Specifically the ones about not saying "that bastard who left me" or "the big

'B.' " For once, I think before I speak and I think that maybe I should use the name his parents gave him in front of my new PA. I mean, I don't want to scare Chris off or anything.

I open my mouth again. "Yeah, that's Brett," I say, then I get suspicious. "How do you know about all that?" I ask him, like I don't already know that Mr. Michael bigmouth is at the bottom of all this. He's obviously given Chris the entire rundown on "the real Gemma," probably including a specially marked calendar of when my period is due so Chris can keep out of the way of my PMS-nasty-type-self.

"Michael told me. I hope that's OK."

Surprise, surprise.

Well, it isn't OK, but there's not a lot I can do about it now, is there? Apart from rip Michael's gossiping bloody tonsils out with rusty pliers the next time I see him.

We eat in silence. Me thinking about Brett and Chris thinking about . . . well, how should I know? I'm no mind reader.

"Exactly how much did Michael tell you about the Brett thing?" I finally ask.

"Um, not much."

"No, really." I can tell he's lying—the guy is practically transparent.

"Well, everything I guess," he grins.

"Typical."

"Sorry?"

"I said that's typical. Michael can never keep his mouth shut for five minutes at a time."

Chris just looks at me in return, a bit surprised maybe.

And yeah, yeah, I know what *you're* thinking, people in glass houses and all that, but I was pretty pissed off that Michael had blabbed all the gory bits of my personal life to my PA. Wasn't I supposed to do that myself as a bonding exercise? Well, if that's the way it was—if Chris knew everything about my personal life, why shouldn't I know anything about his? He hadn't volunteered one single piece of information since

I'd met him. Not one! And here I was, the boss so to speak, and he had all the dirt on *me*. Time for some retribution, I think, polishing off the last of my bagel and brushing my hands together. There was no holding me back now.

"So," I cough, a bit of my bagel still stuck in my throat, "Have you got a girlfriend/fiancée/significant other?"

"No. Not now."

Not now? I smell a fresh breakup. "Is that why you moved?"

He shrugs again and looks away as if something has caught his attention. It's a while before he turns back. "Hey," he says, "I've got a joke for you."

A joke? What happened to my question?

"What do you get when you cross a nun with a computer?"

I look at him like he's crazy. "What?"

"A computer that'll never go down on you!"

He is crazy. "What're you talking about? I asked you a question."

Chris looks at me as if to say, "What question?"

I've had it now. "No more distractions, Chris. I asked you a question. Is that why you moved? Did you break up with someone?"

Even I know I'm pushing it a bit too far now. And when I spit out the bit about breaking up with someone, Chris turns his face up and looks directly at me. "I didn't say there *was* anybody," he says a bit too loudly and people turn and look at us.

I can tell by the tone in his voice that this is the end of the conversation. "I take it it was a messy breakup," I say sourly, still pushing for that last scrap of information (hey, you never know).

"Look," he says, scrunching the rest of his bagel up in its wrapper and throwing it into the bin. "Like I said, I didn't say there was anybody and even if there had been I wouldn't want to talk about it here and now, OK? When you said you were buying me lunch I didn't expect the Spanish Inquisition."

If I'd been in a better mood I would have stood up and shouted the infamous Monty Python line about the Spanish Inquisition, but as it is, I'm too pissed off. Instead, I stand up and throw my bagel wrapper in the bin after his. "Fine!" I say. "Don't talk then. Don't talk about anything." I move in closer to Chris. "I won't know you and you won't know me and I'm sure we'll get along just fine! I'm sure Michael will tell you anything else you need to know about me, anyway," I say, giving my chair a good kick for emphasis.

Chris stands up. "I guess I'd better get going."

Uh-oh, he's leaving. I've done it now—I've scared off my PA. No more dry cleaning and fresh basil for me. I stand up and touch Chris's arm as he walks past me, realizing I should apologize. "Chris, I'm sorry, you don't have to tell me anything, it's none of my business. I just wanted us to go to lunch to get to know one another a little better, that's all."

"Whatever," he shrugs. "It's just that you hit a sore spot. There was someone, but I don't want to talk about it, OK? It's over. That's it. Finito."

I pause. Then, "I know," I say. And I *do* know. I know exactly how Chris feels, even if he doesn't know it, and now I'm sorry I pushed so hard. "So are we, like, OK?" I ask him. I don't want to lose Chris my miracle worker.

"Sure, sure," he nods. "Same time Wednesday?"

I nod back, "Great. I'll see you then."

Chris leaves and I watch him as he goes, still not being able to figure out why Michael thinks we've got so much in common, when we don't seem to. Then I walk three shops up to the liquor store where I buy myself some red wine to drink that night so I won't have to think about anything much anymore. And maybe, particularly, about Brett.

Somehow I think this whole change of lifestyle (read: work) is all getting to be a bit too much.

I drink the whole thing

My third glass into the bottle that night, I sit down in front of the computer to see how the e-mail is plodding along. Actually, I'm quite pleased with the way things are going because (despite this afternoon's little indiscretion) Chris and I now have the site virtually under control.

Virtually. Ha ha. (See what amuses me after more than two glasses of wine?)

But seeing as I've got to do some work on my own tomorrow (unsupervised), I figure I should check out exactly how much I'm going to have to do. (What I mean is, I'm wondering if I can drink the *whole* bottle of wine, or whether I'll have to restrain myself because I have to get up early.)

So I check the e-mail and then quickly read through a few of the entries that have just come in. But as I keep reading, I start to wish I hadn't checked it in the first place, because there's one message, from a girl called Courtney, that blows me away. I don't want to repeat it, because, believe me, you don't want to know. Let's just say it involves a lot of nasty things happening to her and three guys ending up in jail because of it.

One of them is her uncle.

I read the e-mail twice and carefully place my wine glass down on the table, disgusted with these men, disgusted with myself. Here I am wallowing in self-pity and drowning my sorrows with a bottle of wine. What do people like Courtney need? A carton or two, a truck? A truckload of counseling more like it. I look back at the e-mail again, wondering why

I'm so shocked. I know things like this happen, I see them on the news every night, read about them in magazines and the paper. But this is so real. So physical. It's as if I can actually see those guys doing these things to her. I shake my head, wanting to cry, but not being able to.

God men suck.

They really do.

They just take your self-esteem and trash it. Leave it lying in the dirt, crumpled and shaken and begging for mercy.

I keep reading the e-mail over and over again.

And then, with the perfect timing he's always had, that's when Brett calls.

Brett, the ex-fiancé.

Or rather, Brett, *my* ex-fiancé. Aka the big "B," or "that bastard who left me." The ex-fiancé I prefer not to talk about (I guess that's the reason why I "forgot" to mention some of the minor details of our relationship up until now).

"Hi, Gem," he says, chirpy as ever.

"Fuck you and the horse you rode in on, Brett," is what I want to say, and it wouldn't just be the wine talking. But I don't say it because years of manner-bashing at private school tell me I mustn't and I shan't. Instead I opt for a sour, muttered version of, "Hello, Brett."

"So how are you?" he continues.

"Peachy keen," I keep on with the sour motif. "What can I do for you?" I ask. Why else would the guy call me unless he wanted something?

"Well, actually, I don't want anything. In fact, I have something to tell you."

"And that would be . . ." I don't have the time or the energy to play games with Brett. As far as I'm concerned I've played them all already and the last, biggest and most important one I lost.

"I'm engaged!" he says.

My mouth hangs open and I simply don't know what to say.

Brett, engaged? Who'd be so stupid? But then I remember what Sarah told me the night we went out for dinner, something about him seeing a girl for ages, and I think maybe she was trying to warn me.

"Gemma? I said I'm engaged."

Finally I think of something to say. "Again?"

"What?"

I try another approach. "And will you be leaving her six months before the wedding too?"

"Come on, Gem, don't be like that. You'd like her. She's really nice."

Oh great, I think. Not like me. I wasn't "really nice," was I? Not "really nice" enough to stick around for, anyway.

"Gem, are you still there? Gemma?"

"What?"

"I just thought you'd like to know. You know, before the invitation comes and everything."

The invitation? This thing was actually going through? The thought crosses my mind that Brett's being half decent calling and telling me, but there's no way in the world I'm going to thank him for it.

The prick.

Oh, so you think I'm sounding a little harsh, do you? Well, let me tell you, life doesn't look so rosy when you're left to return a wedding dress, sell an engagement ring, and beg to get a refund on your reception deposit. It's a little . . . how should I put it? *Demeaning.* That's it. It's just a little demeaning. So, this is why, a year on, I'm more than a little pissed at Brett. Who, incidentally, is still gabbling on . . .

"Maybe we should get together some time, you, me and Ju . . ."

"Not bloody likely!" I manage to belt out before I slam the phone down. I wasn't going to let Brett go down the "let's all be friends" garden path while I still had a say in things. I look down at the phone knowing I've been ruder than I should have been, but at least it's for a reason. Brett was about to say her name and that's one thing I don't want to know. Maybe because it'd make the whole thing too real. Like it really *is* going to happen, or something. I mean, invitations can always be canceled. I, for one, know that much.

Michael's always trying to fill me in on Brett's latest and greatest, but I've learned to plug my ears and sing *"I'm not listening, I'm not listening"* really loud, over and over so I can't hear what he's saying. It still hurts too much to hear about it and if I don't know, it's easier not to care, if you get what I mean. Which basically describes my whole attitude toward Brett—avoidance.

I sigh and turn around, spying the computer again. Bloody men.

Bloody Chris.

Bloody Brett.

Bloody guys who hurt Courtney.

Oh, bloody everyone.

I pick up my half-full glass of wine (see I *am* an optimist at heart, it's just my life that sucks) and go back to the familiar glow of the computer screen. Taking a sip from the glass, I move the mouse and my flying toasters disappear to reveal the e-mail from Courtney, still sitting and waiting for a reply.

But what to say?

I look back at the phone, surprised that Brett hasn't called back. He used to call back when I'd hang up on him (and believe me, there were more than a few times). But then, that was before he left me.

Ugh.

Left me, I hate saying that. It isn't the finality of it or anything, it's more the emphasis on the final word: me. He left *me.* It is always so much more graceful to be the leaver, not the leavee.

Even now I resent the fact that he got in first.

The bastard.

If it was anybody else pissing me off, I would have called Sarah (not that I'm talking to her at the moment) but the truth is I don't talk about Brett very much. Not to anyone. From the start I've tried to pretend that it wasn't the big deal it so obviously is. But I don't know who I'm fooling, because Brett leaving me hurt. And even now, after all this time, it still manages to twist my guts.

Courtney's e-mail catches my eye again and I turn back to the computer screen. I remind myself I'm supposed to be thinking about *her* problems, not mine—my problems with Brett pale in comparison. I sit and try to think of something to write for ages. Then it hits me—at least I can empathize, tell her about Brett or something. I press the reply button and start typing—quickly, so I won't back out.

To: courtneym@notmail.com
From: gemma@allmenarebastards.com

Dear Courtney,

Thanks for your e-mail which made me think, I mean *really* made me stop and think. Actually, setting up this whole site has made me think about a lot of things. In the past, when I've added guys to the bastard list, I've thought that what they've done is the worst thing that could ever happen to me, you know? But reading everyone else's entries has truly opened my eyes. I just got a call from my ex-fiancé who walked out on me six months before our wedding. That was almost a year ago and now he's engaged. Again. And, funnily enough, not to me this time. Apparently this time it's to someone "really nice."
I know this is nothing compared to your problems, I should be thankful that he didn't beat me or that he wasn't an alcoholic or something, but I can't. You know

why he called me? He called to say the wedding invitation's in the mail.
Gee, thanks. Would you like a little salt with your
wound? My brain tells me that this is a nice gesture,
that he warned me and everything, but I can't be
happy for him. Not yet, anyway—perhaps when I'm
50. Or maybe 85. He wanted me to meet her and play
happy families, so I hung up on him. That's not very
nice, is it? Oh well, I guess I can apologize at the wedding.
If I go, which I probably won't.
Anyway, I hope life's going well for you now and that
you're feeling better about yourself. I think that's the
hardest part—feeling better about yourself. I am, I
think. About eight months ago, there were days I was
so depressed I could hardly crawl out of bed. Things
aren't like that anymore. To be fair, some days I still
think about my ex a lot, but then, other days, I won't
think about him at all.
I like the other days the best.

Gemma

I reread the e-mail, not quite believing how easily it has all
spilled out, especially the part about being depressed. And I
thank God that seems to be over, because it was awful. I just
couldn't cope with anything—not even paying the phone bill.
What I mean is, it wasn't just, "I'm having a bad day" depressed. It was actual, clinical depression. The kind my doctor
wanted me to take pills for. And I haven't told *anyone* about
that. So what was I doing telling a total stranger?

I look at my e-mail, shocked at what I've just confessed. And
then, before I can back out, I press the send button and
watched the blue line zap across the screen, then disappear.
Courtney, whoever she is, wherever she is, has the e-mail.

I push my chair back from the table and sit for a moment before I look at my watch. It's now 2:30 AM, I *have* drunk the whole bottle of wine and I haven't gotten *any* work done. I giggle at my own naughtiness (I'm drunk, OK?), drain my glass, and head off to bed. And, being such a rebel, I decide I probably won't drink any water or brush my teeth, either.

Ha!

But really I'm not such a rebel after all, because I set my alarm clock for 7:30 AM, scared what Chris will say if he arrives on Wednesday morning and I *still* haven't got any work done.

I realize what I have
to do
OR
It comes to me in a
dream

It feels like I've only slept for about half an hour when the alarm starts and I roll over, try to hit the clock radio, miss, and fall out of bed.

Lying on the floor and staring at the ceiling, I gain a whole new perspective on my life.

And it's a bit sad really.

I have a nagging hangover, one of those ones that sticks around all day, however many Panadols, Beroccas, and vitamins you swallow. I also have too much work to do and I'm so worried about what my PA will say if I don't get it done that I'm not about to hang around in bed all morning. So, ten minutes later, I find myself sighing in the shower again (that's sighing, not singing) and lamenting the whole bottle of red wine debacle.

I'd like to stay in the shower till the hot water runs out, but I remember about Courtney and start wondering if she's replied to my e-mail. And, unable to resist temptation again, soon enough I find myself scampering out to the computer, drying my hair on the way, to check my e-mail.

I double click on the "In" box to see what has collected overnight and skim down the list. Boring, boring, boring, boring, another company interested in advertising, great! Boring, boring. Courtney.

Double clicking again, I wait eagerly to read her e-mail.

There's this one part that really hits home:

I'm always asking these questions, asking myself if the whole thing was partly my fault, or maybe it happened

because I didn't handle things right (even though I
know that these things aren't true). I like to think I'm
getting better as every day passes though, because
I'm finding that I'm asking myself these questions less
and less. Hopefully, one day, I won't ask them at all.

I finish drying off my hair with my towel and reread the
part about the questions again. What Courtney had written
really does hit home.

She's so right about the questions. I didn't know other people did that. I thought it was only me, driving myself insane.
The truth was, the first few weeks after Brett left, that was all I
did. Basically I just stayed in bed, staring into space, not sleeping (something I solved by starting to read *War and Peace,*
which would always have me nodding off in no time—I'm still
only up to page 84), and asking myself question after question. Things like, How long had he been waiting to tell me
this? Days, weeks, months, years? How many times did he kiss
me and not mean it? How many times had we had sex and he
didn't mean it? And the big one, Why couldn't I see this coming? It was all I wanted to do, all I could do, really, to lie in bed
and ask myself these questions. I couldn't seem to bring myself
to talk to anyone else about it. Outwardly I just tried to pretend
I knew it was going to happen, that we were going to split up.
But what a big fat lie! Really, I never suspected a thing. Sarah
knew the truth, but I couldn't even talk about it to her, so in the
end she took time off work and just sat with me, making endless plates of buttered toast and cups of tea.

I press the reply button and start typing. I talk about all
these things and more. When I'm done, I lean back in my
chair and click on the send button quickly again so I can't
take anything back. Everything I tell Courtney is completely
true. I tell her how I never spoke about Brett and what had
happened, not to Sarah, not to Michael, not even to Brett
himself. He'd wanted to talk it over when he'd left, had

wanted to sit down and have a big deep and meaningful conversation. But I wouldn't give him the satisfaction. I didn't want to know about his *feelings*. Fuck that. What about *my* feelings? Apparently they didn't count for much, and I sure didn't have any say in what was going on—either way he was going to leave. So I told him to pack up and get out, to piss off and not to call me. Which probably made it worse, but it was the only way I thought I could cope.

Too much typing, too much thinking.

I hold my head in my hands. My little, persistent hangover is growing and I really feel like shit. I glance sideways at the couch. Yes, it's still over there. The couch is over there and I feel like shit. If I feel like shit I should lie on the couch, right? I haul my butt over there before I can tell myself that I should be working, and flick the answering machine to "on" as I stumble over. Imogen's on the window seat curled up into a ball and I suddenly think that looks pretty good. I do the same thing on the couch, hoping that it'll make the effects of the cheap red wine disappear. For a moment, I wonder if that's what Imogen's doing too.

Just as I'm about to fall asleep, the phone rings. I pat myself on the head for having the sense to turn on the answering machine, because if I tried to get up now, I'd probably throw up. I listen as the message runs through and then wait to see who it is. I hope it isn't Chris checking up on me.

It isn't.

"Um, hi Gem, it's me."

It's Sarah.

I open one eye and look at the answering machine, waiting to hear what she's got to say for herself. Maybe it's something nice.

Maybe Barry's been hit by a big, dirty truck.

"Look, I know you're angry about Barry, but he's still getting me lots of work and I'm fine. I wanted to tell you I got the invite to Brett's wedding. Have you gotten yours yet? He put in a note

147

with mine. Can you believe she's a sky slut? What happened to his taste, hey? Anyway, I'm so pissed off—I can't go. I've got a family thing on that day. Shit, can't talk now . . ." and she hangs up abruptly.

I roll over and groan out loud. The invitation to Brett's wedding is probably sitting in my mailbox right now.

I try to ignore it, but it preys on my mind and soon enough I'm rolling over the other way and getting up to go and check if it's there.

It is.

I carry it back inside with two fingers and sit down on the couch and just *look* at it. It's offensive. All that yucky, creamy, thick paper and the lovey dovey wedding stamp to boot. For a minute I think I really *am* going to be sick. And before I know what I'm doing I've ripped it up and thrown it in the general direction of the bin, which is where it belongs.

Then I lie back down on the couch.

Ah, the couch.

The only thing that makes me feel even the teensiest bit better about the whole wedding shebang is the fact that Brett's newly betrothed is a sky slut (Brett and my term for a female flight attendant since the fateful day one of them wouldn't give us four scotch and drys in a row and said she'd *run out* of peanuts. As if! Everyone knows they have a never-ending peanut supply).

The phone rings again and once more I wait for the message to run through. But this time I don't need to think about who it might be—it's obviously Sarah again. I know this because Sarah doesn't make phone calls from work like normal people make phone calls from work. Instead, she talks and talks and talks and then hangs up abruptly like she did before (usually when her boss is walking past because, of course, there are no personal calls allowed at Star Graphics). Then she'll ring up again five minutes later to tell you all the stuff she's forgotten to tell you during the first call. After this, half an hour later she'll ring *again* because she got caught up in talking during her first two calls and has forgotten to tell you the thing she rang for in the first place.

But the phone hangs up instead of leaving a message.

I roll over one more time, praying for sleep and for the phone to stop ringing. And this time I'm lucky, because soon enough I get both my wishes. It isn't a restful sleep, though. My headache is still pounding away and I am hot and sweaty. (Oh, excuse me, the word I'm looking for is *glowing*. According to my mother, ladies don't *sweat*, they either *glow* or *perspire*. I'm sweating.)

And I guess I've been having too many encounters with awful guys, because while I'm asleep I have this really funny dream. Sarah and Courtney and I (don't ask me how I know it's Courtney, it just is, OK?) are getting revenge. We each have to exact ten kinds of revenge on the guys who have hurt us in the past.

And it's the best dream. Probably the best dream I've ever had, because as I play out my revenge on Brett, I really start to enjoy what I'm doing. I don't remember all the things I get up to, but I *do* remember sticking numerous tampons in his nose, ears, and mouth and chasing after him with a golf club. I also remember setting the cat on him, too, saying, "Sic, Imogen, sic!" (If possible, she hates Brett even more than she hates me.)

When the phone rings again, waking me up, I am so very, very happy. I have this big smile on my face that I can't wipe off and I realize my headache is gone. I check the time. It's 2:30 and I haven't done a scrap of work. But I don't care, I just keep right on smiling. I don't think I've been quite so happy for a long time and I think to myself that this whole revenge thing is great, I've really gotten off on it. The message on the answering machine finishes and I wait to hear who it is.

"Gemma? It's Chris, I tried to ring before to see how you were doing. I hope you've got the answering machine on because you're busy working on those slogans, or the editorial or something. Anyway, I'll see you tomorrow."

Knowing I haven't done either and that I'd better get cracking, I sit up and look around, accidentally spying myself in the long mirror over the mantelpiece. My hair is standing on end, I have my daggiest tracksuit on, and a spectacular pair of panda eyes from my mascara. I also still have that silly smile on my face. In a way, I wish I could fall asleep again, just to keep on going with my sweet revenge.

Oh yes, it had been sweet.

And how!

I stare at myself in the mirror and wonder why it was so great. And all I can come up with is that it gave me some of my power back, my mojo! Up until now, Brett had had all the power—he was the one who told me it was over, he was the one who left, he was the one getting married. And me? I'd just gone along with it all, letting him decide how my life was going to be. Until my dream, that is. And even if it *was* just a dream, I still felt better, like I now had some say in our relationship, even if it was over. I had a bit of power, and I *loved* it.

I glance over at the computer and for some reason remember Courtney. Maybe that was what she needed, too. Some kind of revenge, a way of getting her own back. Then I think of all the other women who have put entries on the site. Maybe it was what they all needed, too.

Empowerment, that was it, the word I was looking for. Empowerment.

And I can't believe I haven't worked it out sooner. Isn't that why we'd made the bastard list in the first place? To empower ourselves, to say *we* had the control. That we had the control to get rid of the guy and get on with our lives. And that was why people were writing into the site, wasn't it? For empowerment, or for closure, to tell themselves that yes, this bad experience with a man had happened to them, but now they were putting it behind them and moving on. So what's so wrong with a little revenge along the way? It's healthy, cleansing even!

Right?

I stand up, amazed. Empowerment is the key. Empowerment with a little revenge mixed in along the way.

Yes!

And suddenly, I know what I have to do.

I jump off the couch and grab a notepad and pen off my desk. Then I run back to the couch and start writing. This is the same notepad that sat blank all weekend, but now I quickly fill it with line after line of my messy handwriting. When I finish covering the first page, I flip it over and start on the next one. Then another and another until my stomach grumbles so noisily that I'm forced to look up and check the time.

It's 7:30. Seven-thirty and I'm still on the couch in my daggy tracksuit (the really bad one with holes in the knees and dead elastic in the waist). But I've gotten the work done and now have hundreds of fabulous ideas for the site written down on paper. I breathe a sigh of relief and stand up to go and make a big pot of coffee and a pile of toast, because something tells me it's going to be an all-nighter.

And an all-nighter it is.

I work straight through, only stopping to call for a pizza at 10:30. When I push back my chair from the computer, eyes bleary, it's 3:15 AM. I stretch my arms above my head, exhale loudly, and then smile at what I've done. In the space of eleven hours I've worked out three designs for the T-shirts and stickers we'll be having made, written an article, and researched a couple more. I can't wait to show Chris everything—I've been stuck for ideas for so long I think we'd both given up on me. But this is it, all the work's now in my hand thanks to my little couch revenge dream. I head off to bed exhausted and happy, dodging Imogen, and pulling up my non-elasticized tracksuit pants as I go, and I tell myself that if the rest of my life is going to be like this, one thing's for sure: I really, really need to invest in some new clothes.

http://www.allmenarebastards.com

Ten great ways to get back at your ex (please, try not to end up in jail).

1. Sign up his parents to one of those porn "picture a day" sites. Get the site to send a card saying the subscription is an early (or late) anniversary gift from their beloved son.

2. You know those toy bags of plastic soldiers? They make great car dioramas. If your ex loves his car more than he loved you, make it even better for him by supergluing your own re-creation of Waterloo (or your own personal favorite battle) onto the hood. Got some glue left? I'm sure he'd appreciate having his windshield wipers glued down too.

3. Sign him up for a subscription to *Reader's Digest.* Feel smug in the knowledge that they will never, ever leave him alone again until they sight an original copy of his death certificate.

4. Send a letter to customs in his name. Ask them if it's OK for him to import another eleven pounds of heroin because he's almost run out of the last lot he brought into the country. PS: inquire whether they can do anything about the street price—in case they haven't noticed, it's horrendous!

5. If you've still got his house key, sneak into his house when he's away for a few hours and place a few prawns in strategic places. Spots where you know he won't look (probably from years of experience), like the washing basket, under the kitchen sink, and in the linen closet are the best.

6. For some added fun, place a stock cube or two in his shower head. Mmmm . . . soup! Or, for a sweet surprise, jelly crystals would be nice.

7. While you're in the bathroom, you may as well add some fast-acting hair remover into his bottle of shampoo to give him the scare of his life. (Tip: don't get greedy and add too much—it smells.)

8. Don't have his house key anymore? Try this instead: wait until you see him enter the house after a hard day's work. Later that night, slip a note under the door saying something along the lines of, "Tonight is the night you shall die." Ring the doorbell or knock so he'll be sure to find the note and read it. Now, keep a good watch on the house to see that he doesn't go out. Then, at 3:00 AM, when he's finally asleep, set some fireworks off on his lawn and see how he reacts!

If you're lucky enough to work together, these next two are especially for you:

9. Stick a notice up on the office noticeboard stating that he'd like everyone to know that he's entitled to use the women's toilets and other facilities now that he's officially a transsexual.

10. Send his boss a fax telling him/her that he's had a way better job offer in another state. Then tell the boss exactly what your ex thinks about him/her (include every single little bad thing you can remember your ex ever saying about his boss—it'll make the fax oh-so-much more realistic).

Chris is right on time

As per usual, Chris is right on time. I've managed to scramble out of bed ten minutes before he's due (only hitting the snooze button three or four times) so when I open the door I've at least had a shower and lost my morning doggy breath.

Well, a girl does have to make herself presentable.

"Hey," Chris says when I open the door. I can tell by the way he avoids looking at me that he's still embarrassed about our little confrontation the other day. I'm surprised, because it's something I'd almost forgotten about, but then, unlike Chris, my life is full of little confrontations.

"Coffee?" I ask, making my way down the hall so we can skip the awkward doorway greeting scene.

"Great."

Chris sits at the kitchen table as I putter around the kitchen getting the coffee ready. I mustn't have said anything for a while because after five minutes or so Chris pipes up.

"A penny for them?"

"What?"

He smiles. "A penny for your thoughts."

This is something I haven't heard anyone say in ages. Years even. Decades. I shake my head and try to remember what I was thinking about. The truth was I'd been mentally constructing a grocery list, which wasn't very exciting. Then I'd thought about Sarah for a second and how I should call her, connected this to tampons and then went on to debate whether or not to try one of those new "mixed packs" of tampons, or buy the two separate boxes like I usually did (probably details of my life you really don't need, or want, to know). I'm not about to go into the pros and cons of this with Chris, however, so I try to think back to the thing I'd been thinking about *before* that. Which had been partly about Chris and how he was still embarrassed about our little confrontation and also about Sarah. Yeah, that's what it was, about that time Sarah went away to the coast for a week with my family. I look at Chris's face, still waiting expectantly for my answer, and decide to do a little quick story editing.

"I was thinking about my family, actually," I say, passing him his coffee.

He takes a sip. "What about them?"

"Well, you know Sarah, right?"

Chris nods.

"One Christmas, Sarah came down the coast with my family for a week."

Chris nods again.

"She was supposed to stay with us for two weeks, but after the first week she wanted to go home."

"Why?" Chris asks.

I shrug. "I pressed her and pressed her to try and find out, but she only came up with lame excuses, like her mum would be missing her and she had to feed her budgie. In the end I gave up."

"So what happened? Did you find out why she wanted to go home?"

I nod. "Yeah, about five years later! My *family* was the reason she wanted to leave!"

"What about them?"

I snort. "Well, you don't know my family, but we're kind of loud."

"I can imagine."

"Hey!"

"Sorry," Chris grins.

"Anyway, I think we kind of freaked Sarah out. You see, her parents are kind of quiet. She said that being with my family for a week totally stressed her out."

"But what actually happened?"

"Oh, I don't think it was any one thing," I shrug. "It was just the whole situation. I guess my family's known Sarah forever, and we just treat her as one of our own. I think the main problem was that my family members are yellers."

"Yellers?"

"You know, we scream and rant and rave, and within five minutes it's all forgotten. Sarah's family isn't like that. I don't think I've ever heard them raise their voices. But with us, we'll yell about anything—who's got the TV remote, who ate the last packet of chips, it doesn't matter."

Chris nods.

"So I guess that's why I am the way I am. So if I say anything stupid, don't take it to heart, OK?" I hope Chris understands my rather pointed "moral of the story" reference. He must, because he nods again and then busies himself at draining his coffee.

"Let's get cracking," he stands up.

I look up at him. Is he nuts? I haven't even finished my first cup of coffee for the day yet and I usually need at least three before my brain kicks in.

"Well?" Chris says, still waiting for me to get up and skip joyously out to the computer.

"What did your last slave die of?"

"Exhaustion," he laughs, and suddenly I know it's going to be a long, long day. To break it up, I decide to wait until just before lunch to surprise Chris with all the work I've done.

In retrospect, I needn't have bothered.

At 12:30, when we're both getting tired, I pull the papers out of my top desk drawer and hand them to him.

"What's this?" he asks.

"Oh, just a little something I whipped up last night."

159

Chris flips through the papers, skimming the articles. He stops after he's read the T-shirt and bumper sticker designs and looks up.

"What?"

"Um," he looks back down at the designs again.

"No, tell me what it is. Why is everyone so scared of me for Christ's sake!"

Chris pauses.

"Tell me what it is before I rip your bloody arms off!"

"OK, OK. It's just that I think the slogans are a little over the top."

"Over the top?" I repeat. "What do you mean?"

"Gemma, come on. Don't you think that 'I speed up for men' is just a little on the subversive side?"

"No, not really," I cross my arms and sit back in my seat.

"And, 'Women are from Venus, men are just a penis'? What's that supposed to mean?"

"You figure it out."

"I just think it's all a bit much. I think you've been reading too much Heidi Killman on the weekends," Chris shrugs and hands the papers back.

"It's what women *want*," I say.

Chris just looks at me.

"And what's wrong with Heidi Killman? Women love her!"

He shrugs slightly.

"Look," I try to make him see my point. "Like a lot of women who come to the site, I've been pushed around and trodden on one too many times. This kind of thing is what I want—what I need—right now. It figures that it's what the rest of them want too." I pause to see how I'm going, but Chris remains silent, so I try another approach . . .

"It's therapeutic to hate men after they give you a hard time. It warns you off them for a while!" I point at the computer, "Just look at some of the entries we get. Those women don't want closure, they want revenge, they want blood!"

I can see Chris still doesn't believe me, so I come out with my trump card: "Anyway, it's my site" (a variation on a theme I learned in kindy). I consider adding the all-time Gemma favorite, "You're not the boss of me" (another kindy favorite), but at the last moment decide against it as this might come across as a little too childish at the age of twenty-seven, even for me.

Chris turns back to his computer. "You're right," he says. "It is your site." And he just keeps right on working.

Now, don't get me wrong. I like the part Chris said about me being *right,* I just don't like the tone of the sentence overall. For the rest of the afternoon I sit at my desk, a couple of feet away from Chris, and seethe. How dare he tell me how to run my site? Where does he get off telling me what the women coming to my site want? What does he know about slogans and bumper stickers and T-shirts? And, while I'm at it, why is he still so damn secretive about his personal life? Michael had been *so* wrong when he said I had a lot in common with Chris, because we have nothing in common. Nothing at all!

Chris plods away steadily on the computer all afternoon. And every little sound he makes, every slurp of his coffee, creak of his chair, or hit of the return key makes my blood curdle. By 4:00 I'm sitting on 99 degrees and am ready to boil over.

But if Chris knows I'm pissed off, he doesn't say anything. So, on the other side of the room, I try to keep my cool by slowly grinding my teeth and digging my nails further and further into the palms of my hands.

And then, at 5:00, Chris just gets up and leaves like he usually does.

"See ya!" he says, making the quickest dash for the door I've ever seen.

See ya! As if nothing is wrong.

When I hear the front door close, I get up and run to the

window. I watch as Chris makes his way to his car, gets in, and drives off. And then I kick a couple of chairs, throw some cushions, and get straight on the phone to Michael.

"What the fuck is his problem anyway?" I say when Michael picks up the phone.

"Let me guess . . . is it Gemma?"

"Of course it's me. I don't know why you thought we had anything in common, because *we do not!*"

Michael sighs. "What happened? What did you do?"

"What did I do? What did I do?" I splutter. "*I* didn't do anything! It was all *him*. Apparently what I want to put on my site isn't good enough for *him.*"

"Gemma," Michael says, "I think you're getting a little overexcited."

"A little overexcited my arse! And he won't tell me anything about himself either. Who does he think he is? Some kind of a mystery man? An international spy or something? He doesn't even like Heidi Killman."

"Gemma, you're the only person I know who likes Heidi Killman. And Chris just likes to keep his private life private, that's all. He's had a hard time lately and he probably doesn't need you on his back about it. Anyway, there's more to it than you think."

"Oh for God's sake, is anyone ever going to tell me what it is we've got in common, or do I just have to guess for the rest of my life? What is it? He takes size eight and a half shoes? He likes his coffee with two sugars and milk? What?"

"I'm sorry, Gemma, I can't tell you. He has to tell you that."

This is getting ridiculous. Chris the international man of mystery. What a load. "You've got so much in common with him, Gemma." Yeah, right. All I really know about him is that he lived in the most boring place on Earth, now he doesn't, and that at one stage or another he was seeing somebody. Somebody who probably dumped him. So all I can see that we have in common is that we've both been unlucky enough to get ditched. And hasn't everybody at some time or another?

"Look, to change the topic, I'm sort of glad you called," Michael says.

"And why is that?"

"Because I've got some news for you."

I don't like the sound of this. I sit down on the couch to prepare myself. "Don't tell me you're getting married too."

"Unfortunately, no. White's not my color, anyway. But I managed to get you an interview for tomorrow on *Triple J*."

I'm glad I decided to sit down now, because this is big news. "Do I have to?"

"Yes! It's great publicity and it's free too."

I groan, because I know if I'm going to be interviewed on *Triple J* I'll have to be hip and funky and go out tomorrow morning and have my hair dyed blue or something. Then I have a panic attack about what I'm going to wear, before I realize that this is radio—it won't matter.

Michael gives me the details, where to go, what to do, and what to say. He also says I should take Chris along with me, just in case. Just in case what, I don't know.

Just in case I get attacked by a pack of wild dogs?

Just in case I get abducted by aliens?

Who knows?

"And Gemma . . ." he says, right before he's going to get off the phone.

"What?"

"Behave."

I poke my tongue out at the phone and blow a raspberry before I hang up. I'm sick of people telling me what to do. First Chris and now Michael. I blow another raspberry for good measure.

I sit for a bit thinking about the day's events, then go over to my desk and grab the T-shirt and bumper sticker designs and pull out the Yellow Pages. If I'm going to get all this free publicity, it's probably time I got serious about this site and do what *I* want to do with it, not what everyone else thinks I should do. It's time to get some quotes for the merchandise. And right after I do that, I'm going to write a new article for the site. Because, finally, I think I'm beginning to find out what women want, or I hope I am. Anyway, I know what I want—some therapy. Some therapy of the written kind, an article straight from the heart. It's going to be called "Brett— The Downfall of a Bastard," it's going up on the site tonight, and it isn't going to spare any details.

Not even the gory truth about his hemorrhoids.

My radio debut

I thought Michael was joking when he said he was sending Chris as my watchdog to the radio interview.

He wasn't.

Half an hour before I'm due to leave home, I hear the chug, chug, chug of Chris's old yellow car pull up in front of the house. I don't even need to look out the window to check if it's him anymore. I can tell simply by the sound. It's unmistakeable—especially the way it gurgles and dies when he turns it off.

As soon as I hear the familiar sound I roll my eyes in exasperation. Can't I do anything by myself anymore? What's so hard about turning up to a studio and giving an interview?

"It's open," I yell from my bedroom when I hear Chris climbing the front steps.

He comes in and stands in the doorway. "Hey! Are you ready?"

"No." And I'm not. Before Chris's arrival I'd been busy jumping around my room doing some weird calisthenics. My favorite pair of jeans had been in the dryer and are now uncomfortably tight (definitely the fault of the dryer and not of all the bagels and cream cheese I've been eating lately).

"You'd better hurry up, or we'll be late."

"*We'll* be late? I thought it was just me giving this interview."

"That was what Michael sent me for—to make sure you *get* to the interview so that there is one."

I push past him. "Yeah, I guessed as much—thanks for the vote of confidence." I grab my bag in the hallway and head for the door. "Well, what are you waiting for?" I turn around and look at Chris. "You're the one who's so eager to go."

He looks a bit startled that I'm ready and that he hasn't had to drag me out of bed or anything. "Oh, OK," he says, heading for the door. "Let's go."

It's a fifteen minute drive to the radio studio and on the way Chris tells me that Drew Watson is going to be the presenter, which is a bit of a bonus. Drew's really funny and has the most gorgeous voice you've ever heard. He used to be on in the mornings and I'd hear him all the time then, but since he moved to an afternoon slot I haven't caught his show as much. I wonder if his face will match his voice while Chris blathers on and on about what Drew might ask me.

"Are you listening?" he finally asks when my intermittent nods and "mmms" become just a bit obvious.

"No."

"Well, you should be. Don't you want to know what kinds of questions you're going to be asked?"

I shrug. "What can Drew ask me that I won't be able to answer?"

"Probably nothing. But if you think about your responses beforehand, you won't be so nervous."

"I'm not," I say indignantly.

"Yes, you are. You're twisting your hair around your little finger again."

He's right. I am twisting my hair around my little finger—something I always do when I'm nervous. Instantly I pull my finger out of my hair and it gets stuck. "Ow," I say, yanking it out. "I'm not, I wasn't, I mean, I'm not nervous."

Chris grins at me.

"Oh shut up," I say and look sulkily out of the window, before I crack a smile. I hate it how I can never be mad for long around Chris—it's so annoying. Meanwhile, he keeps right on chattering about what questions I might be asked. I almost tell him to stop fussing—that I know everything's going to be all right because I'm wearing my lucky red undies. But after some thought I decide not to: we need to keep a *little* mystery in our relationship, don't we?

Finally, we get to the studio and the guy on the gate tells us where to park and which building to go to. Inside, we're met by the producer who shows us where the interview will be held (no prizes for guessing—it's the studio with the big, red, lit-up ON AIR sign). Inside, I can see the back of a guy's head, which I guess must be Drew, but nothing more. The producer tells us to take a seat and then asks us if we want a coffee while we wait.

"I told you we'd be early," I hiss at Chris as the producer leaves.

"It's better than not being here at all," he hisses back.

We quit fighting as the ON AIR sign turns off, the studio door opens, and a guy sticks his head out.

Cue: instant drool.

Because Drew is absolutely, stunningly, magnificently, statuesquely, and everything else-ly gorgeous.

This is no DJ with a face for radio.

He should be on television. Mine. All day. Only him.

"Hey there," he says, and I try to look normal and not like one of those cartoon characters who's just been hit over the head with something made by ACME. "I'm Drew Watson. Are you Gemma?"

I nod.

"Cool. And?" he looks at Chris.

I turn and look at Chris too, who, for a moment, I'd totally forgotten was there.

"Oh, right. That's Chris. My PA."

Drew shakes his hand and then holds out his arm to me. "Ready?"

Oh yeah, I'm ready.

He pulls me up and I only just remember to pick up my tongue and throw it over my shoulder as I follow him into the studio. He closes the door behind us.

"A male PA, hey?" he says. "You must be a real ball-buster!"

I have no idea what he means by this, but I laugh anyway. "Yep. That's me, ball-buster extraordinaire."

"Take a seat. I've still got some stuff to do, but I thought you might like to come and watch for a bit, you know, get used to being in the studio and everything. It freaks some people out a bit."

I nod and dreamily think how I could listen to that voice all day.

Drew fiddles around a bit and then holds up one finger to his slightly parted, wet lips (sorry, got a bit carried away there), indicating that I should be quiet. Then he starts talking into the microphone. While he says something about what track he's just played, I take a good look around the room. Then I tune in properly because he's started talking about what's coming up this afternoon. "We'll be chatting to Gemma Barton who runs that oh-so-popular Web site all-menarebastards.com. So why don't you spend the next five minutes checking it out, because we'll be taking calls and talking to Gemma right after this . . ."

I wait till Drew's taken his headphones off. "We'll be taking calls?" I ask him.

"Sure will."

"From people out there?" I nod in the direction of the street, and I can feel my eyes growing wider and wider.

"What's the matter?"

"Well, I have to warn you, the people out there," I nod in the direction of the street again, "they don't like me very much—the guys that is."

"I find that hard to believe," Drew says with a smile.

I decide to give him a frank example. "Usually they tell me to go and get myself a good fuck."

170

"Sounds like good advice to me."

I wonder if he'd oblige, but decide it's a little too early on in the piece to inquire about this. I think about asking him if they're going to screen the calls—but I guess the guy knows what he's doing. He's done interviews like this one hundreds of times before, hasn't he? I let it go.

"So have you ever been on radio before?"

I shake my head and Drew gets up and comes around to my side of the table. "A radio virgin, hey? Well, it's pretty simple. You just have to put these on," he says, picking up a pair of headphones and placing them on my head (ecstasy!). "And speak into the mike. Don't shout though, just speak normally."

"OK," I say, moving the headphones into a better position and out of the corner of my eye I see Chris peering in the window. Drew notices him too.

"So is he your boyfriend as well as your PA?"

I shake my head a little more vigorously this time and even add in some wavy hand movements too—I don't want Drew to get the wrong idea. "No way, he's my PA, that's all."

"Oh, right. Is he good?"

I have to be fair about this. "The best. He does his work and my work besides."

Drew laughs. "I might have to steal him off you if he's that good.

I look over at Chris, still standing near the window and wonder what I *would* do without him. Probably die a lonely, horrible death slumped over the keyboard of my computer from poor nutrition. I give him a little wave and he smiles and waves back.

"By the looks of him you don't have to worry," Drew says. "It's not me he's interested in."

I swivel on my chair, turning away from the window. "What do you mean?"

"Oh, come on, Gemma. Look at him. That's not a caffeine high he's having out there."

171

I turn around and take a look at Chris again. He doesn't look any different than usual to me. "He looks completely normal," I say to Drew.

"Maybe he always looks like that, I don't know. But I can guarantee you 100 percent that he likes you in ways that a PA shouldn't," Drew wiggles his eyebrows suggestively.

I take one more look to make sure. Chris looks like, well, like Chris drinking coffee. I shrug and tell myself that Drew just doesn't know us very well. Chris and me? I don't think so. Especially after the last couple of weeks—it's practically an impossibility. I decide to change the subject.

"So can you do a submarine noise?" I ask Drew.

"What?"

"A submarine noise and then put a goat over the top of it."

Drew laughs. "Either you have a good reason for asking me to do this, or you're a complete loon."

I guess it *is* a kind of strange request, so I try and explain. "I'm not a *complete* loon. It's just that a couple of years ago there was a radio school that used to play an ad on this station. And it was really funny—they started out by saying something about how you could do all this stuff on radio that you couldn't do on TV. Then, as an example, they sent a submarine noise across the top of the ad, *beep! beep! beep!* and then they put a goat inside the submarine, *beep! beep! beep! baaa, baaa, baaaa, beep! beep! beep! baaa, baaa . . .*" I trail off, realizing I'm making rather a fool of myself. Meanwhile, Drew is busy pressing buttons.

"And that folks is the enigma that is Gemma Barton, the creator of the site allmenarebastards.com. We're going to be speaking to her this afternoon, but I thought you'd like to hear that as a little introduction. Now I'll take you back to your song."

I stop cold and watch Drew who looks like he's about to wet himself he's laughing so hard. "You're joking right? You didn't really put that on air, did you?"

Drew nods, still laughing. "Sorry, I just couldn't help myself. It was too good to waste. You're wrong—you *are* a loon."

I think he's probably right. I try to be angry, but it doesn't work—the laughter's infectious, and soon enough I'm laughing right along with him. I laugh so hard that I snort and Drew and I both stop laughing and look at each other for a second and then start laughing even harder again.

When we calm down I have to wipe the tears out of my eyes and take a few big, deep breaths.

Drew shakes his head. "The thing is, it just doesn't make sense—why would you want a goat on a submarine?"

"Maybe they were trying to attract the navy crowd—I guess if you were on a submarine for months and months at sea a goat might come in very handy!"

And we start up again.

When I've finally gotten over this one, I notice Chris at the window again. He's obviously seen us laughing and he holds his hands up as if to say "What's going on?" I wave back again and smile. This whole interview thing is going way better than I thought it would and I'm glad I got Drew and not someone else because we seem to get on really well together.

Drew exhales loudly. "You're going to have to make me stop laughing now, because otherwise we'll never get this interview done. We're already five minutes behind schedule."

I follow his gaze up to the clock on the wall. Five minutes, hey? I guess this is a big thing for a DJ, but five *hours* behind schedule is more like a way of life for me. I shrug, ready for anything Drew can throw at me. "OK, let's do it then."

"I have to warn you, strange things can happen in interviews, so just play along the best you can, all right?" he says. And then, before I can register this and protest he holds up his finger again, telling me I should be quiet.

Shit. Strange things? Now I am nervous.

"Sorry about that little interruption before, but as I said to Gemma, I just couldn't help myself. I hope you've been busy

173

surfing the Net and checking out allmenarebastards.com, because that's what we're going to be talking about this afternoon. With us is Gemma Barton, creator of the site and specialist submarine and goat-noise maker. How are you doing today, Gemma?"

"Fine, I think. At least I was before the whole goat debacle."

"No one's going to hold a goat or two against you."

I just can't help myself. "What's the point of having a goat on a submarine if you can't hold it against you?"

Drew laughs and points his finger at me. "Don't start. This girl has had me in stitches for the past fifteen minutes—I was laughing so hard I couldn't breathe. If she starts up again can someone please come and save me? Please? *Please?*"

"You know you love it, Drew," I say in my best husky voice.

"Yes, well, I have to admit that's true. But anyway, down to business. This site of yours, allmenarebastards.com, seems to have taken the world by storm in the past couple of months—from a list on the fridge to twenty hits a day on your home page to over 2,000 hits a day now. Is that right?"

"Well, actually, it's over 3,000 hits a day now, but I won't be picky."

"Right. For those of you who don't know, and there can't be that many of you with the site getting so many hits a day, allmenarebastards.com is basically a place where you can write in and tell the world about the bastards in your life and what they've done to you. So, Gemma, tell us what kind of entries you get. For example, who's the worst bastard on the site?"

I have to think for a moment. "I guess, technically, they're all the worst, each person's own private hell, but there are a few that stand out. The guy we like to call the 'loose screw' is pretty bad."

"Go on."

"Basically, over a period of ten years, five of which he was married, he managed to screw not only his wife, but also his sister-in-law, his mother-in-law, an aunt-in-law, and two cousins-in-law. They only found out about it all after he died."

"Let me guess, of an STD?"

"Strangely enough, no. He was run over by a car. In her entry, his wife said that she was sorry it happened that way because if she'd known, she would have run over him herself, not let some stranger get all the satisfaction."

Drew laughs.

I remember something else. "I'd also like to mention another one of our worst bastards, Dr. David T. of Boston, Massachusetts, who put a lawyer onto me. I'm probably not supposed to say that, but somehow I doubt he's listening. Anyway, you're scum, David!"

"He put a lawyer onto you?"

"Yep. He wanted his entry taken off the site, but he can't do anything about it while his surname's not there, so I haven't taken it down."

"OK, now tell us about one of the funniest entries."

I have to think for a moment again, but I come up with one entry in particular pretty quickly. "That'd have to be the one we call 'ex Ms. Piggy.' "

"Tell us about her."

"Well, this guy and his girlfriend had been seeing each other for over a year when they decided to move in together. The problem was, they couldn't have pets in the apartment they were moving into and he was really attached to his pet potbellied pig, who apparently went by the name of 'Josie.' But he decided it would be OK, he'd leave Josie at his family's home with his brother's potbellied pig where she'd be happy and he'd go over and visit her a couple of times a week. So he and the girlfriend moved out and everything was OK, for a while, until he really started to miss Josie. Things got worse and worse and then, when the girlfriend came home from work one day, all the guy's stuff was moved out and there was a note on the table saying he just couldn't live without Josie and that he was moving back home. He left her for a pig!"

Drew laughs again. "A pig, hey? And a potbellied one at that. But how do you know that all the entries are true?"

"How do you know that what your listeners tell you is true?" I counter.

"Well, I don't know about you, but I use the bullshit-o-meter . . ."

"Yeah, I've got something like that too, but even the really far-out stories that are hard to believe, like the 'loose screw'— they're still funny even if they aren't the whole truth."

Drew starts pressing some buttons and I wonder what's going on. "OK, we might take a break now, so why don't you go and check out www.allmenarebastards.com and we'll take a few calls from you right after this . . ." He presses one more button and then pulls his headphones off.

I pull mine off too.

"That was great," he says. "I really like the one about the potbellied pig. You think that one was for real?"

"I think so. She seemed pretty pissed off."

Drew gets up. "Well, I've got to, you know . . . it's the bane of the radio announcer's life."

Ah, the radio announcer toilet run. I've always wondered about that. It must be awful working on radio and having to hold it in till you can take a break. And what would you do if you needed to do a number two? You'd have to play a really, really long song like "American Pie."

Sorry, that was disgusting.

When Drew's gone, Chris pokes his head around the door and gives me the thumbs-up. "This is great," he says, "you sound really good."

I think about what Drew said before, about Chris liking me in ways a PA shouldn't, and take a good look at him. Nothing.

He still looks completely normal—not like he's lusting after me at all. "Thanks."

Chris and I chat for a moment or two before Drew comes back in, then we sit down and put our headphones on and he presses a few more buttons. I realize I have absolutely no idea what any of those buttons do, but remind myself to behave in case one of them is an ejector seat.

Drew holds his finger up again, which by now I know means "shut up, Gemma," or something like that. I smile, thinking that, if they saw this, I bet my friends would wish the signal would work for them, too.

"So, did you manage to check out allmenarebastards.com during the break? I hope so, because we're taking your calls now. Our first caller today is Troy."

"Hi, Troy," I say. "And what do you think of the site?"

"I think your site sucks. You must be one really ugly bitch who needs a good fuck . . ." he trails off, either having hung up or been cut off.

"Lovely," Drew says as I give him the I-told-you-so look. "That's just what the world needs, more constructive criticism. Let's see if we have better luck with caller two. Susan?"

As I'd guessed, Susan loved the site. As did the next three callers, all women.

"Our final caller for the day is Amanda. Let me guess, Amanda, you loved the site too?"

"Hardly. I wanted to say that I think the site's all a bit sad, really. I mean, getting revenge, especially this way, is a bit childish—isn't it healthier to just move on?"

I look at Drew, not knowing how to answer this one, but he throws it right back at me. "What do you think, Gemma?" he urges.

"Well," I try and think up something on the spot. "Of course we all want to move on after we get dumped—it's not like I'm advocating this as an alternative to therapy or something. It's just a bit of fun, an added way to wash-that-man-right-out-of-your-hair kind of thing. If you read how the site started out, as a list on our share-house fridge, then you'd see that."

"I still think it's puerile."

"OK then, you move on, and I'll get my puerile revenge and we'll both be happy, hey?" I look at Drew and motion for him to wind things up.

He gets the hint.

"Thanks for your comments, Amanda, and to everyone who called today, sorry we couldn't get through to all of you. And also a big thanks to Gemma Barton, creator of www.all-menarebastards.com for coming in and talking to us today. Don't forget to check out the site. Now, staying true to our theme, here's a little song I thought you might like . . ." he presses some more buttons.

"What is it?" I ask, taking my headphones off.

"It's this new song, 'You Can't Never, Never, Never Trust a Man.' Hey, sorry about the 'ugly bitch' guy."

"I warned you," I say, standing up.

Drew stands up too and comes around to my side of the desk. "You did. Anyway, if it's any consolation you're definitely not."

"Not what?"

"Definitely not an ugly bitch."

I laugh. "That's very reassuring," I say, and before I know what I'm doing, I reach out and touch his arm. "I had a great time. Thanks."

Drew gives me a big smile in return and I almost melt. "Anytime, Gemma. It was fun."

Oh my God. I could look into those sparkling eyes, count those dreamy teeth, and drink that milky white skin in all day. And as he smiles at me I get the guts to do something I've never done before. Go for it, Gemma, go for it, my mind gives me a mini pep talk.

"Um, are you doing anything this Friday night?" I blurt out.

"Oh, right. Um, sorry, I would if I could," he says, and then holds up his left hand, "but I'm married."

It's only then I notice that the finger's got a ring on it and I kick myself for not looking beforehand.

I try to act breezy, as if I ask married guys out all the time. "Oh well, c'est la vie!"

"I've got to get back," Drew says, pointing at the console. "The airwaves call . . ."

"Yeah. Thanks again," I say, then head for the door.

Fast.

Outside, Chris and the producer are waiting.

"That was great," the producer beams. "You did really well."

"Thanks," I say and we chat for a bit. Just as we're about to leave, I see the ON AIR sign switch off and Drew sticks his head out of the studio door. "Hey, Gemma," he says. "Is this it?"

And then this noise reverberates around the whole building . . .

beep! beep! beep! baaa, baaa, baaaa, beep! beep! beep! baaa, baaa, baaaaa . . .

It's the submarine and goat noises, but not the ones from the radio. Drew must have whizzed in then and made them up.

And even though I've been embarrassingly turned down by the most gorgeous guy in the universe, I can't help but laugh out loud.

The cleansing

Sitting in the passenger seat on the way home, I remember Drew's comments about Chris and decide to test out his theory once and for all.

"I asked Drew out," I turn and say to Chris.

"You what?"

"I asked him out, like on a date."

"Why?"

"Duh. Because I liked him, because he was cute, because he had a great body and a very sexy voice . . . tell me when you get the picture."

We stop at a red light. Chris looks at me. "And?"

"And he's married."

"Oh well," Chris says with just the tiniest hint of a grin on his face.

"You needn't be so happy about it."

"Who said I was happy?"

"I can tell. You like it when the shit hits the fan in my life."

And from this back and forther, all I can think is that Drew's theory is wrong. Totally wrong. Because if Chris really *did* fancy me, then he would have taken offense to all the stuff about Drew being cute and having a great body and a sexy voice, etc. and me asking him out. Wouldn't he? Still, it was a pity Drew was married.

Not that I'm looking for anything like that, of course.

But dinner might have been nice.

Or a movie.

Coffee even.

Anything, really.

Chris drops me off and tells me he'll see me on Monday. He also tells me to have a good weekend, which I'm not sure is just Chris being nice or Chris having a laugh that I'm not going out with Drew. Probably the latter. So I stomp up the front stairs, let myself in the house, and, before I do anything else, turn on the radio. Then I flop onto the couch and listen to the rest of Drew's show, which makes me feel a hundred times worse than I already do. "Why are all the good ones already taken?" I ask myself over and over again as I listen to his voice for the rest of the program.

And soon enough I work it out. Duh.

The good ones have all been taken because I spent five long years with Brett. And during this time, all the other girls did the legwork. They weeded out the good ones and left the dregs for the likes of me, one of the ditched-before-thirty category. If Brett had had the decency to tell me he was going to leave me at the ripe old age of twenty-seven, things would've been different. I'd have had the smarts to get out there and snare me a date with a Drew or two.

But did he have the decency to tell me?

No.

The bastard.

Drew's show finishes and I use the remote to click the stereo off. It's so quiet without it on and I realize that it's Friday again, which means cocktails. My eyes flick to the answering machine as I think about Sarah and I see that the red light's flashing. There's a message. I get up and press the button, wondering if it's her.

It is.

"Hi Gem, it's me. I wanted you to be the first to know that I've ditched Barry. I know you're probably still pissed at me, but it's cocktails tonight and I really want to go—with you, of course. So, can we? Please? It's 5:30 now and I'll be at work for another half an hour, so give me a call, OK?"

I check my watch. Five-thirty. It's 6:00 now.

I pick up the phone and dial Sarah's work number, trying not to think too hard about the whole Barry thing. It was stupid us fighting like that and I've really missed cocktails and Sarah in general—especially her favorite drunken line: "Gemma, you're beautiful!"

"Sarah Peters-Masterson."

"Hi Sar, it's me."

"Gemma! I didn't know whether you were home or not."

"I just got home. I've been on the radio with *Drew Watson*."

"*Drew Watson*, cool! What was he like?"

"Oh, pretty gorgeous. I asked him out, actually."

"You asked him out?"

"Yeah, and he was married, just my luck," I say flatly. "I'll tell you all about it tonight at cocktails, hey?"

We decide to meet at 6:30. I hang up and then have to run around getting ready because it's going to take a good half an hour at least to get a taxi and push through the traffic at this time on a Friday. I change into whatever I find looks like it's actually been ironed at least once in its lifetime and slap on some eyeshadow and lippy. I'm out the door in seven and a half minutes flat (a new Gemma-getting-ready record).

I was right. It took exactly thirty-seven and a half minutes from my phone call to the taxi pulling up outside our old haunt. And when I walk in the door, Sarah's already there (a first for Sarah), symbiotically attached to the end of the bar, drink in hand (not such a first). I'm a little pissed off that she's started without me, but can't help breathing a sigh of relief when I spot her. It's like some kind of stability has come back into my life, even if it's just getting plastered on cheap margaritas on a Friday night.

Sarah waves and orders me a margarita as soon as she sees me, and by the time I've arranged myself on the bar stool, the drink is in front of me.

Now *that's* service.

"Thanks for waiting."

She shrugs. "I figured you'd understand."

It's only then that I notice how down she looks. I get straight down to the details. "So what happened with Barry?"

"The bottom line was he wanted me to get a $4,000 nose job."

"What? What's wrong with your nose all of a sudden? No one's ever said anything about it before."

Sarah leans over and puts her nose right in front of my eyes. "You see this?" she asks, pointing to something on her nose.

"See what?"

"This," she points again. "This bump."

"I don't see any bump. Where?"

"Beats the shit out of me, I don't see it either."

I snort. "But Barry does, right?"

"Yeah, and so does Barry's friend the plastic surgeon."

This was too *Barry* for words. "I bet he sees it. I bet he sees all $4,000 of it poking out there."

"And more besides. Apparently my eyes could 'use a little work' too," Sarah says, draining her glass.

I swivel on my chair a bit and look at her front on. "So how come you got all this modeling work before and now, suddenly, you need plastic surgery?"

Sarah points with her finger again, this time to the outer edge of her eye. "Wrinkles. I'm getting old. *Apparently.*"

She's crazy. For a start she's twenty-seven years old and there aren't any wrinkles where she's pointing, not that you could see without a magnifying glass. And frankly, I'm not surprised I can't see any, because since she started modeling at the age of thirteen, Sarah's always taken perfect care of her skin. Even if we go out till five AM and fall out of the taxi onto the footpath when we get home, Sarah will still spend half an hour taking her makeup off and applying various gravity-defying lotions and potions. And she wears an SPF30+ moisturizer like religion, even if she's just stepping outside to get the mail.

"Anyway, Barry says I don't have the 'look' anymore."

"That's bullshit, you've got heaps of jobs this year."

"Heaps of tampon commercials I've hated doing, you mean. If I'm not designing covers for the bloody boxes at work, I'm dancing around half naked as a model extolling their virtues."

"So you ditched him, hey?"

Sarah nods, pulls her new margarita toward her, and then downs the whole glass in one go.

"Slow down!" I tell her. "How many is that?"

Sarah bites her lip and counts off. "Three. No wait, four."

"I'm surprised you're not drinking them from under the bar by now."

"Yeah, well, I've got something else to tell you. I haven't just ditched Barry, I've ditched the whole thing. No more modeling for Sarah."

"Really? Are you sure?"

She shrugs. "It's not like it's asking much to give it up. I only ever seem to get the tampon commercials now and they'll even stop asking me to do those soon. You either have to be thirteen and perky and wear a lot of lime green and bright orange, or twenty and disgustingly active, running around on the beach in winter with a big blown-up ball like some kind of a wacko. And you know how I hate the beach. All that sand, yuk."

I listen to Sarah saying all of this, but my brain's stuck on one thing. I can't imagine Sarah not modeling, not thinking that owning all the newest and most expensive shades of nail polish is more important than paying the rent. It just wouldn't be, well, it wouldn't be *right*. "But do you really mean it? That's it? Forever?"

Sarah shrugs. "For now, anyway. For a long, long time I think. Maybe I'll do some of those incontinence ads when I'm sixty."

I ask the obvious question. "So if that's what you want, why are you so unhappy?"

"I don't know. I should be partying, shouldn't I?"

Instinctively, I know what I have to do. "Pete, hey, Pete!" I call out to the bartender and he comes over. I whisper in his ear what I want and he nods and walks away. There's some rustling from over the other end of the bar and when he comes back, he's carrying a big metal bowl that he places in front of Sarah.

"What's this?" she asks.

"Salt and vinegar chips, your favorite. I considered barbecue, but I thought the flavor might clash with the margaritas. You need to think about these things you know, now that you can eat again."

Sarah stuffs a handful of chips in her mouth and eats them. Then she does it again. And again, more and more handfuls. Finally, she turns to look at me, shocked and wide-eyed. "These taste fucking great!" she says after a while, her mouth hugely full. "This is just what I needed—I feel better already."

I knew it.

I knew that it would work again, this rediscovering of food. You see, I had to do the same thing to her last time she quit modeling. On the way home from somewhere or other I'd had a craving for Baskin Robbins, so we stopped off. Sarah hadn't really wanted any, but I coaxed her into getting a single scoop of cookies and cream. I can still remember her expression as she tasted it for the first time and this look of total wonderment came over her face. "This tastes nice," she'd said, staring at the spoon and she'd put on such a show of eating the rest of it that I'd had to put mine down and watch her eat the rest of hers before I could continue. In hindsight I should have sold tickets, because a couple of passers-by stopped and watched her too. The owner even gave her another free scoop, she was so good for business.

Now, watching her with the chips, it's like the scene from *When Harry Met Sally* all over again. You know, the one in the diner.

Sarah and food have this love/hate relationship I'll just never understand.

But Sarah and alcohol—well, that's another thing entirely. That I can understand no worries at all. And as if to prove my point, in the course of an hour and a half we both manage to get totally and utterly and completely smashed on half-price margaritas.

As we drink, I tell Sarah about Drew and my theory on how the good ones have now all been snatched up. That all that's left for us are the dregs of manhood. "That's what I reckon anyway," I slur. "And I'm sticking to it."

Sarah agrees with me wholeheartedly, and then, to make ourselves feel better, we do what we always do when we've been ditched, slighted, or otherwise maligned.

We start in on the man jokes (we kind of collect them and store them up for occasions such as these).

"Ooh, ooh, I've got one for you," Sarah says.

"Yeah?"

"Yeah."

Silence. "I can't remember it."

"Well, I'll tell you one then while you're remembering. What's the difference between a man and a catfish?"

"Beats me."

I have to concentrate to get it out right. "One's a bottom-feeding scum-sucker and the other's a fish."

Sarah's face looks confused for a moment as she works it out. Then . . .

"A fish! A fish!" she cackles and everyone in the bar turns and looks at us. "Now that's a joke," she points at me. "That's a joke."

189

"I've got another one," I say. "If you're up to it."

"Hang on, I'd better go to the toilet first."

"You're joking."

"You don't want me to have an accident, do you? I'll be right back." And Sarah clambers off the bar stool and runs in the direction of the toilets.

I finish off what must be my tenth margarita and soon enough, as promised, she comes trotting back.

"All better?"

"Yes, thank you. Now tell me the joke."

I have to think for a minute to remember it, but eventually it comes to me. "OK. What do you call an intelligent, good-looking man in Australia?"

"What?"

"A tourist!"

She laughs. "Good. But not as good as the fish one."

This reminds me of a joke someone sent into the site the other day, which I've been dying to tell to Michael. I haven't told him, though, because I was still a bit pissed off about the last-minute radio interview. But seeing as things have gone so well today, combined with the fact that I'm completely and utterly smashed, now means I am a more amiable person all-around. I pick my bag up off the floor and start searching around in it.

"What are you doing?" Sarah asks.

"Trying to find my cell. I have to ring Michael, I've got a joke for him."

Sarah pulls on my sleeve, "Tell *me* the joke!" she says in her whiny little girl voice, complete with pout.

"That only works on guys, Sarah."

"Oh, right," she says, straightening up. "I forgot. Do you want my cell?"

I can't find mine, so I give in and take her cell instead. I dial Michael's number.

"Hello?" a voice answers.

"Michael, why is it so hard for women to find men who are sensitive, caring, and good-looking?"

"I don't know. What's happened?"

"No, it's a joke."

"Oh, OK. Why is it so hard for women to find men who are sensitive, caring, and good-looking?"

"Because those men already have boyfriends!" I screech into the phone and watch as Sarah practically wets herself laughing (it's probably a good thing she went to the toilet when she did).

He laughs. "Is that Sarah I hear in the background?"

"Yep."

"Are you girls at cocktails?"

"Yep."

"Are you drunk?"

"Oh, yep. Definitely, yep. Yep, yep, yep."

"Well, I'd better let you get back to your margaritas."

"OK, bye." I hang up the phone.

"Didn't he want to chat?" Sarah asks.

I shake my head and give her the phone back. And full up to the top of my head with margarita as I am, I completely understand why. Drunk people are hilarious when you're drunk too, but when you're stone cold sober it's a different thing entirely.

I busy myself with my drink and when I look at Sarah again she's got this somber expression on her face.

"What's the matter?" I ask.

"It's a pity that joke's true. We'll never find any decent men. You know what I resorted to the other day? I bought a book on witches' spells going cheap for two dollars because I thought it might help."

"Witches' spells?"

"It's got all these spells you can do for different things. There's one for increased wealth and one to help your career—there's even one to help you find the right man."

191

"Really?" I'm getting interested now. "What do you have to do?"

"Oh, just burn some stuff from your past relationships and then say something—'So mote it be,' I think—whatever that means."

"Did you do it?"

Sarah looks at me as if I'm crazy. "Get real!"

I get that overwhelming urge to *do* something. You know that urge you sometimes get when you're drunk? Not the one to hurl everywhere (or "ride the porcelain bus to woof city," as Sarah likes to call it), but the one to get up and get busy. For me, this urge usually involves running—something I would never, ever do if I was sober (for the simple fact that it would then be called exercise, which is something I don't believe in). A couple of years ago, in one of my less finer moments, I had found myself on quite a busy road intent on running along the white line. It had taken three people to stop me.

I grab Sarah's arm. "I think we should do it. If there's a spell specifically for finding the right man, it's the spell for us. We need all the help we can get, right?"

Sarah shrugs. "I guess so."

"Come on then, let's do it!"

Sarah looks completely uninterested, but she shrugs again and I decide to take this as a yes.

"OK, let's swing by your place and pick up the book and some of your past relationship stuff and then go back to my place for the cremation."

"Can we get some food?"

"Of course we can get some food. What a stupid question."

"Gemma?"

"What?"

"You're beautiful!"

So we leave. And when we've found a taxi, we climb in and cajole the driver into stopping off at a service station on the way over to Sarah's.

Except that, at the service station, he very rudely kicks us out and screams off to the smell of burning rubber, just because we were playing a little game in his taxi. Nothing bad . . .

We were only coming up with as many terms as we could for wanking (don't ask how we got onto this subject). I thought we were doing quite well, actually, for two drunk girls. This is what we came up with on the way:

1. to make the bald man puke;
2. to wrestle the walrus;
3. to free Willy;
4. to burp the baby;
5. to feed the chickens;
6. to audition the finger puppets;
7. to tickle the pickle;
8. to charm the snake;
9. to fondle the fig;
10. to clear the snorkel;
11. to knock on wood;
12. "I'm just checking for testicular cancer" (Sort of counts because this is the excuse Sarah was given once when she caught a boyfriend at it in her bathroom. He swore that, as a policeman, it was something he had to do routinely because of the radar guns.);
13. to converse with the one-eyed trouser snake;
14. to yank the yam;
15. to paint the ceiling;
16. to shake hands with the unemployed;
17. to hold the sausage hostage;
18. to flog the log;
19. to meet Ms. Palmer and her five daughters;
20. to beat the bishop;
21. to slap the salami;
22. to cuff the carrot;

23. to polish the rocket;
24. to shine the pole; and
25. to sling the jelly.

Trust us to get the born-again Christian taxi driver.

So we call another taxi (this time we specifically ask the woman at the call center for a non-Christian driver as we may offend). And then, while we wait for the taxi to show, we buy one of everything that Sarah's probably never tasted in her life, including a vile-looking orange hot dog that looks like it's been rotating in its glass case for around a century or more.

When we get to Sarah's place, it takes her quite a while to hunt through her bedroom to find things from past relationships. I figure this is simply because she hasn't had many relationships that have gone on long enough for the guys to give her anything except flowers. Eventually, we find a few letters and an old shirt she never gave back to one poor guy, and decide this will have to do. We grab the witch book and we're off.

At my place I sit Sarah down in the living room with her junk food and head off to find stuff I can burn. Unlike Sarah, I've got plenty to choose from. I have a whole plastic shopping bag worth of letters from Brett and heaps of other stuff besides. I pick a couple of letters out at random (I'd need a backyard bonfire to burn them all) as well as this grubby-looking teddy bear he'd won for me at a fair once. When he'd given it to me, I'd thought it was so cute, but somehow it wasn't quite so endearing now. I head back to the living room with my stuff and dump it on the floor in front of Sarah who's lit a candle, cleared some space on the floor, and found a metal bowl to put our burnt offerings in. For a second I worry about two drunken girls being in charge of a lit candle, but then tell myself not to fuss, putting it down to watching too many fire safety videos in grade three.

Stop, drop, and roll, girls!

194

Sarah looks up at me, half an orange hot dog in one hand. "Gem, I don't feel so good. I think I ate too much."

She does look kind of green. "It's OK, I've got a remedy for that," I say and sprint out to the kitchen. I return a minute or so later, glass in hand.

"Here, drink this," I pass it down to Sarah.

"What is it? It's all fizzy."

"It's a special drink that lets you eat too much and then get away with it, no upchucking required. It's called Eno."

"Eno?" Sarah says, eyeing the glass, before she shrugs and downs it all at once. Then she hands me back the empty glass and looks at her stomach. She burps. "Hey, this stuff's great, I'm starting to feel better already."

"Good," I reach over and grab the rest of the hot dog. "I wouldn't advise you eat the rest of this, though. Stick to the packaged stuff, grasshopper."

Sarah burps again and then nods wisely. "I think I'm getting the hang of it." She pats the floor beside her. "Now come and sit down here and I'll read you the spell."

I sit down.

" 'This spell will help you to find the man you are looking for by encouraging you to put the past behind you and move forward in your life. The first step is to find objects from your past relationships (this can include such things as letters, personal effects, or anything that you think signifies your relationship as a whole). When you have collected these things, write the person's name who gave them to you somewhere on the object. Now clear a large circle in front of you and light a candle, placing it in the center of your space. Clear your head and inhale deeply. Then, as you burn each object in the flame of the candle, think intently about the person the object came from and imagine them slowly fading into the background. Do this with each object and when you are finished say the words "So mote it be." The next man you see will point you in the right direction.' "

195

Finished reading, Sarah places the book on the floor.

"What's that supposed to mean?" I ask her. "The next man you see will point you in the right direction?"

"Beats me."

"What's he going to do, point us to true north or something, like a compass?"

Sarah sighs. "Look, this was your idea. Do you want to do it, or not?"

Time to get started. I grab the candle and move it into the center of the circle. "Now, take three deep breaths," I say.

We take three deep breaths in unison.

"Pick up one of your objects and think about who gave it to you."

We both pick up a letter to start with.

I think hard about Brett, about him writing the letter, how long we were together and what life was like as a couple. How I really thought we'd get married and have kids, but how he obviously didn't feel the same way. I pause. "Now burn it and imagine him fading into the background," I say, and on cue we both reach out and light our letters.

Quietly, we watch the letters burn, each thinking our own thoughts. Soon enough, the flames get too close to my fingers and I flip the rest of the burning letter into the metal bowl. A few seconds later, Sarah follows suit.

"Shall we?" she asks, picking up the shirt. It's only then that I recognize it as John's, this guy Sarah went out with for a good year or so before he moved overseas. They tried to keep the relationship going long distance, but it didn't work. Sarah was quite upset about it if I remember correctly.

I select the grubby-looking teddy bear. "Let's do it."

We take another three deep breaths before lighting our respective objects.

Except that as soon as mine catches alight I realize it must be made of polyester, because the next thing I know there's this whooshing sound and the whole bear is covered with flames.

"Shit!" I say, throwing it into the metal bowl and then inspecting my hand for any damage.

It's only then that I notice Sarah clambering to her feet, this huge burning *thing* flying around in front of her, flames licking out in all directions.

"HOLY CRAP!" she yells, and throws it on the wooden floor, trying to stamp it out with her feet.

"Not on the fucking floor!" I yell back, thinking of my bond money. I reach down and grab the shirt, which is still burning, despite Sarah's efforts. I pick it up and decide the best thing to do will be to get it outside.

But as I make my way toward the door, several things happen at once. (If this were a movie, now would be the point where everything starts moving in slow motion.) This is what happens:

1. the smoke alarm goes off;
2. the living room curtain catches alight; and
3. Sarah starts screaming hysterically.

I manage to get to the front door and throw the stupid shirt out onto the front lawn. Then I race back inside, pull the curtain down, and stomp on it a bit. And, unlike the shirt, it goes out quite quickly.

Which makes Sarah stop screaming.

But doesn't turn the smoke alarm off.

So I run off again and grab the broom out of the kitchen, take it into the hall, and start poking the smoke alarm in the hope that it'll stop its incessant screeching noise. I poke it and poke it and poke it, but this doesn't seem to work.

So I start beating it instead and eventually it falls onto the floor and I keep right on beating it.

And then some.

Until it gives one last, half-hearted screech and dies.

I give it a good kick and it goes sailing out the front door, onto the lawn, and lands right beside the still-flaming shirt.

And in spite of my heart beating right up into my throat, the smoke choking me, and sheer terror making me shake, I'm still able to admire my great kick.

"Cool," I say.

But my happiness is wiped away all too quickly because that's when I hear it.

This *wheer, eer, wheer, eer, wheer, eer* sound.

A sound that's all too unmistakeable.

And it's getting closer.

Wheer, eer, wheer, eer, wheer, eer.

It's a fire engine.

"Oh shit," I turn and look at Sarah. "We'd better go outside." I make it halfway down the front steps before I realize Sarah's not with me, so I go back inside.

Where she's still standing in the same spot as before, paralyzed with fear.

"Come on, you hopeless fool," I grab her hand and lead her to the front door, down the front steps, and onto the lawn (if you can call it that, maybe "patchy grass" would be more appropriate).

I sit Sarah down and stomp on the last few sparks the shirt is giving out.

"There," I say to her. "All done." And my work finished, there's nothing to do but sit down beside Sarah and listen to the fire engine get closer and closer.

"Hey, you," I hear a male voice call out from the footpath. "Are you all right?"

I look over. It's a guy, probably sixty or so, obese, wearing an old blue trucker's singlet, blue stubbies, and blue thongs (obviously a carefully matched fashion story). "It's Merv," he says, coming in the front gate, "from next door. I heard yer smoke alarm and saw flames at the window, so I called the fire brigade."

I consider giving Merv a piece of my mind because this is going to cost me a fortune, but then I see it from his point of view. He probably thought we were dying in there and the spell *was* a pretty stupid thing to do, especially when we were drunk.

"Thanks, Merv, it was just a little flaming shirt problem," I say sourly, suddenly feeling very, very sober.

"Are youse both all right then?"

"We're fine, thanks, Merv. Just fine. You can go back to bed now if you want. I'll deal with the fire brigade."

"You sure?"

"I'm sure," I have to yell, because the fire engine's coming down the street now and as Merv turns to leave it pulls right up in front of the house.

A couple of guys run out and Merv goes and says a few words to them, his hands waving as he tells the whole story.

Two of the firemen break off from the others and come through the front gate. One of them goes past us and into the house and the other stops beside us. "Are you girls OK?" he asks.

"We're fine, thanks," I say.

Sarah struggles to get to her feet and the fireman bends down and gives her a lift up. She loses her balance a bit as she stands up and he has to hug her for a second to set her right.

"Sure? You don't need an ambulance or anything?" he says, still holding onto Sarah's arm.

"No, really, we're fine," I get up and brush a bit of Sarah's hair out of her eyes. "She's just a bit shocked, that's all."

"OK, if you say so. I'm James, by the way."

We all turn as we hear the other fireman come down the front steps. "Everything's fine," he says as he passes James and keeps going. James turns and follows him, giving us a wave.

"Thanks, James," I say as he heads back out the front gate

to his fireman buddies. They get back onto their truck and leave. Merv watches them go. "I'll be off then, too," he says.

I give him a small wave. "Yeah. Thanks again, Merv."

"Thanks," Sarah says, finally speaking.

When he's gone, she turns to me, a troubled look on her face.

"What's wrong?" I ask her.

"That guy, Merv."

"What about him?"

"We don't have to count him as the first guy we saw after the spell do we? The only direction he's going to point us in is the way to the local."

I flop back down on the ground and laugh.

Sarah continues, "We can count James the fireman as the guy we saw first instead, right?"

I grab Sarah's hand and pull her down. "Guess what?"

"What?"

"We forgot to say the thing. The end of the spell thing. What was it again?"

"So mote it be," Sarah says.

"OK, then. One, two, three."

"SO MOTE IT BE!" we yell together. Then we lie right down on our backs and laugh till our stomachs hurt, while Merv watches us out of his front window.

Three phone calls and
a storm

The feature in *The Australian* was published the day after the fire and the one in *Wired* was published the week after. With all this publicity, I decided it was time to get moving. The T-shirts and bumper stickers had been ordered and I figured that if I put them up for sale early, a few would sell and I could send them out as soon as I got them. So I put the merchandise up on the site.

Every single item sold out in two days, a week before I'd even received the goods.

After this, I guess you could say I went a little crazy with success. All of a sudden I felt like I had this power—I knew what women wanted. And now that allmenarebastards.com was getting down and dirty, they seemed to be sucking the marrow out of the site's contents more than ever. They were angry. I was angry.

I decided to give them more.

So, I added this program to the site called Bobbitt-choppit where there were a number of pictures of faceless men, a selection of instruments of torture, and their members, trouser snakes, penises (whatever you like to call them), and you could—well, I'm sure you get the picture. It was inspired by Heidi Killman's latest column, which I thought was one of her best ever. It was all about her son, Buster, and his crown jewels. She went on about how she thought Lorena Bobbitt had it right when she cut it off because the things are just too much hassle, especially on kids. As she said, "One minute they're peeing on you when you thoughtfully change their diapers and the next they're grown up and are sticking it into all kinds of places it shouldn't be."

And as if I wasn't busy enough doing all of this, Monday turns out to be a day of phone calls. Three biggies in a row to be precise. The first is Brett who isn't all that impressed with the kiss and tell hemorrhoids article. In all truth, after the "cleansing" thing, I'd been going to take it down—a therapeutic gesture if you like—but then I got sober again and remembered he was getting married.

The bastard.

The conversation runs a little like this:

Brett: "What's all this shit about me doing on your site, Gemma?"

Me: "It's not shit, it's all true. Name one thing I've said that isn't true."

Brett: "I don't care if it's true or not, just take it off, people from work are reading it for Christ's sake."

Me: (rolling eyes) "That was kind of the whole point."

Brett: "So you're not going to take it down?"

Me: "No."

Brett: "You refuse to take it down?"

Me: "No, I mean, yes."

Brett: "Well, you can forget about coming to the wedding then."

Me: (laughing evily) "Oh, really? Such a disappointment, especially considering I wasn't going to go anyway."

A pause.

Brett: "What's your bloody problem, Gemma? Why are you being such a bitch?"

Me: "Why am I being such a bitch? Well, I guess I'm just doing a little better at looking after *me* these days. Let's face it, you weren't much chop at it, were you? So if you think the article's being taken down you've got another thing coming, baby."

Brett: "Is that right?"

Me: "Yeah, that's right."

Brett: (sneeringly) "OK, fine, whatever, it's your choice, but while you're so busy on the Net, why don't you go take a look at my home page? You never know, you might like mine as much as I like yours."

And with this he hangs up. Naturally, the first thing I do is whiz over to the computer and load up his home page. He's right. I don't like it. I don't like it one little bit.

The first thing to greet me is a little peal of bells and then Wagner's "Bridal March."

Dum dum dum-dum, dam dum dum-dum . . .

And then a chintzy-looking photo of Brett and, I guess, his *new* fiancée loads up. One of those really *sick* photos where the happy, freshly engaged couple are sitting in a café, sucking out of the same milkshake and gazing into each other's eyes like possums into the headlights of a Holden Commodore on a dark highway. The photo's been taken too far away to get a good look at her and she's wearing a raffia hat, so I have to squint and pretend I can see what she looks like.

But it's not the photo that pisses me off the most. What Brett had meant me to see was the site itself. He knew that this would get to me because having a wedding site had been *my* idea. All my idea. But, the problem was it had been Brett's *responsibility.* He was going to do it, except that he hadn't, even when I'd nagged, cajoled, and begged for months on end.

But he'd done it for her.

His little fluffykins, his little honeybunny, his little Ju-Ju . . . whatever her stupid name is.

I pick up whatever I can find off the desk and throw it at the opposite wall.

The stapler—*You bastard!*

The hole punch—*Conniving bitch!*

205

My pencil case—*I hope your children all have clubbed feet!*

The cell—*And expensive, put-the-orthodontist-on-speed-dial buck teeth!*

And just as the cell is about to hit the wall, it starts to ring. Too late.

It hits the wall with a thud and bounces back onto the floor, landing in two pieces.

But it keeps ringing, which quite surprises me, and I forget I'm angry for a minute. I go over, piece it together, and pick it up.

"Hello?"

"Oh, hello, Gemma, darling."

It's my mother. Conversation two.

"I thought I'd get the voicemail. You always seem to have it on."

"No, it's me," I say, thinking that she's right, the voicemail usually is on—mainly to avoid calls like this.

"Yes, well," obviously she'd *wanted* to get the voicemail. A pause. "So, how are you?"

"Fine."

"Well, I guess I should get to the point," she says. And I know instantly, at that very second, that it has something to do with my father. I can tell by the sigh in her voice.

"Has something happened to Dad?" I ask brightly.

"Um, yes and no. Well, the truth is, your father's getting divorced."

"Again?" I ask, wondering if you can get divorced more than once in the same year. "What happened to Susan?" Susan was Dad's fourth wife, I think. I'd decided I wasn't going to keep track anymore.

"You know what happened to Susan."

"No, I don't."

"Yes, you do."

"No, I don't."

She pauses, unsure if I'm putting her on or not. "I told you. Susan ran off with Patricia."

I'm getting lost now. "Patricia?"

"The mistress."

I'm taking a slug of coffee when she says this and unfortunately I can't swallow it in time. Most of it comes out my nose. The rest of it I choke on. I run over to my desk and search blindly for a tissue as I sneeze twice, splattering coffee everywhere.

"Gemma, Gemma, are you there?"

"Yes, I'm here," I say, laughing, and it's the funniest thing I've heard for a long time. "Are you joking, or what?"

"No, I'm not joking," she says snippily in that don't-talk-to-me-in-that-tone-of-voice mother speak. "He's moving in here for a while, until he gets everything sorted out."

Now this I *don't* believe and I'd check my watch to see if it's April Fools' Day, except I know it's already July. "Let's get this straight," I say. "Dad, my father, the oppressor of women, is moving back in with you."

"Don't call him that."

"What, Dad? I know he doesn't deserve it."

The universal motherly sigh of disappointment is all I get in return.

"I don't see why this is so hard for you, Gemma. It's not like you bother to see either of us as it is."

Funny that. Maybe it's because they moved to the Bahamas five years ago and I wasn't invited. I didn't even get one of those sad T-shirts that read "My father was extradited and all I got was this lousy T-shirt." Now their aims seem to be to dodge tax, unite the world through racism, and marry and divorce everyone on the entire island within a decade or two, all while drinking copious amounts of piña coladas and strawberry daiquiris.

"I didn't call you for your opinion, Gemma. I just thought

you might like to know. You may call when you're a little more civil. Good-bye."

And she hangs up too. Which is strange, because while I end most conversations with my parents this way, it's usually *me* who does the hanging up.

By now I'm getting a little bit sick of all the hanging up this morning, so I throw the cell at the wall again for good measure. The wall nearest the front door, that is. It misses Chris, who's just walking in, by centimeters, hits the wall, and breaks into three pieces this time.

"My father's moving back in with my mother while he gets his fourth divorce," I say to Chris by way of explanation, though I don't think Chris knows anything about my parents and their life's work to piss me off.

And then, remarkably, the phone rings again. Not the cell phone—I'm afraid that's beyond repair. This time it's the normal phone and I suddenly regret that extra phone line I put in.

Conversation three.

Chris goes to grab it, but I get there first. "No, no, please, let me," I say. "This should be interesting."

It's Michael.

"Hi, Gemma," he says, quite unaware of my current state of being.

"Ugh," I grunt.

"Just checking if you want to go out tonight. Thought we might hit the clubs, what do you reckon?"

"Couldn't you find anyone else to go with?" I ask sourly.

"Well, I thought *you* might like to go."

"Why?"

"Oh, I don't know, for a good time? Some people have them you know."

"Not me."

"Come on, Gem, you're my lucky charm!"

Suddenly, I get it. "Oh, now I see. You want me to go as your little *fag hag*, right?"

"What are you talking about?"

"I'm not some little piece of fluff to hang off your arm when you want to pick up, you know."

"Gemma, what's the matter?"

"Nothing's the matter."

"Get up on the wrong side of the bed this morning, did you? What's your problem?"

"What's my problem? I'll tell you what my problem is, it's bloody men. My ex is getting married and my mother's letting my father move back in. I've just about had it. The fewer men in my life the better, I'd say."

"Well, how about I become one less then?"

And for the third time that day I get hung up on. Shit. I look at the clock and do some quick math. It's only 9:30 AM. At this rate, about a hundred more people could hang up on me today if they feel like it. I want to laugh like a crazy thing, lie down on the floor and belly-laugh at the ceiling, kick my legs around and lose it, but I can't. I only remember feeling like this a few times before in my whole life and it's always when my temper gets way out of control. It doesn't feel good. In fact, I feel not-quite-right. I can almost see the wrinkles growing on my face as each moment passes and my stomach is rolling over and over. If I had to describe it I would have to call it all-over body constipation.

Very strange.

I turn around and spot Chris leaning in the doorway, a smirk on his face.

"That was Michael," I say.

"Yeah, I figured as much," he says.

The phone starts ringing again.

"Why don't you let me get it this time?" Chris says, sprinting for it.

I let him. It's probably for the best.

Chris picks it up and turns his back on me as he mutters for a bit. I can't hear anything he says and a minute or so later, he puts the phone down.

"Who was that?" I ask.

"Um, no one."

"Who was that?" I ask again, but this time I narrow my eyes into that you're-my-PA-and-I-can-fire-you-right-now-if-I-want-to stare.

"It was Sarah, actually," Chris gives in. "She wanted to know why she couldn't talk to you herself, so I told her that Gemma wasn't here today and that an evil clone of Gemma has taken her place. She seemed to understand—she said she'd call back when she gets home, she's off on a business trip some-where."

I stomp past Chris and into the kitchen. He follows me, laughing.

He's not supposed to laugh. This isn't funny. There's noth-ing to laugh about.

"Don't piss me off, OK?" I say, pointing at him. I open the fridge and grab the peanut butter.

"You keep your peanut butter in the fridge?" he asks.

I eye him warningly as I open it up and poke a finger in.

Chris reaches into his bag, pulls out a brown paper packet, and offers it to me.

"What's that?" I ask.

"It's a salad sandwich. All you've been eating for weeks is peanut butter and coffee and, very occasionally, toast. It can't be very good for you."

I take the bag and rip it open, taking a look inside. It is, in-deed, a salad sandwich.

"It's got beetroot on it," I say ungratefully. "I don't like beetroot."

"Pick it off."

I wonder about his motives. "Why are you being so nice? Do you want a raise or something?"

"Well, if you're offering . . ." Chris says as he picks up his coffee and makes his way out of the kitchen. To do some work I suppose.

"I'm not offering!" I yell at his retreating back.

Square, I think nastily when he's gone. Geeky computer boy.

"I know what you're thinking," he calls out from the hall, making me sit up straight.

How did he know what I was thinking?

God, I hate men.

I put my chin on the table and sigh one of my poor-Gemma-has-such-a-terribly-hard-life sighs, eyeing the salad sandwich, but not wanting to give Chris the satisfaction of eating it. Finally, it gets the better of me. I open up the top layer of bread and peel off the beetroot, then stick the whole thing back together again and take a big bite. Just as I'm halfway through chewing, I hear Chris's footsteps in the hall. Quickly, I shove the rest of the sandwich back into the bag and try to look innocent.

Chris stands in the doorway and looks at me and then down at the sandwich bag.

"You know, I'll never understand you," he says, shaking his head and walking over to the coffee machine for a refill.

Gracelessly, I show him two fingers (no need to specify which ones) and then watch his movements around the room until he's back in the doorway again.

"So, are you going to have a shower and do some work today? Or are you just going to sit around with lettuce all over your face?"

I wipe the lettuce off my chin and grab the sandwich bag for another bite of wholesome Chris goodness. If he knows, he knows, right?

"Well?" Chris tries again.

I swallow. "Well what? I feel like shit, OK? Not a good day for Gemma."

"People have bigger problems than you, you know."

"Yeah? I'd like to bloody well meet them then," but as I say this I think of Courtney and feel a bit guilty.

"Just hurry up," Chris says and goes back to his computer.

Mr. Boring, I think, shoving the rest of the sandwich in my mouth and scrunching up the packet.

"I heard that, too," Chris calls out.

I poke my whole wheat salad sandwiched tongue out at the wall, hating everyone, everything. Brett for being happy and finding someone else so soon, my mother for being weak and letting my ever-philandering father in the house, and Michael for nothing really at all—for being in the wrong place at the wrong time, I guess. I sit and think about what I'm going to do about it all. Then I think some more.

And a bit more.

And a bit more after that, until, finally, I realize there's nothing I *can* do.

However many hissy fits I throw, Brett is still going to get married.

My mother is still going to let my father move in.

Poor old Michael is always going to be in the wrong place at the wrong time while I'm still breathing.

So I do what Chris tells me to do and get up and have a shower.

But I'm still not completely happy about it.

And I *do* feel a bit better after the shower. I even go to the effort of putting my pj's in the washing machine (note: this is a big deal) and fish out a *decent* pair of jeans and a *clean* jumper for the working day. And by the time I sit down at my computer to do some work, I am almost a non-angry version of Gemma again.

212

Except that when I sit down at my desk, the first thing I see is that Chris has sorted out the day's e-mail and, to be read first, is twenty-four hours of post-*Wired* article hate mail (which I liked to call hate *male,* because, inevitably, that's who it's from).

My little black cloud of anger reappears and rises a little as I minimize the e-mail program on my computer, deciding to deal with it later.

Which seems like a good idea until I find out that underneath I haven't gotten rid of Brett and Ju . . .'s Web site. The cheesy-looking photo slaps me in the face one more time. I turn and look at Chris, ready for a rant, ready to fling my arms around a little and put on a show.

On the other side of the room, Chris ignores me.

So I turn back to the computer and, as I look at the site, the little black cloud turns into a storm cloud and covers the space directly above me and my computer. And then the lightning starts.

My own little thunderstorm.

But I know what I have to do to make myself feel better. I have to do what I always do when things go bad—I have to ignore them! So I throw myself into my work until the late afternoon.

Except that I don't do the work I'm supposed to.

I write an article about ex-etiquette instead and put up some FAQs on the site.

And Chris ignores me right up until he leaves at 5:00, except to tell me that Michael e-mailed and has arranged a "little something" for me. The fact that the "little something" might be a firing squad crosses my mind, but it turns out that Chris and I are going on a quick plane trip next week. I'm going to appear on *Noon* with Mary-Anne Melody for a panel discussion on the topic: "Men, are they as hopeless as they make themselves out to be?"

Heidi Killman's going on too. I'm excited about that.

But, shit. Everyone knows the camera piles twenty pounds on you.

http://www.allmenarebastards.com

allmenarebastards.com top five FAQs

1. Why do you hate men?

I don't hate men, I just hate most of the things men do most of the time.

2. Are you a lesbian/dyke/lemon/les/lezz/lezzy/muff diver/carpet licker?

No. Although it would probably make my life a lot easier if I was.

3. Why don't you stop wasting your time on this site and get a real job?

I had a real job once. Believe me, it's much more fun wasting my time on this site.

4. Did your father molest you as a child or something?

No, my father was never around enough to molest me as a child.

5. You say that you reply to all your e-mail, so how come you haven't replied to mine?

Because I'm a slack arse and my personal assistant does most of my work as well as his. We get over 50 e-mails a day and it's hard replying to all of them, but we promise we'll reply to yours soon. If you've been polite, that is.

I experiment with
home cocktails

I don't talk to Chris much on Friday and I certainly don't do any work. Instead, I skulk around the house, feeling crappy at life in general. Chris avoids me (I think he knows his powers aren't strong enough to bring me out of this one). Even Imogen wisely keeps out of my way—I have replaced her and am now the Queen of the Shits. As Chris gets into his car and pulls out onto the road, I run over and take a look at what he's done all day. I'm kind of hoping that he's been taking too many coffee and biscuit-dunking sessions and hasn't done much work, basically so I can rev the shit out of him. I'd like to do this because he's the only person who doesn't hate me at the moment and with any luck I'll be able to complete the record and make everyone hate me at the same time.

But he hasn't been a slacker.

He hasn't been a slacker at all.

Not only has he dealt with the advertisers and just about *all* of the feedback e-mail, he's even started work on the merchandise orders, which was what *I* was supposed to have been doing today.

I feel guilty for all of five seconds.

Then I go and pour myself another cup of coffee out of my third pot for the day and sit down at the computer. My article on ex-etiquette is coming along nicely. Basically it's a list of dos and don'ts for the recently exed. If you think about it, there's truly a need for a whole book like this, outlining the ex-etiquette for every situation. Let me give you an example:

A few weeks after Brett and I had split, he called in the middle of the night begging me to come over to his flat. When I got there he was doubled over in pain on the floor. I'd had to use all of my strength not to give him a good kick in the guts myself, but I'd resisted and eventually shoved him in the car and drove him to the hospital. As we'd made our way to accident and emergency, me driving and Brett rolling around in agony on the backseat, I'd worked out this little fantasy of what would happen on our arrival. It went something like this:

Doctor: I'm very sorry to inform you, Ms. Barton, that Brett is dying. All that we can do now is make his last moments less painful. Would you mind holding this wet flannel on his forehead to relieve some of his pain?
Me: Um, no. I don't think so. Kinda busy actually.

Sadly, my little fantasy didn't quite go as planned, because Brett was diagnosed with nothing more serious than appendicitis.

But the hardest part of all this was the ex-etiquette. Once Brett was safely installed in the hospital, I hadn't known what I should do with myself. Did I stay and hold his hand? Should I go and remain impartial? Or would it be better to stay for, like, half an hour and *then* go? In the end, I just left. He'd looked a bit confused when I said I was going, but then the pethidine knocked him out and everything was fine. The last thing he said to me before I walked out was: "Brad isn't Hayley's father, it's Mike, he fell in love with Susan when they were trapped in the cave after the big earthquake. You've got to tell her before it's too late." He was quite insistent about this and when I asked him about it later, he said he'd been watching some awful late night soap because he was in pain and couldn't sleep.

But even I know my recent dilemma about whether or not to go to the wedding is a bit bigger on the ex-etiquette scale than the hospital drama—though I seem to have gotten out of making a decision now that Brett's told me I'm uninvited (yeah, right). However, there's still some part of me sending off the warning that I'll be more conspicuous by *not* showing. If I go, at least I'll look like I'm the stronger person, that I'm over it all and everything's all right.

I sit, fingers poised, thinking about all this before I remember what I'm supposed to be doing. Then I get down to work and quickly finish off the article. When I've proofread it, I sit back and smile smugly because I'm actually quite proud of myself. Women need to know about this stuff, this ex-etiquette. For example: *Do* "accidentally" burn his 300+ collection of *Playboy* magazines. *Don't* take him up on his offer to have casual sex for convenience's sake until you both find someone better. *Do* stop buying his favorite foods, even the ones you like too. *Don't* send him birthday and Christmas cards in the six months after you break up (these things can be misconstrued). *Do not send Valentine's Day cards at any cost.*

"*Do* stop buying all his favorite foods, even the ones you like too" makes me stop and think for a moment. For the first month or so after Brett had left, I'd come home with the shopping, unpack it, and find all the things I'd been so used to buying for *him* over the years—I now just put them in the cart automatically. Cheese and onion–flavored chips instead of my favorite salt and vinegar ones, apple juice instead of orange, blue gel toothpaste instead of the white stuff. Even his favorite *condoms* for Christ's sake (this shows you how strong the force of habit is). So, the next time I went shopping I very carefully changed the brand of just about everything I used and treated myself to all of *my* favorites besides (oh yeah, and I left out the condoms because I wouldn't be needing them anymore, would I?).

I post the article to the site and surf around on the Net for a while before I realize I'm bored. It's 6:30 on a Friday night and I'm bored. How pathetic is that? Usually I'd be having cocktails and endless bowls of peanuts with Sarah right now, but as she's away on business, we won't be doing the cocktail thing again until she gets back.

In the kitchen I check out the food situation. It's not good. Unless I'm interested in concocting something out of half a packet of stale corn chips, a tin of ham-flavored baked beans, those silver balls you put on top of cakes, and various out-of-date spices, I'm out of luck. I think about going back to the computer, but that seems boring too, so I sit down on one of the kitchen chairs and decide I'll try being bored in the kitchen instead.

Kind of like a new experience.

I say it out loud so it's more real.

Bored, bored, bored.

And then I try something different.

Hungry, hungry, hungry.

Put them all together and what have you got?

Bored, bored, bored, hungry, hungry, hungry.

I continue like this for about five more minutes until I realize it's even *more* boring being bored. I start to fantasize about the good old days of cocktails and what we'd be doing if Sarah and I were there right now.

Naturally, we'd be perfectly made up, dressed in new outfits, and casually leaning on the bar, men surrounding us and buying us drinks. Not the cheap happy hour margaritas, mind you, but the good shit with the cocktail umbrella and the maraschino cherry and the chunk of pineapple on the side. Maybe mai tais. We'd be engaging in witty repartee, dazzling everyone around us. Our hair would sit perfectly all night and our lipstick wouldn't come off on the glasses or our teeth. Yes, that's what we'd be doing at cocktails if we were there now.

But I can't go with Sarah, as I said before. And I can't call someone else to go out with tonight, because I distinctly remember pissing off most of the people I know earlier in the week. Besides that, if I went without Sarah, it would probably put the time continuum out of whack. But I really could do with that margarita . . .

I lick my lips. A margarita and a bowl of peanuts would really hit the spot right about now.

I get up and go over to the cupboard to check out what I've got in the way of alcohol. Who knows? Maybe I've got the ingredients to make a margarita myself (not that I've been to the supermarket lately—I'm hoping that the margarita fairy might have brought them). I don't have any tequila, but I *do* have some warm, pineapple-flavored vodka, and I know I've got half a moldy lemon in the fridge and plenty of salt in the cupboard.

I put all the ingredients on the table, find a cocktail glass, and get cracking. I don't have any egg white to stick the salt to the glass, so I lick the rim instead, put the salt on a piece of paper and turn the glass upside down.

It sticks.

So far, so good.

I splash a substantial amount of pineapple vodka into the glass and squeeze in the parts of the lemon that aren't so moldy. Then I stir it with my finger and give it a go.

I've never tasted anything so disgusting in my life.

Well, what did you expect?

But it's alcohol, so I force myself to swallow it ("don't waste good alcohol" is something I learned in my college days).

I sit down, still gagging, and look at what I'd just made. It's amazing how desperate you can get on a Friday night at home. I've made the Frankenstein's monster of cocktails and I wonder how the hell I even lifted it to my lips to taste it.

Naturally, the next thing I do is mix another one.

And after the fourth one, they don't really taste so bad anymore.

I still haven't solved the hunger problem, though. So, before I have any more, I make a quick trip to the shops and pick up dinner. The biggest packet of tomato salsa–flavored corn chips I can find. Then, with dinner covered, and nothing else to do for the evening, I fix myself another drink, grab the corn chips, and settle down in front of the warm glow of the computer.

Dumped2

First, I check the e-mail.
There's only one message:

To: gemma@allmenarebastards.com
From: dumped2@notmail.com

Hi Gemma. I'm your number one female fan and have been since the very beginning of your site. It really used to give me a laugh, reading your new articles—I liked the one about the ways to get back at him best. But Gemma, what's going on? Some of your articles have gone a bit dark. And that article, the one about the ex-fiancé with the disclaimer down at the bottom saying that none of it's true and that the ex-fiancé's name has been changed to "Prett" to hide his real identity. That was your ex-fiancé you were writing about, wasn't it? I could tell. Isn't that a bit mean? Anyway, I just wanted to say that I know what you're going through. And I really do like your site. It could definitely go places if you get back on track. Why not talk to someone about your problems? It can be really helpful, you know.
Dumped2

By the end of the e-mail I am fuming. My articles a bit dark? Being mean to "Prett"? Telling me to "talk to someone"? And pardon me, but I thought my site already *was* going places. Where did this chick get off?

Usually, I wouldn't bother replying to this kind of e-mail, but tonight it really, really pisses me off. By now, the alcohol's kicked in and it's all I need to spur me on.

To: dumped2@notmail.com
From: gemma@allmenarebastards.com

Well, thanks for your input Dumped2. I guess you're right. My articles have gone a bit dark lately, but yours probably would too if:

1. your fiancé walked out on you, decided to marry someone else, then asked you to the wedding;
2. your mother took your father back for about the fifth time, while he got another divorce; and
3. you pissed off all your friends in quick succession because you were a nasty bitch (apparently it's just a phase I'm going through).

So, if I've been a bit mean these past couple weeks, please excuse me.
I'm sure you understand what I'm going through, you understanding person, you (why does everyone tell me this?).
Oh yeah, and as for the "talking to someone," I don't think I really need a psychiatrist, thanks. I haven't gone quite that loony.
Yet.
I'll let you know when I do.
Gemma

I send the message, cross my arms, and sit back. Ha! Take that. I open up the corn chip packet and dig in heartily, ready to ingest copious amounts of fat and maybe play a few games on the Net to fill in the rest of my Friday night.

But then, just as fast as I've sent my message, one comes whizzing back.

To: gemma@allmenarebastards.com
From: dumped2@notmail.com

Gemma! No need for the sarcasm. I didn't mean you needed a psychiatrist, I just meant that you should talk to a friend, something like that. Oh, and I'm not one of those awful people who pat others on the back and say they understand. I really do understand because the same thing that happened to you, happened to me. Let me explain.

I got engaged to the person I thought was the "love of my life." My wedding date was set and we'd planned everything to perfection over a whole year. Sure, we'd had our ups and downs and there was almost a time when we canceled the wedding because he wasn't sure of his feelings for his ex, but we worked this out and everything seemed fine. Except that, an hour before the wedding, just as I was getting ready to leave for the ceremony, his brother showed up to tell me that he wouldn't be coming (this was supposed to be the "nice" way of telling me). He'd taken off with the ex who, apparently, he'd been seeing behind my back for months.

They got married two weeks later in Hawaii.

So, you see, I do understand.

Hey, I've got an idea. Are you doing anything right now? Want to chat? We could IM if you want. E-mail me back if you want to.

Dumped2

Poor Dumped2, I think, stuffing more corn chips into my mouth. What a bummer! The groom makes tracks on the actual wedding day and then goes off and gets married two weeks later to his ex. In Hawaii, too. That makes it doubly bad.

But do I want to IRC?

I stuff even more chips into my mouth as I think. Why the hell not? Isn't that what all single people do on a Friday night these days?

Greasy-fingered, I e-mail back to say yes. Then I quickly finish off the corn chips, wipe my hands on my jeans, and wait for the little flashing message that means someone wants to speak to me (about time, eh?).

Flash, flash.

I press on the message and wait.

D2: Gemma?

I hold off from replying for a second while I try and find out where this person is from. You see, on some programs you can trace where the other person is. I know you can do it on this program too, but I'm out of luck—she's blocked the information (not that this is strange or anything, I do the same thing myself when I'm IRCing—there're some real weirdos out there roaming the Net).

D2: Gemma?
Gem: That's me.
D2: Oh, there you are. I guess I should start by saying that I didn't mean to be rude about your site. I just wanted to know why it's changing all of a sudden.
Gem: Like I said, it's changing because I'm a nasty bitch.
D2: I'm sure you're not a nasty bitch.
Gem: Want to try me out?

D2: OK, I believe you, but why?

Gem: Why what?

D2: Why are you being such a nasty bitch?

Gem: I just can't seem to help myself. All the men in my life suck. I'm majorly pissed off at just about everyone.

D2: Everyone?

Gem: Almost. So what's your real name?

D2: Sorry, can't tell. Nothing personal, there're just a lot of crazies on the Net, you know?

Gem: Yeah, I know, I was just thinking the same thing myself. But don't worry, I know what they're doing. Most of them are busy twenty-four hours a day e-mailing my site. You should see the hate mail I get! Can you at least tell me how old you are/what you do?

D2: I'm a 21-year-old telemarketer.

Gem: Really?

D2: No, it's just what all the guests say they are on the talk shows on TV, so I thought I'd go along with it.

Gem: Aha! You're in the States.

D2: Maybe, maybe not. Anyway, let's get back to the men thing. All the men in your life can't suck.

Gem: Want to bet?

D2: Come on . . .

Gem: Come on, what? I'm telling you, all of the men in my life suck. Like the site says, "all men are bastards."

D2: No they're not.

Gem: How can you say that? You got dumped just as bad as I did, worse even.

D2: That doesn't mean that all men are bastards, just that mine was!

Gem: Close enough. So obviously yours and mine are either representative of the species or they're working in collusion.

D2: But men get dumped too.

Gem: Sure. Have you ever personally heard of a woman leaving a man at the altar?

D2: Actually, yes.

Gem: Well I guess that blows my theory. But I still think they're all bastards.

D2: Look, I'll prove to you that all men aren't bastards.

Gem: Yeah? And how are you going to do that?

D2: I don't know.

Gem: Well, that's not much of a start, is it? Let me rephrase the question, *why* are you going to do that?

D2: Because it's true—they're not all bastards. Just because your fiancé and your dad let you down doesn't mean you should lose hope. There's some really nice guy for you out there. I'm sure of it. But if you close your mind, you close your eyes, too.

Gem: Spare me the new age shit.

D2: Nice!

Gem: OK, so did you find your guy yet?

D2: Well . . . not yet. But I'm going to. I really am. And I want you to as well. I really detest those man-hating women, they've got ugly personalities and a definite lack of faith. Don't become one of *them*.

Gem: I think I already am one of them. So, go on then, prove it to me. Prove it to me that all men aren't bastards.

D2: Now?

Gem: Yeah, now. Go on.

D2: Only if you tell me your argument first.

Gem: What argument?

D2: That all men *are* bastards.

Gem: Oh, so now I have to give you an argument, do I? This is all starting to look like work—like some kind of bad high school public speaking event.

D2: It's only fair. Then I can tell you why they aren't.

Gem: Good luck.

D2: I can! How about if we IRC at the same time
tomorrow? Then we'll both have a day to think about
it.
Gem: I wouldn't miss it for the world. I'm looking for-
ward to hearing this argument of yours.
D2: So am I.
Gem: OK then, see ya.
D2: Bye.

I get rid of all the IRC stuff and think about how cool that
was. Dumped2, whatever her real name is, seems really nice.
It's strange how easy it is for me to open up to people on the
Net. I guess it's the anonymity of it all. And I have to say it
feels good to talk to someone who's been through the same
thing. After all that not-talking-about-Brett to Sarah, to
Michael, to my parents, even to Brett, it is kind of therapeutic
to finally let some of it out, to talk about it to someone like it
really did happen, that it matters, and that it isn't some fig-
ment of my imagination.

I go to bed a much happier Gemma.

Brett relents

A n e-mail from Brett greets me over my morning cereal:

To: gemma@allmenarebastards.com
From: bretth@notmail.com

Dear Gemma,
Although I'd still like you to take that article down off
your site, I'm sorry about yelling at you the other day
and also that I told you to look at the wedding site like I
did. I've tried to see things from your point of view and
I understand why you're angry. I know this is a bit late,
but I'd still like you to come to the wedding on
Saturday if you can make it. You were a big part of my
life for a long time and I know I handled things badly,
but I'd still like us to be friends.
Anyway, give me a call or e-mail or something if you'd
like to come. I'll be keeping a place for you and anyone
else you'd like to bring.
Brett.

Dumped2 –
the showdown

S even-thirty the following night:
Flash, flash.

D2: Hi, Gemma!
Gem: Hi. Guess what. My ex sent me an e-mail. He's reinvited me to the wedding.
D2: You should go—it'll make you look like the better person.
Gem: I was thinking along those lines too. But then I'd actually have to go.
D2: Well, yes.
Gem: And it's this weekend. I've got nothing to wear.
D2: Buy something. Buy something totally cool and expensive and go. And take someone with you. That way you can't back out at the last moment.
Gem: Like who? You think I've got this never-ending dance card?
D2: Isn't there anyone you can take?
Gem: Unless you think a) a gay guy, or b) an escort is a good idea, then no.
D2: Actually, an escort would be great. You can hire one of the expensive, luxury models (the ones that come with a brain attached to the looks) and show him off.
Gem: I can see the possibilities, but it's too gross!
D2: Isn't there anyone else?
Gem: Nope.

D2: Absolutely no one at all?
Gem: No one.
D2: Come on, there must be someone. How about someone from work?
Gem: "Work" = me and my PA.
D2: No good, it has to be a guy.
Gem: My PA is a guy.
D2: No way! Your PA is a guy? Go girl! Isn't that supposed to be a power thing?
Gem: Apparently, but he's the one with the power over me. You should see how he makes me work. Like a Spartan slave or something.
D2: So ask him.
Gem: Hmmm . . .
D2: Go on.
Gem: Well . . .
D2: Do it!!!
Gem: Maybe . . .
D2: You better :o)
Gem: Stop it, I hate those things, they make me ill.
D2: OK :o(
Gem: Ugh. Stop it, I said!
D2: Anyway, time for your argument.
Gem: I was waiting for that.
D2: So?
Gem: OK, I've written a list—you'll have to give me a moment to type it out.
D2: I'm waiting . . .
Gem: All men are bastards because:

- they leave the toilet seat up;
- they all say they want a woman who has "personality plus," when what they really want is a woman with a "personality" *plus* the body of a Barbie doll, *plus* the reproductive eagerness of a bitch in heat;

- they all know those three very special little words "let's be friends" and use them like a "get out of jail free" card;
- they have complex and involved relationships with their penises, so much so that they need to give them ego-boosting names like "Sam the Slayer" and "Huge Hugo";
- they leave the toilet seat up;
- they gawk at good-looking women and like to think they're being discreet;
- they leave the toilet seat up;
- they whine like they're on death's door when they get a little cold, and when we have the flu, they complain that we haven't done the shopping;
- they leave the bathroom smelling like something recently died in it; and then, when they're done
- they leave the toilet seat up;
- they complain about women drivers when everyone knows the stats say women are *better* drivers than men (apparently these stats are "rigged");
- they eat the last piece of chocolate cake and lie about it;
- they leave the toilet seat up; and
- they leave the toilet seat up.

There. I'm finished.
D2: Wow.
Gem: So? Counter argument?
D2: Um . . .
Gem: Don't tell me you're going to flake out on our deal.
D2: No, it's just that yours is better than mine—that toilet seat thing is pretty convincing. Can you give me two extra days? Please? I'm begging you.
Gem: Cheat!!!

D2: It'll be worth your while, I promise.

Gem: It better be. It's my birthday tomorrow—don't piss me off on the day after my birthday.

D2: Happy birthday! I promise it'll be good. The birthday *and* the argument.

Gem: You shouldn't make promises you can't keep. Same time then?

D2: You got it. And ask your PA to the wedding.

Gem: I didn't read that.

My birthday turns out better than expected

Naturally, I wake up early on my birthday. This is simply because I've got nothing to do and nowhere to go and this way I can torture myself about it. At 7:30 I lie in bed for half an hour waiting for the phone to ring, but knowing that this is unlikely to happen since I've managed to piss off just about everyone I know. I give myself a quick update and count off the people who aren't speaking to me on one hand. First of all there's my mother, then Michael. And I guess Imogen makes three, because I doubt she'll make an effort to stop trying to kill me on my birthday, and my father makes four because he probably doesn't know when my birthday is anyway. At least I've made up with Sarah, otherwise I would have to start counting everyone off on two hands (and after that it's toes time). But even Sarah's not going to be much good to me today, because she's still away on business.

I roll over and check the little red numbers. Eight o'clock. If Chris was working today he'd be here in an hour or so.

But he's not working today.

I roll right back over again and try to think of something exciting I could do on my birthday that will make everyone else extremely jealous that they missed out.

I could go to a theme park and ride a roller coaster all day.

And be sick by myself.

I could go and have a first-rate lunch at the best table in the best restaurant in town.

And sit by myself.

I could go on a movie marathon and see four movies in a row.

And eat Jaffas by myself.

See a link here?

By 8:30 no one's called and I start to truly believe they're not going to. So I get in the shower and am shampooing my hair, just about to make an executive decision on what to do today, my twenty-eighth birthday, when the phone starts ringing.

Aha! I knew they couldn't resist.

I wash the shampoo out as fast as I can, grab a towel, and sprint to the phone.

Which naturally stops ringing just as I pick it up.

But no fear, I pick it up and do that new whatsit-thing where you can dial back the phone numbers of calls you've missed. There's no way I'm missing a birthday call.

I copy the number down and look at it for a minute, trying to work out whose it is. It's familiar, but it's definitely not Michael's number or Sarah's cell like I'd expected. Then I remember who it belongs to.

It's Chris's number.

So it's not a birthday call after all, because I don't think Chris even knows when my birthday is. He's probably calling about work or something.

I consider going back and finishing my shower, but I'm already standing here with the phone in my hand, so I call him back right away.

"Hello?"

"Hi, Chris, it's Gemma. Did you just try to call me?"

"Um, yeah. I thought you weren't home."

"I was in the shower."

He laughs. "Sorry. Anyway, happy birthday."

Happy birthday? How did he know? But before I get a chance to speak, Chris answers for me.

"Michael told me."

"Oh," I say. "Thanks."

"So what are you doing today?"

I try to think of the correct answer to tell my slave driver PA. "Um, working, I guess."

"Gemma, you're allowed a day off on your birthday."

"Yeah, but to do what? And with whom, if I may ask?"

Chris pauses. "Aren't you doing anything? Aren't you going out tonight with Sarah?"

"Not likely. Sarah's still away and I'm not talking to Michael, or he's not talking to me, or something. So it's Imogen or nothing. And if that's what it comes down to, I'll take nothing. Gladly."

"Oh, right. I thought you'd be busy."

I wrap my towel around me a bit tighter. "This is my twenty-eighth birthday—to be remembered in history as the birthday no one spoke to me. I'm not going to be very busy."

"Well, do you want to go out or something?"

"With you?"

"If it's not too beneath you or anything."

I'm floored. "No, I didn't mean . . . well, OK. What should we do?"

"What do *you* want to do? It's your birthday."

I tell him about my roller coaster/best restaurant/movie-marathon birthday-type fantasies and how I haven't been great at coming up with something to do so far.

"Fine then, I'll think of something," he says eventually. "All you have to do is be ready in half an hour, OK?"

"OK," I say back, and as I hang up the phone and run back to the shower, I catch a glimpse of myself in the mirror. I see me with a big smile on my face.

I'm dressed and am drying my hair off in the bathroom when Chris arrives. I turn the dryer off for a second and stick my head around the door. "It's open," I yell. "I'm in here."

I worry for a second that it's not Chris and that I've just invited a vampire or an ax murderer into the house. But sure enough, it's Chris who turns up in the bathroom doorway.

Carrying Imogen in one hand and a present (!) in the other.

"Hey," he says, putting Imogen down with a pat. "This is for you," he holds the present out.

I gingerly take a step over Imogen who hisses at me and runs off down the hall. While I'm watching her departure, Chris leans forward and kisses me on the cheek. "Happy birthday."

I'm flustered for a second, not expecting the kiss, or even the present. "Um, thanks," I say, taking more than a few steps back and almost tripping over the bathtub. I sit down on the toilet lid and open the present.

It's chocolate. A big box of milk chocolate Lindt balls.

My favorite.

I open the box as quickly as I possibly can and unwrap one, popping it in my mouth.

Oh yes. I can practically feel my eyes rolling into the back of my head.

When it's all over, I remember my manners and pick another one out, unwrap it, get up, walk over to Chris, and pop it in his mouth.

I wait for the reaction, but it's just not the same.

"Don't you like them?" I ask him.

He shrugs. "It's chocolate. I can't tell the difference between that stuff and Cadbury's really."

I look at him in complete non-comprehension. Men. They just don't understand chocolate. I remember this boyfriend Sarah had for a while who, for her birthday, sent her the largest chocolate basket I'd ever seen. He didn't understand chocolate either. Not only was ten pounds of chocolate a very *bad* choice of present for a model, he also displayed his complete ignorance of the female chocolate-coated mind. Sarah and I ate some of that chocolate and we came to agree that it was the worst chocolate we'd ever tasted in our lives. The guy just didn't understand that two ounces of Lindt was a better gift any day than ten pounds of gritty crap. In the end, Sarah gave the chocolate to a thirteen-year-old cousin who ate it happily, because being thirteen and male he didn't understand chocolate either.

I open up the box again and offer it to Chris who shakes his head. "It's wasted on me," he says. "But you have another one."

As if I needed any encouragement to eat chocolate. I put one more in my mouth and do the eye rolling thing again. When I come back down to earth, Chris is still standing there, leaning against the door frame and watching me in amazement.

"So where are we going?" I ask.

"I thought we might go for a drive in the country, have lunch somewhere, and check out a few galleries."

I don't know about the gallery thing, but the lunch sounds good. "Great," I say and squeeze past Chris to get into the hallway. I pick up my bag and put the chocolate box in as Chris watches me. "In case we get hungry," I explain with a grin.

"Good thinking," he says and steers me down the hallway by the small of my back.

Outside Chris opens the car door for me (how gallant), we get in, and we're off.

As we drive through the city, it's funny seeing people rushing around. I have to remind myself that it's a normal workday for them, a day spent at the office with half an hour to grab a sandwich somewhere in the middle. And that's what they're doing now, running out to buy their sandwich. I smile for a moment, remembering how I used to be the same and that the one big decision I would make for myself on a workday was whether to have ham and salad or pastrami and salad and whether or not I could afford to buy a juice and a muesli slice as well. I hated my job and I'm glad my life's not like that anymore.

"What's so funny?" Chris asks.

I tell him about the sandwich thing and as we stop at a set of lights we take a good look at the people walking past.

"He's definitely a meat pie or sausage roll kind of guy," Chris says, looking at one man in particular. "Look at that stomach, there's no way he could keep that up on a sandwich for lunch."

"And her," I say, pointing to a woman across the road. "She's a falafel roll kind of girl."

"Chips and gravy at twelve o'clock," Chris says, looking directly in front of him.

"Oh yeah, you're right. He's a chips and gravy kind of man. And a Coke." I look at them and shake my head. "I'm so glad I'm not a worker bee anymore," I tell Chris as the lights change and we move off.

"A what?"

"A worker bee. This guidance counselor I had once, the first question she asked me was whether I was a worker bee or a bossy bee. Believe me, I had no idea what she meant, either. But she explained that there were two kinds of people in life—bossy bees, the ones who tell people what to do, and worker bees, the ones who do the work. And for years and years I was the worker bee. And now I'm a bossy bee. Being a bossy bee is great."

"Gemma, I can't imagine you being anything *but* a bossy bee."

I give him the evil-Gemma look. "Remember whose birthday it is?"

"How could I forget?"

I settle back into my seat and watch the world go past my window. And as I'm sitting, I think that for what seems like the first time in a long, long while, I'm actually having a good day.

Half a box of chocolates later, we're in the country. Chris tells me it's my job to count the cows and his to count the windmills, which he explains is some kind of family tradition, so I play along. It's nice and sunny outside and very country-ish. So countryish it's hard to believe we're only forty minutes outside of the city. It takes us twenty cows to get there (this is my new method of measuring distance in the country—in cows).

Chris finds a park and we hop out of the car, eager to stretch our legs and move around after our long drive.

"Now what?" I ask Chris.

"Let's have a look around," he suggests. "We can do the whole main street and by then we might even be hungry."

I doubt it after all the chocolate I've eaten, but I tell myself it's my birthday—I'm supposed to stuff myself. Calories don't count on your birthday, right? If I had my way, calories on my birthday would be negatively geared.

We start the trek up the main street, stopping in all the little galleries and holding delicate, beautiful, and some just plain strange things up for each other to see. Chris is particularly taken with some gorgeous handblown and decorated glass balls. The fudge shop with its great slabs of multicolored and flavored fudge is more my style, but I'm too full of chocolate even to consider buying some at this stage. Farther up the street I stop and drool over some rice bowls. They're perfect, just like some I saw a while back in this lifestyle magazine I buy sometimes (I don't know why I do, though, because every time I read it, it only makes me feel inadequate). I think about buying the bowls, but then stop myself because if I did I'd then have to redecorate my whole house to go with them. So I sulkily turn away and we head back down the street again and find a café to have lunch in.

Chris finds us a table and tells me he'll be back in a minute. While he's gone I read the menu and decide on a warm prawn and mango salad and a glass of chardonnay, which I know is so eighties, like cappuccino, but so what?

I like chardonnay.

I like cappuccinos too.

The Wham shirts and the fluorescent socks I can give up.

Chris comes back and sits down, placing something on the table—something gift wrapped.

"What's this?" I ask him. "You already gave me my present."

"It's a little something extra," he says, smiling. "Go on, open it."

I open it, already knowing what it is.

And I'm right.

It's the rice bowls, two of them.

I turn them over in my hands, admiring them. They really are beautiful. The lightest shade of blue with a crackled glaze and little indentations in the top to rest your chopsticks in.

"You shouldn't have, Chris. They're so expensive." And they were expensive. Almost forty dollars each.

"I saw you looking at them, I couldn't resist."

I tell him about the lifestyle magazine drool-fest I put myself through every now and again.

"You don't want a house like that," he says when I'm finished. "They're not real, it's like no one lives there. Your house is much nicer. It looks . . ."

"Like a bomb hit it?" I butt in.

He laughs again. "I was going to say lived in."

Lunch is perfect and halfway through I almost have to stop and pinch myself, I'm having such a good time. I'm really surprised when Chris tells me a bit about his brother and his sisters and his family life. After all this time he finally seems to be opening up a little, although he doesn't say anything about the ex I think he had, and I don't try to push it this time—I don't want to spoil things. After coffee and a shared piece of mudcake we realize it's 4:00 and decide to head back.

"I have to go to the toilet first," I lie, and I sneak off and pay the bill and then make a quick dash to the shop three doors up where we saw the glass balls. I buy the nicest one and sprint back to the café where Chris is waiting by the door.

"You shouldn't have paid," he says.

"Gotta be quick," I tell him and we make our way back to the car.

I think I fall asleep on the way home, full of prawns, chardonnay, mudcake, and cappuccino, because all of a sudden Chris is pulling up in front of my house.

"Home again," he says.

"Did I fall asleep?" I'm a bit worried I've done the whole head nodding and mouth hanging open thing. But Chris doesn't seem disgusted, so maybe I didn't.

"All the way home."

"Sorry."

"That's OK."

As I pick up my bag I remember the glass ball. I take it out and hand it to him. "For you. Thanks for taking me out."

Chris opens it up and I can tell he already knows what it is too. "Thanks. It was my favorite one," he leans over and kisses me on the cheek again. And this time it doesn't feel so weird.

I get out and wave as Chris drives off, then check my mailbox.

Where I find a Telstra bill.

And three cards. One from Michael, who says he misses me, one from my mother, who says she kicked my father out after two days, and one from Sarah, promising she'll be home soon, complete with present.

http://www.allmenarebastards.com

The guy who lives up the road (Sydney, New South Wales, Australia) I don't know his name, but there's this guy who lives up the road from me who definitely deserves a listing on this site. Why?

255

Because he actually has one of those "no fat chicks" stickers on the back of his car. Ugh.

Danny (Houston, Texas, USA) Danny wasn't really a bastard, though he did show some bastard-like qualities now and again. What Danny really was was whacked in the head—the guy needed some serious psychiatric help. He had this weird Star Wars fetish and his house was full of packaged Star Wars stuff (which only his trusted Star Wars buddies were allowed to touch). He even had these life-size cutouts of the actors all over his house which would totally freak me out every time I turned around because someone or other's light saber would be pointing in my face. At first I thought, fine, OK, it's nice the guy has a hobby etc., but I soon learned it wasn't a hobby, it was more like a way of life. The sex was fantastic though, which is probably why I stayed around for so long. Or, that is, it was great until he wanted to start calling me Star Wars character names. Princess Leia I could handle. But Yoda? That's just too kinky.

Donald (Edinburgh, Scotland, United Kingdom) Donald had this little game that he liked to play throughout the five years we were married. I worked and he didn't and he seemed convinced (for the last year of our marriage anyway) that I was having an affair with someone from work. Some days I think he must have sat around our flat for hours thinking about nothing else and searching through my stuff, because when I'd come home, he'd put all his "evidence" in front of me (dockets, movie stubs etc.) and ask me to explain myself. Eventually he got so psychotic that I *did* have an affair with someone from work. Funnily enough, though, he never found out about that.

Sean (Perth, Western Australia, Australia) Because we went to the movies and halfway through the movie he took my hand and put it where I don't think a lot of girls have been before, or are likely to go in the future.

The post-birthday
blues

I've got the post-birthday blues on Tuesday morning. I always get this way after my birthday. For one day a year I get everything I want and everyone's nice to me and then I'm supposed to fit right back into the real world?

I don't think so.

So, every July 28 I'm grumpy. Like clockwork.

Grumpy as I am, I put an hour aside to call Michael and my mother to kiss and make up, but neither of them is home. I leave a message for both of them, knowing that we'll probably end up playing answering machine tag before we get to speak properly.

When Chris arrives I try to be a nice person, especially after our day out and the beautiful rice bowls that I used last night and washed up so carefully. But the nice thing doesn't work for long, so I relegate myself to the couch and try to keep out of his way. I've taped a whole week's worth of *Noon* with Mary-Anne Melody and have allocated Friday to sitting on the couch, eating Redskins, and studying the show intently, as if by doing this I'll be prepared for my appearance on Monday.

Naturally, Chris pretends that there is nothing wrong, that everything is as usual. He does all his usual "hellos" and "how are you this mornings," gets us both a coffee, and then, when he doesn't get much of a response to anything, he just sits down at the computer and starts working.

And while I fast-forward, and rewind and watch Mary-Anne Melody make a giggling ass of herself like she does every day, Chris works.

And works.

And works.

Which means he pays no attention to me. Little by little I start to think this is funny. Me on the couch in my post-birthday bad mood. Chris working away on the computer and pretending not to notice. So I make it into a game. I decide to see how much I can piss him off before he actually reacts. First, I chew and slurp on a Redskin very loudly. Then I turn the volume on the TV up louder, then a bit louder, then a bit louder again.

No reaction.

So I turn the radio on as well.

Imogen jumps off the TV, hisses at me, and takes a swipe at my leg with one paw as she passes, but from Chris there is . . .

No reaction.

I turn the radio off and start watching the program again. And I can't believe my luck. Mary-Anne has some chick on singing a Celine Dion song.

Perfect.

Every girl knows that Celine Dion songs are, to guys, like those high-pitched whistles you buy to scare off dogs. I turn to Chris with an evil smile and say, "Gee, I love this song," and then, still looking at him, I turn the TV up really, really loud.

It works.

Chris jumps up off his seat and his mouth moves.

I turn the sound down for a second. "What?"

"I'm going to get some lunch," he says, heading for the door.

He's almost there when I speak up, "Hey, what about me?"

"Scavenge," he says and slams the door behind him.

The bastard.

I might have deserved the slammed door, but withholding food is taking it a bit far.

I turn the TV back down again and flick channels until I hear Chris's car downstairs again. Then I turn Mary-Anne back on and pretend I've been watching intently the whole time.

He comes back in carrying a brown paper bag that I know is from the bagel place down the road. He's been to the bagel place, my favorite lunch place, and he hasn't brought me back a bagel. I turn the TV up louder again, hoping the Celine Dion singer will do an encore, when Chris throws something onto my lap.

"What's this?" I ask, not opening it.

"A bomb," he says, sitting back down at the computer.

I open it up gingerly (who knows, it could be a bomb) and look inside. It's a chocolate chip bagel.

As you must know by now, my favorite.

"Gee, thanks," I say sourly, because I was all set to be in you-didn't-buy-me-a-bagel-and-now-I'm-pissed-off mode, and turn the TV down just a little bit. I bite off a big chunk of bagel and practically choke, so I go out and grab the milk carton from the fridge. I bring it back with me into the living room and stand beside Chris at his computer thinking that since it doesn't look like I'm going to get a Celine Dion encore, maybe I can gross Chris out to get a reaction.

"Whattya doin'?" I ask, sprinkling crumbs over the keyboard and taking a big swig of milk from the carton.

He looks at me steadily. "Replying to the feedback e-mail."

That's my job. "Oh," I say and wipe my mouth on my pajama sleeve like I don't know it's my job. Then, patronizingly, "Keep up the good work." I go back and fling myself on the couch.

He stands up and looks at me and I get the feeling I'm about to get into trouble. "Look," he says, "why don't you go out and buy yourself something to wear to the wedding on Saturday?"

I sit up. "How do you know about that?"

He stops dead. "Um, Michael told me."

"Michael doesn't know."

He looks at me. "Of course Michael knows, everyone knows."

I point my finger at him. "But Michael doesn't know Brett reinvited me. So how do you know? Did you read my e-mail?"

Chris pauses for a moment and shrugs. "OK, so I read your e-mail, it was just sitting there!"

Aha! I knew it! Finally, I've caught him doing something he isn't supposed to do.

I'm ecstatic.

I get up off the couch and go over to him. "So, you've been reading my e-mail, have you?" I ask, walking around him in circles.

"Only that one," he says.

I stop circling him and move my face in closer, eyes narrowed. "*Only* that one?"

"Only that one," he repeats and I can tell he's trying not to smile.

I move in closer again. "How can I believe you?"

He's really trying not to smile now. "I guess you can't. So are you going to go out or not?"

I lean over and switch the desk lamp on, and move its position so it shines up in Chris's face. "*Ve* vill ask ze questions!" I say in my best German accent. Then I return to my former line of questioning. "I said, how can I believe you?"

"Well, I don't know your password," Chris says.

"Is that so?" I circle him again, then stop directly in front of him. "And what is *your* password?"

Chris pretends to look around, like other people are listening. "I'll have to whisper it," he says. "The walls have ears." He grabs my arm and pulls me in closer so he can whisper in my ear. The collar of his linen shirt brushes against my neck and he smells divine, a cologne I know, but can't remember the name of.

Then he says, slowly but surely, "If I tell you I *vill* have to *keel* you."

I start to laugh at his bad German accent, but then realize how close we're standing and immediately try and take a step back. But I'm stuck. Chris is still holding my arm. Surprised, I turn my head to look at him and he moves in just a fraction closer.

As if . . .

As if . . .

As if he's going to kiss me.

Chris, kiss me!

I wrench my arm away and take a step back, fast.

"What the fuck are you doing?" I yell at him.

Chris takes a step back too. "Nothing, why? What did you think I was doing?"

I stare at him like he's crazy. "I thought you were about to . . . I thought you were going to . . ." I try, then realize I don't want to say it. "I don't know!" I yell, throwing my hands up in the air.

"What are you talking about?" he asks and I start to doubt myself. Maybe he wasn't going to kiss me at all.

I stomp off to my room to get dressed and by the time I resurface, I've almost convinced myself I dreamt the whole thing up. I grab my bag and head for the door. "I'm going to go and buy myself an outfit," I say, starting to pull the door closed behind me. Then I remember I haven't actually invited Chris to the wedding yet like Dumped2 told me to. I turn and poke my head around the door, so he can hear, but not see me. "You are coming to this stupid wedding thing, aren't you?" I ask him.

Silence, then . . . "I guess I don't have much choice," he says. "But I want a raise—twenty-five dollars an hour."

"Twenty-five bucks!" I yell, but then I think about all the work he's been doing. All my work, that is, and I feel a bit guilty. "Twenty-two fifty," I try.

"Twenty-five."

"Twenty-three."

"*Twenty-five.*"

I poke my tongue out in his general direction, knowing I'm not going to win. "Fine, twenty-five dollars an hour, bleed me dry why don't you?"

And as I slam the door behind me I think that all the "wedding" stuff that Brett and Ju . . . will be sure to have (i.e., a choice of either overcooked or salmonella-infected chicken, lumpy gravy, disgusting fruit cake, cheap grog, and numerous tacky dances) will just about be punishment enough for Chris.

Dumped2 tries to win an unwinnable argument

I buy my new outfit (a grey shift dress and jacket that are tres chic and very I'm-not-the-ex-he-dumped), chug a small black coffee, pick up a TV dinner (they're very sophisticated these days, you know), and head home. I've got to be ready to go at 7:30 PM for Dumped2's argument. I manage to have a shower, don the trusty old pj's, and shove the dinner into the oven just in time.

Flash, flash.

D2: So, did you ask your PA to the wedding? (Say yes.)
Gem: Yes.
D2: Did you really?
Gem: Yes.
D2: I take it he's going.
Gem: Yes, yes, and double yes. Get off my back already.
D2: So, what does he look like? Will he make a big splash?
Gem: Not unless he dazzles them with his wit and charm.
D2: That's not very nice.
Gem: OK, so he's not that bad.
D2: But you get on with him, don't you?
Gem: Sure, we get along just fine. He works and I watch. On good days I even manage to piss him off.
D2: I'm sure you don't. I'm sure he thinks you're a great boss.

Gem: Yeah, so great he tried to kiss me, or at least I think he tried.

D2: What?! He tried to kiss you?

Gem: I don't know. I'm not sure. I think I'm trying to talk myself out of believing it.

D2: Maybe there's hope for you! Do you like him?

Gem: I don't know. A bit. Maybe. No! Anyway, I'm not looking for anything like that. I've had it with men.

D2: So you keep saying. But maybe something inside you is saying they're not all bastards after all.

Gem: If that's your argument, I'm leaving now.

D2: It's not.

Gem: Besides, just because we can't help fancying some men doesn't mean they're not all bastards.

D2: Hmmm . . . logic is falling a little short here.

Gem: My logic! Let's hear yours then.

D2: Ah, so you want to hear my argument?

Gem: Yes. And you've already lost five marks for handing it in late. There'll be no gold stars or "warm fuzzy" stickers for you.

D2: Oh well, here it goes then. So, the "all men are bastards" thing? It simply can't be true because it's a generalization. How can all men be bastards? You may as well say that all blondes are dumb or every woman is a bad driver, and I'm sure you don't believe those things. I think all people are bastards to other people at one time or another, men, women, children, old people, young people. So it should be "all people are bastards" not "all men are bastards," right? Wrong—this can't be correct either because not everyone can be a bastard all the time. You were with Brett for five years, weren't you? That's a long time to spend with someone who's a bastard all of the time. There must be more good times you remember than bad, there has to

270

be. And the same goes for everyone—it was the same with my partner. So, I guess it should be "some people are bastards some of the time," because it certainly isn't true that *all* men are bastards *all* of the time. I guess you could say a subset of men are bastards . . .

Gem: Yeah, but it just doesn't have the same ring to it, does it? "Asubsetofmenarebastards.com." I think I'll pass on this one . . .

D2: Don't butt in! Look, answer me this question. Do you really think that just because the two most important men in your life let you down, that every single man in the world is like that and will let you down too?

Gem: But they all seem to, sooner or later.

D2: Come on! Are you telling me every man in your life has let you down?

Gem: You sound like you think there are a lot of men in my life.

D2: What about friends?

Gem: I've only really got one good male friend and he's not speaking to me at the moment, so I guess he's let me down too.

D2: Why isn't he talking to you?

Gem: Basically because I'm a mean bitch.

D2: So who let who down, was it him or you?

Gem: No comment.

D2: You have to agree with me then. Not every man in your life has let you down.

Gem: Fine, then. I agree.

D2: Your PA hasn't either by the sound of it, has he?

Gem: No, I guess not.

D2: Then I think you should sit down and have a really good look at your life and what you're doing. You're only hurting yourself by dealing with your breakup this

way. I can't see how crucifying all the men in the world
is going to help you get over your ex and get on with
your life.

Gem: I thought I *had* gotten over him and gotten on
with my life.

D2: Really? Do you really think that?

Gem: Yes.

D2: OK, let me ask you this. When you guys first
started up the bastard list, when you were share-hous-
ing, how much time did you spend on it? In the first
couple months how many hours would you have spent
sitting down and writing guys in?

Gem: I don't know. Maybe five?

D2: And then what did you do? Did you go about your
business, not thinking about the list or the next person
who was going to go on it?

Gem: Sure. We were at college, we had plenty of
other things to do.

D2: Well, that's just it, Gemma. You see, that's how
other people see your site. It's something they do for a
laugh. They write a couple of guys in, then they get up
and get on with their lives.

Gem: So? That's what it's for.

D2: I know!!! But you're spending twenty-four hours a
day on your site, compared to the five hours a month
you used to spend. It can't be good for you. It's like
watching a news channel that's only bad news all the
time.

Gem: But it's my job . . .

D2: Yes, but you take it so *personally.* Even as an out-
sider I can see the anger building in your site. It used
to seem like a bit of fun, a way to vent some frustra-
tion, nothing serious. But now you're trying to hurt
people like your ex with your site, and that's not going
to make you feel any better in yourself, it's just petty

and spiteful. It seems even your friends have had
enough of it. Isn't it time to stop?
Gem: Geez, why don't you tell me how you really feel?
D2: Gemma, I'm not trying to get at you, maybe you
should talk to someone about your problems instead of
trying to be "strong" and cover them up. You should
talk to your friends, at least. It doesn't sound like
you're telling them much at all and what's the use of
turning your friends away? We all need help from people at some time or another—that's what friends are
for. They might be able to help steer you onto the right
track. I mean, this hatred of men seems to be seething
from your every pore and while it's OK to hate Brett,
for a while, you can't hate *all* men for what he did forever! It's unreasonable.
Gem: I've got to go.
D2: Gemma, I . . .
Gem: No, I've really got to go. My dinner's burning.

And it is burning. I pull it out of the oven and hopefully in-
spect the damage.

But it's burnt. Not scrape-off-the-black-bits burnt, but really
truly burnt, as in burnt into a piece of charcoal.

I swear and throw it into the garbage. It's going to be
muesli for dinner again. Imogen comes in and I feed her one
of her expensive little one-serve tins that cost $1.50 each and,
as I do so, I realize her dinner's costing more than mine.

I'm sure she thinks that's the way it should be.

I sit down with my pathetic bowl of muesli and an even
more pathetic plastic cup and spoon because I haven't done
the dishes (except for the rice bowls) since Chris did them
last week. And as I'm eating I remember something a friend
at college told me once. She'd said, "You know, if you didn't
have Brett, you'd be a real man-hater."

And I guess she was right, because I am. I mean, my whole

paycheck is based on it, so I must be one. But it sounds like such an ugly thing to be. And all that stuff Dumped2 said about the site taking over my whole life, about me believing in it too much and it not being fun anymore, at least that's bull-shit.

Isn't it?

Or is that just what I keep telling myself?

Cocktails—again

I toss and turn the whole night in bed, thinking about what Dumped2's said. A few phrases in particular keep popping up in my mind:

Not everyone can be a bastard all the time. It just doesn't work that way.

Do you really think that every single man in the world is going to let you down?

You're trying to hurt people with your site and that's just petty and spiteful.

You can't hate all men for what Brett did to you.

It gets so bad that at two AM I wake up repeating the phrase "petty and spiteful" over and over again in my head. I have to get up and drink a glass of water and I can't get back to sleep until 3:30.

And it continues like this all day. And all the next day—I just can't stop thinking about it. I consider calling Sarah for a chat and telling her about it, but something stops me. Maybe it's the fact that I've never spoken to her about the breakup before. Or, maybe it's because I can't tell her about Dumped2—how would she feel about me confiding in someone I don't even know when I can't talk to her, my best friend?

But it keeps right on grating at me. It's like I know some of the things Dumped2's said are true, but I can't admit it to myself that they are, or won't admit it. So I push the thoughts to the back of my mind and work away on replying to all the feedback e-mail. Then I take a well-deserved nap in the afternoon to catch up on my missed sleep. I'm hoping that Sarah will make it back from Melbourne in time for cocktails, because all I want to do is go out and forget about the whole thing.

Sarah calls me at 6:00, just as I'm losing hope.

"I'm back, I'm back!" she says.

"About time," I humph. "I've been sitting here dressed and waiting for over an hour."

"Oh, very nice. I hope you appreciate this, I had to sprint to catch the plane—I didn't think I was going to make it."

"So where are you now?" I ask.

"I'm in a taxi heading for my place. How about if I just drop my stuff off at home and then meet you at the bar?"

"About half an hour?"

"Great, see you there."

I hang up and quickly go back and finish off the shirt I was ironing (I was kind of lying about the "sitting here dressed and waiting for over an hour" thing). Then I put the shirt on, add a bit of lipstick and a squirt or two of perfume, call a taxi of my own, and I'm off like a vomiting barn rat (oops, how did that get in there?).

With some superb timing, Sarah's cab pulls up right behind mine outside the bar. She comes over and takes my arm and we head inside. "God I need a drink," she says. "I only had $2.50 and a Cabcharge on me so I couldn't get one on the plane."

"Bad flight, eh?"

"I'll say. They sat me between two guys and for the whole of the flight the one on my left kept trying to hit on me and the one on the right used his sick bag, my sick bag, and the guy on my left's sick bag."

"Lovely. And did he give them back when he was finished

with them? You wouldn't want to miss out on all that dis-counted film processing."

"Thankfully, he didn't. The discounted film processing I can go without for once."

We sit down at the bar. Sarah catches Pete the bartender's eye and holds up four fingers.

This is Pete's signal that it's been a bad day, we need four of his best, and to make it snappy.

He does.

Sarah takes a long sip of her drink as soon as it comes, then sighs. "That is *so* much better." She reaches down, pulls some-thing out of her bag, and then straightens up again. "This is for you," she says, handing me a small parcel. "I got you some-thing extra special because I couldn't be here for your birthday."

I tear off the wrapping paper to find a very familiar-looking little box. It's familiar because I've got plenty of these boxes at home—they come from my favorite shop in Melbourne, this tiny little Russian shop that sells gorgeous jewelry and all sorts of other drool-worthy objects.

I open up the box to find the most beautiful pair of amber earrings.

"Thanks, Sar," I say, giving her a big hug. "They're just what I would've chosen." I take off the earrings I have on, put the amber ones on instead, and push myself up on the bar. I dodge the bottles on the shelves opposite me so I can see my gorgeousness in the mirror. "They're beautiful! So how was Melbourne?" I take one more admiring glance at myself be-fore I sit back down.

Sarah polishes off her first margarita and starts on the sec-ond. "Very, very boring. Don't want to talk about it."

"That bad?"

"Worse. To give you an idea of how bad it was, the hotel was full and I had to share a twin room with Stinky Stacey from ac-counts."

"Oh no." Stinky Stacey was, as her name implied, stinky. We could never work out whether she'd just never discovered deodorant, whether the deodorant she wore didn't work, or whether her funk had just seeped into her clothing over the years. What we did know was that she was stinky with a capital "S." The girls at Star Graphics had tried various tricks to get Stinky Stacey to wear deodorant over the years. Leaving bottles of the strongest varieties around the women's bathroom had been a favorite, as had hopeful Christmas gifts of Impulse and other body sprays.

Nothing had worked.

"So how'd it go?"

"What do you reckon? She stank. The hotel room stank. I stank. But enough about that, tell me what's been going on here."

I shrug. "Nothing."

"Nothing! I bet I've missed out on heaps. Isn't the wedding tomorrow?"

"Don't remind me."

"Are you taking Michael?"

"No, Chris actually."

"Really?" Sarah's eyes widen and for a moment I think she's going to make some comment about Chris. The same kind of comment Drew made.

I think up something quick to stop her. "So what happened to that guy?"

It works. "What guy?"

"The one from here, from the bar."

"Oh, him. Dumped him," she shrugs. "But I'm seeing someone else."

Surprise, surprise.

"Who?"

"Well, you know James?"

"James?"

Sarah gives her margarita a quick stir. "James the *fireman*."

"Oh my God, don't tell me you're seeing him."

"I am seeing him. I called up and got his number the other day—he seems really nice."

"You don't waste any time, do you? Why didn't you tell me?"

"I was going to! I haven't even been out with him yet, we're going out for lunch tomorrow."

Aha! Now I see why she didn't tell me and I give her The Look. "I thought you had a family thing tomorrow. I thought that was why you couldn't come to the wedding."

"Well . . . it was canceled and I'd already sent a non-acceptance card and everything."

"Yeah, thanks for the moral support, *best friend*."

"You'll be all right . . ."

"Yeah." Then . . . "Maybe," I say a bit more quietly. And Sarah must see it in my face, the fact that I've let my guard drop just a little. The fact that it might just be OK to ask.

"How do you . . . how do you feel about going?"

I shrug. "I feel OK about it, I guess. I don't want to go, but I have to, really. And it won't kill me to act like it doesn't matter for a couple of hours."

Sarah pauses. "But it does matter, doesn't it?"

I look her straight in the eyes because I can't say anything. If I do, I think I might cry.

She takes one of her hands and tucks it under my chin. "Don't you worry, chickadee. He just didn't know a good thing when he saw it. You'll be fine. And if you want me to come with you, just say so. I'll cancel with James."

I take a deep breath as Sarah digs around in her handbag and hands me a tissue. "No. It's OK. I'll go with Chris."

"You sure?"

I nod. "I'm sure."

"Gemma?"

I know what's coming, but decide to play along with it for her sake. "What?"

"You're beautiful!"

And even though I've heard her say it a thousand times before, I know that this time she really means it.

The wedding

I wanted to look stunning. I wanted to look on top of the world, but carefree too, like I always breezed out of bed on a Saturday morning and thought "Hmmm, I wonder what's on the agenda today—oh, that's right, my ex-fiance's wedding. I almost forgot."

Yeah right.

So, knowing I'll need both a good night's sleep and an hour and a half's preparation for the stunning, on top of the world (but carefree) look, I go to bed at three AM after my massive binge drinking session with Sarah.

Pathetic, I know.

The wedding's at two PM and Chris calls me at one. I do my best to sound as if I'm not still in bed and he tells me to get out of bed, he's on his way over. Chris only lives ten minutes away, so I have the quickest shower in history (surprisingly, for what must be the first time in my life, I don't have a hangover) and am drying my hair when he lets himself in.

I stick my head around the bathroom door, banging myself on the open top drawer of the bathroom cabinet as I go. "Ow. Almost ready," I lie over the noise of the hair dryer.

I hear his footsteps on the wooden floor. And then I look down and I panic. There, right in the middle of the top drawer for everyone to see is the packet of pills the doctor gave me. The ones I never took. For the depression. Instantly, I realize I don't want Chris to see them. Out of everyone, I don't want him to know. Quickly, I shove them up the back, close the drawer, and pull my bathrobe tighter around me as the footsteps come right up to the door. There's a pause.

"Coffee?" he asks.

"Yes thanks."

The footsteps move into the kitchen, I breathe a sigh of relief, and keep getting ready. I just hope he hasn't seen them already.

I finish drying off my hair, which looks like shit, and slap some makeup on. Things aren't going well. I've got a volcanic zit on the end of my nose, which I cover up with loads of foundation before I realize I've now got more makeup on than Lenin's corpse. I miss with the liquid eyeliner and get some in my eye, which kills and instantly goes red. Then, to top it all off, I use too much blush. The whole effect looks something like Beppo the clown after a big night out and I end up having to tissue most of it off. I tell myself at least my clothes are right, but it's quite sunny outside and when I put on the grey shift and jacket, I feel hot and uncomfortable. I pull my brand-new expensive magic "figure-controlling" tights on, which I find aren't magic at all—they just rearrange your internal organs to make you *look* skinny. And while I'm pulling them on I manage to rip them right up the back with one of my well-bitten nails.

That's it. I pull them off and stalk out to the kitchen.

Chris is sitting at the kitchen table. He looks up at me as I come in.

"I'm not going," I say, flinging the pantyhose into the bin.

"What's the matter, Gemma?"

"Well, for a start, I look hideous. I've got an eruption happening on my nose, my hair looks like a bird nested in it, I don't have any tights, and I'm hot," I say, pulling off my jacket and dumping it on the table. "It's not supposed to be hot. It's still winter for Christ's sake."

"If we don't get going, we'll be late."

"I just said I don't want to go. Anyway, what's the point?" I grab an apple out of the fruit bowl and a knife and chop it straight on the bench. "I'll just be embarrassed to be there, I won't have a good time. No one will talk to me, they'll just point and stare and whisper and we'll be put on the losers table at the reception. In fact," I say, pointing the knife I'm holding at Chris for emphasis, "I'll look like an idiot."

Chris stands up and takes the knife off me. "Gemma, you'll only look like an idiot if you *don't* go."

I don't have anything to say to that, so I shove a piece of apple in my mouth while Chris stares at me. Eventually it wears me down. "What?" I ask, with a mouthful of apple.

He laughs. "You are a bloody mess, aren't you. Come on," he grabs my hand and pulls me down the hall to my bedroom. For a freakish moment I think he's going to seduce me, but he pulls me past the bed and stands me in front of my wardrobe.

"Right," he says. "Where're your scarves?"

I point to one end of my wardrobe and Chris kicks aside some clothes on the floor to get to it. He pulls the scarves out and lays them on the bed, then selects a delicate pink one, ties it around my neck, and jauntily turns it so that the knot sits at the side.

"There," he says. "That solves you being hot. You can just take the jacket and wear it tonight when it's a bit colder. Now, pantyhose. Where do you keep them?"

I point to one of my dresser drawers. Chris goes over, opens it up, and rummages around. "I can't find any pantyhose," he says after a minute or so.

"That's because I don't wear pantyhose. But if I had any I'd keep them in there."

"What's this then?" he says pulling something out for me to look at. "Or shouldn't I ask?"

It's a pair of black fishnets.

"They're from jazz ballet, all right?"

"Sure."

"For God's sake, I was twelve! I couldn't wear them now even if I wanted to."

He's smirking. "Let me rephrase the question. Do you have any *normal* pantyhose?"

"I just *said* I don't wear them."

"Doesn't matter, women always seem to have a drawer full of them whether they wear them or not. We'll buy some on the way. Now, shoes."

I point again and Chris moves over to the bottom of the wardrobe. He picks out my favorite pair of black mid-heels, the ones with the strap. I'm surprised he's chosen them—most guys would have picked the slutty-looking stilettos. The boy obviously has taste.

"Handbag?"

I point and he chooses my little black clutch.

"Earrings? Perfume?"

"In the bathroom."

He grabs my hand and pulls me up the hallway. In the bathroom I open up my jewelry box and he picks out some pearl studs. Then I show him my perfumes and he chooses "Happy" by Clinique, my favorite.

"Happy," he says, looking at the label as he sprays it on me. "I wish."

When he's finished spraying he stands back and takes a look at me. "Hair stuff?"

I open up one of the bathroom drawers and Chris searches through it. Finally he pulls out a large black hair slide, a brush, and a can of hairspray.

"Turn around," he says, swiveling my shoulders so I've got my back to the mirror.

I'm too shocked to do anything but comply.

Five minutes later he swivels me around again and I get to see the end result. He's pulled my hair up and used the slide and hairspray to give me the kind of French roll I can never do myself, even leaving a little wisp of fringe and some hair at the sides like the hairdresser does.

"Sorry I can't do anything about the zit," he says. "I don't do makeup."

I'm speechless.

"Now," Chris says, grabbing my hand one more time, "come and have a look."

He drags me out and stands me in the hall where there's a full-length mirror, positioning me in front of it.

"Can we go now?"

I take a look in the mirror. Grey shift dress, pink scarf, pearl earrings, French roll, black shoes, and bag. I look kind of like Audrey Hepburn on a fat, zitty day, but I tell myself the zit and lack of stockinged leg give me the natural look I've been seeking.

"How did you do that?" I turn to Chris, stunned.

"I've got three sisters—it was the only way I could ever get in the bathroom. So, what do you reckon?"

I turn 360 degrees and take another look. "Good, great even." I stop and smile as a thought enters my head.

"What's so funny?"

"Oh, I was just thinking that I've never been dressed by a guy before. Undressed, yes, dressed, no." Then I go red because I remember what I'd thought as Chris had dragged me into the bedroom.

He doesn't notice, or if he does notice he's polite enough not to say anything. Instead he goes and gets my jacket and the present and we scramble out to the car, already fifteen minutes late. On the way, we stop at the 7-Eleven for pantyhose (plus a spare pair that Chris makes me buy—just in case) which I pull on in the car while holding the map and giving the worst directions ever.

When we get to the gardens, I just have time to give my pantyhose a final hitch and find us the last two seats before the ceremony begins.

After we sit down I get busy sorting myself out, smoothing my skirt, picking up the program, and fussing around (I'm also hoping that no one asks to see our invitation because I've got Sarah's—mine got "lost," remember?). In fact, I'm so busy that it's only when I sit back five minutes later that I get to have a good look around. I'm surprised at how tasteful everything looks. I thought there'd be numerous gold cherubs and tacky hearts and miles and miles of cheap netting. But there's not. The chairs are covered with a white, plain material with hot pink organza bows and the ends of the rows are decorated with multi-colored gerberas in pots. There's a runner down the aisle, but it's just some plain white fabric, not at all like the tacky red velvet ones I've seen before. There's a string quartet, too. Everything is really nice . . .

And then I see her.

Ju . . .

The sky slut.

And she's not at all what I thought she'd look like. She doesn't look like a sky slut at all.

I thought she'd be one of those tall, frizzy blondes. The ones with the fringe that looks like they spray it with a whole can of hairspray and then rub the palm of their hand over it really fast to make it stand up—complete with red lipstick and too many gold chains or a charm bracelet or something. And she'd have the "princess for a day" dress on, big and fluffy and white with lots of beading and sequins—nothing tasteful at all.

But she's not.

She's wearing a very plain white shift dress, quite like the grey one I've got on, with some kind of a translucent wrap on over the top. She's got short, dark hair in a miniature bob, the kind of cut I've always wanted but unfortunately don't have the bone structure for. And she's carrying a large bunch of multi-colored gerberas. I check the shoes. You can always tell

290

a girl by her shoes. And they're little and white, very plain. Just what I would have chosen. She looks beautiful and happy and what scares me the most is that she looks, well, nice. Like a nice person. Like she could be one of *my* friends.

It's only as she nears the top of the aisle that I catch a glimpse of Brett. I have to strain my neck to see around the lady sitting in front's hat. It's him all right. He looks the same, all spruced up, but the same. He's got that silly smile of his on his face. And as he turns around, I wonder if he'll look at me, but of course he doesn't because he's only looking at one person, there's only one person on his mind, one person to smile at.

Ju . . . smiles back at him. And it's not a normal smile, but one of those smiles that makes her show her teeth and get that "look" in her eyes—one of those "I can't help but smile" smiles. And me? I feel winded. Because he smiles back at her in the same way and in all our time together I don't ever, ever remember him looking at me like that.

I try to hate her.

I try really, really hard.

I try to squeeze the hate out from the bottom of my black little heart.

But I just can't do it. I can't hate Ju . . . She looks like the kind of flight attendant who *would* give me that extra bag of peanuts, and maybe another one to keep for later.

I look down at the ground and Chris leans over and pats my knee.

"Are you all right?" he asks.

I nod, still looking at the ground.

"It's OK to be sad," he says.

This perks me up a bit. "I'm not sad," I hiss back and manage to sit up and pull my shoulders back, ready to watch the ceremony.

It's over before I know it.

The string quartet start playing again and Brett and Julie (I finally find out her name during the vows) walk back up the aisle to the click of many a camera.

Funny, I seem to have forgotten mine.

There's a break of an hour and a half while they have their photos taken somewhere, so Chris and I go out for a coffee. And even though we have a great time talking, we watch the time and head off to the golf club, where the reception starts at 5:00, like the good little guests that we are. I'd had a bit of a snicker when I saw that the reception was going to be at a golf club, but it's not what I imagined at all. I thought it would be one of those meat, three vegetable, and gravy sit down dos, but it's not. It's a cocktail style, standing reception and as we enter and put our present on the appropriate table, someone hands us some champagne. I take a quick look around and breathe a sigh of relief. At my cousin's wedding there had been a little alcove near the entrance and every guest had had to sit down and say something on video to the bride and groom. I'd been a bit worried that Brett and Julie might have done the same thing. Thank God they hadn't though, as I had absolutely no idea what I would have said.

I take a sip of champagne and look at Chris. "Now what do we do?"

"We mingle," he says, grabbing my hand for what must be the thirtieth time that day and dragging me off again.

"No, wait," I say, and he stops.

"What?"

"I don't want to. They're all Brett's friends, he took them with him when he left. They'll just laugh at me."

"No, they won't."

"Yes, they will."

"Don't be ridiculous," he says, grabs my hand, and we're off again. He pulls me into the middle of the crowd and stops a passing waiter to grab us some hors d'oeuvres. "Now, tell me who they all are."

I look around. "Well, over there," I point, "that's his best friend, Sean."

"Great," Chris says, polishing off a piece of sushi and grabbing my hand. "That's where we're going then."

I don't even have time to argue, because Sean's spotted me. All I can do to protest is dig my fingernails into Chris's hand and hope it hurts.

"Hey, Gemma, how are you?" Sean asks and I'm surprised that he seems genuinely happy to see me, not like he's laughing at all.

"I guess you didn't expect to see me here," I say.

He looks confused. "No, Brett told me you were coming."

I want to make a joke of how I always thought I'd be at Brett's wedding, just in another capacity, but I don't.

"Um, this is Chris, my," I pause. What is he? He's obviously not here as my PA. I try again, "My friend, Chris Patterson."

Sean shakes his hand and then Chris says he'll go and find us all some more drinks. I curse him for leaving me, but Sean asks me about the Web site and, well, you could write a whole book on that, couldn't you? So, as it turns out, we've got plenty to talk about.

And the whole night works out pretty much the same. Chris and I talk to lots of people who keep calling him my boyfriend by mistake and eventually I stop correcting them. We drink too many cocktails, eat too many hors d'oeuvres, and even dance a bit (I was wrong, they didn't do any tacky dancing, not even the chicken dance or the macarena). Finally, when we're winded from dancing so much, Chris pulls me off the dance floor and we decide to go outside for a minute to catch some air. I'm not drunk, but definitely tipsy, and I'm being very careful not to fall over as we walk off the dance floor because I've seen too many of those "funny video" shows and I know what happens at weddings. I don't want to end up displaying my knickers on national television.

It's nice and cool outside on the balcony and I go and sit

down on one of the many benches and take my shoes off. My feet are killing.

Chris sits down beside me. "It hasn't been so bad, has it?" he asks. "The ceremony was nice, the reception's great, and everyone's been really happy to see you."

I don't say anything, just lean back against the balcony and look up at the stars. It's true, what Chris said. It has been a nice day, and I'm still surprised everyone's been happy to see me. Even Brett's parents. Somehow I figured that everyone would avoid me, make fun of me, or brush me off, but it hasn't been like that at all. I thought Brett would have turned them against me, telling them terrible stories about the breakup.

The same kind of stories I told about him.

I think about what Dumped2 said again, the thing about being "petty and spiteful" and feel more than a little ashamed of myself. I sigh and look over at Chris and smile a bit in answer to his question—it really *hasn't* been so bad after all. And then the smile drops off my face because over Chris's shoulder I see Brett coming right this way. I stand up in shock and Chris turns around to see what I'm looking at.

"Gemma," Brett says when he reaches us. "I've been looking for you."

"Oh," I say before I remember my manners. "Congratulations. It's a nice wedding."

"I just wanted to say thanks for coming. I know it must've been hard. And I wanted to give you this, too," he says, passing me a small, hardcovered book.

"What is it?" I ask, turning it over.

"Look inside."

I open the book and flip through the pages. It's full of stubs from movie tickets, little notes, boarding passes, things like that. Then I look more closely. The movie stubs are from the first movie Brett and I saw together, that's my handwriting on the notes, and the boarding passes are from the holiday we took to Bali. And the book's full of things like this, things Brett and I did together. I keep flipping through, remembering, astounded at all the little things he's kept. A straw, a ticket from a car park, a plastic ring. Half of the things I don't even recall being important, but they must have been important to Brett for him to keep them for so long.

"I want you to have it," he says.

I stop flipping through the pages and look at him. "I never knew you had this, I had no idea."

"In the past few months I've been thinking a lot about what happened and I'm really sorry things ended the way they did."

I go to say something and Brett stops me, "I just want to say this, OK?"

"OK," I say, looking back down at the book.

"It's just that I know I could have handled things better than I did, and I'm sorry for that. But from reading that article you wrote about me on your site, it seems you've got some kind of impression that I never cared about you, and that's just not true. So I wanted to give you this and to tell you that I wish you all the best, I hope things work out better for you and Chris than they did for us."

I'm floored by this. By the book, which I never knew about, and the fact that Brett's taken the time to bring it tonight and give it to me. Now I really do feel ashamed.

I go to open my mouth to tell him that Chris and I aren't together, that I'm sorry about the article on the site, that I'm sorry about everything really, but nothing comes out.

Finally, Brett speaks. "Well, I've got to get going." He gives me a quick peck on the cheek before he turns and walks back into the reception room.

Just as he's at the door, my voice returns. "Brett," I say, and he turns around. "Thanks."

He smiles and waves before he disappears inside.

I sit back down and place the book in my lap, rubbing my

fingers over the textured cover, trying to squeeze back any tears that might be trying to make their way out.

"Well, he doesn't seem to be the bastard you made him out to be," Chris says. "It's a beautiful book, he must have really cared about you. You didn't know about it, did you? You weren't just saying that?"

I shake my head and suddenly I realize why everyone's been so nice to me tonight. It's because Brett *didn't* tell them terrible things about me like I told my friends about him. And that fight I had with Sarah in the restaurant? I was starting to get the feeling she might have been right, that maybe I hadn't quite been telling things like they were—instead, I was telling them how I *wanted* them to be. I look over at Chris and shake my head. "I didn't know. I just didn't know."

There's silence for a moment and then Chris picks up my shoes and slides them back on my feet. "I forgot to ask you—what did we get them as a present?"

This makes me laugh. "At first I got them a chip and dip. The ugliest one I could find. But then I felt guilty and took it back. In the end they got a waffle maker. Brett used to love waffles."

Chris doesn't say anything, but smiles and then quickly holds out his hand. "Come on, let's go dance."

I crane my head so I can see the dance floor. The first people I see are Brett and Julie smiling and laughing at each other. They look happy, but I don't feel the stab I felt before when he smiled at her. And from all those self-help books I've read in the past year, I realize that what I'm feeling is closure. I even hope their waffles don't burn. So even though I know I've already drunk too much and that I'll get blisters if I dance any more, I get up and let Chris lead me inside. We eat and drink and dance and laugh all night.

I work my butt off
OR
The house gets an
overhaul

For some unknown reason, I wake up at 7:30 Sunday morning feeling really, really good and can't get back to sleep (believe me, this would never happen on a weekday). So I get up and make myself a big batch of pancakes and then spend the rest of the morning applying large amounts of Savlon and numerous Band-Aids to my feet and worrying about my TV appearance tomorrow.

When all my tacky teenage video clip shows have finished and my stomach is all pancaked out, I'm up for some distraction. Perhaps because of my encounter with Brett last night, I'm in a very making-up kind of mood, so I try and call Michael and my mother back, who by now have returned my calls, but all I get are the answering machines again. I end up watching my Mary-Anne tape one more time, trying to prepare for the kinds of questions she might ask. I know she's a ditz and that she's unlikely to ask me anything too difficult, but, hey, you never know, do you? This is TV and anything's possible.

By 12:00 I'm done with Mary-Anne and am starting to get bored. I figure this is simply because I have no idea what normal people do at this time of day. It's midday on a Sunday—a thing usually unknown to me. Late Sunday afternoon I can almost comprehend, I usually manage to stagger out of bed by at least 2:30 PM. But midday Sunday?

Sorry, no idea.

I take a guess at what might be going on outside. People are probably working in their gardens, regrouting their bath-rooms, doing the laundry, baking bread, things like that—homey-type things (things that don't usually get done at *all* in my household).

Looking around me, it becomes rather obvious that I need to do one homey-type thing in particular. The house is a pigsty. My clothes from last night are scattered from the door-way, down the hall, into the living room, and then out to my bedroom. There's even a pair of pantyhose slung over my computer (don't ask how they got there, because I don't know). There are dirty coffee cups on my desk and even a crumb-encrusted plate balancing on top of the modem. I de-cide it's time to get up off the couch and clean up. But just to make sure I'm doing the right thing, I pick up the remote, turn the TV on again, and have a quick flick through the channels. No, there's nothing on.

Fine, cleaning up it is, then.

I start by moving all of my clothes from last night into my room where they should be. And I *do* make an effort—I spend a good ten minutes looking for my left shoe before I find it. Or half of my left shoe, because the other half is sticking out from under Imogen. She's curled up on the window seat, in a little patch of sun, sitting half on and half off my shoe. For a moment I consider pulling out the shoe from under her (maybe she won't notice), then I get real and decide to leave it.

Why wake the sleeping beast?

Anyway, I figure she'll move fast enough when she hears the vacuum cleaner (Imogen hates the vacuum cleaner—ap-parently all cats do).

When I've moved everything to where it should be, I'm left with the task of emptying out the handbag I took to the wed-ding. The first thing that falls out when I turn it upside down is the little cake bag they'd given to all the guests as we left the reception. It's now a very squashed little cake bag, containing a very squashed little piece of cake. Second to fall out is the book Brett gave me and third is everything else, a mishmash of girly stuff. I ignore the girly stuff, pick up the book, and flip through it quickly, then take it and the piece of cake over to the couch and sit down.

The tidying up can wait.

I tear open the little cake bag, pick off the icing, and suck on this as I start on page one of Brett's book.

By the time I get to the end of it, two hours have passed. The cake is well and truly gone, and more than a few laughs and tears have been shared with the turning of the pages.

I stare at the last page for a long, long time. And after a while, I realize I'm still feeling the same sort of closure I did last night when I saw Brett and Julie together. It doesn't seem to matter so much who left who now, or how it happened, just that it's over. I close the book and take a look around me, at the place in which Brett and I used to live. Some days everything looks so much the same that I expect him to come walking through the door at the end of the day. And as I look around me, I suddenly don't like this feeling—that Brett's presence is still here.

But then something happens.

A strange thing, something that has never happened to me before (and probably won't happen again in my lifetime).

I get the strange and overwhelming inclination to get up off my lazy butt and spring clean the house. To redecorate, to change everything.

To have a fresh start.

To make this place "mine," all mine and no one else's.

And before I can talk myself out of it, I stand up and get going like a thing possessed.

The first thing to go is the picture of Brett on the mantelpiece, then the assortment of birthday cards and notes from him that are still stuck on my pinboard.

After this, I go through each and every room in the house

collecting things that remind me of Brett. Magnets off the fridge, an old pair of sneakers left on the back veranda, a beer in the cupboard, two prints we bought together, etc. When I've collected everything, I put it all in a pile on the living room floor and sort through it. Most of the things I decide I don't want to throw out (except for the sneakers and the beer—I'm not that sentimental). So, I go out to the kitchen and grab the biggest plastic bag I can find and put everything in there. This goes into the top of my wardrobe along with my plastic shopping bag full of letters from Brett and the book he gave me last night. I slam my wardrobe door closed.

Finished.

Done.

Then I start on the living room. The furniture gets rearranged. Anything I don't like gets chucked out.

And after this it's my bedroom, everything in there gets moved and thrown out too.

Nothing is spared.

When this is done, I decide to do what other, normal people do on a Sunday and head out to the biggest homewares store I can find to give my credit card a workout (the closest thing to exercise I'm going to get). I buy a rug, a few scatter cushions, a screen, two new prints, and a big vase for the living room (oh yes, and some new non-fire-damaged curtains). Next, some dinky plastic trays and drawers for the office find their way into the cart. Then I move onto stuff for my bedroom—a new bedspread, more new curtains, another print, and a big, industrial-size hamper with three separate compartments to organize all my dirty clothes in. I choose bright colors for everything. Oranges, pinks, purples, greens—colors I love but never used to buy because Brett hated them. He said they made his eyes sore.

I go a bit crazy actually.

And as I wait in line at the checkout, I even make an impulse buy, something I don't usually do (that's why they have those confectionery free checkouts at the supermarkets—for people like me). I pick up two aromatherapy burners and some lavender essential oil, all on sale, and throw these in my cart too. And as I wait (mentally adding up everything in my cart) I tell myself that it's OK I'm spending this much money. Most of it's for the office, which means it's a tax deduction, right?

Right?

And then I almost have a heart attack when they total everything up.

You don't want to know how much it comes to.

So I put one of the aromatherapy burners back before I sign on the dotted line.

See, I *do* know how to budget!

Then I make my way happily home again, only stopping to buy a bunch of irises from a lady on the side of the road, before I get busy with my new purchases.

By 7:30 PM, I'm done. Everything has been rearranged, thrown out, put up, washed up, dusted, vacuumed, and polished to within an inch of its life.

Everything, that is, except the bit around Imogen who I still don't have the guts to move.

I step back into the hallway and admire my work for a moment. The house looks fantastic. Everything looks so bright and cheerful—not cluttered and gray and drab like it used to.

I stand and look around me for a whole minute and a half before I flop onto the couch, exhausted.

And all in all, I feel kind of good, except for the fact that the house looks spectacular and I look like . . .

Well, like shit, really. There's no other word for it.

So I try and squeeze out a bit more energy to clean up *me*. I have to look good for TV tomorrow, don't I?

I get up off the couch one more time and head for the

bathroom, picking up the aromatherapy burner and oil on the way. In the bathroom, I run a big, long, hot bath and light the burner. I even put a few drops of oil in the bath and slap on a face mask for good measure before I climb in.

And I can practically hear my muscles thanking me as I soak in the bath for the next hour. It's not every day I ask them to get up off the couch and actually do something *phys-ical*—the poor things are probably a bit overwhelmed by the whole experience. I console them with the fact that it was definitely worth the pain to get the house looking so great and to achieve the goal I set this morning.

Which brings me back to thinking about the goal itself—to change everything, to give myself a fresh start, to make the place "mine" and no one else's—to get rid of Brett.

And the redecorating has obviously worked, because it doesn't feel like Brett's presence is here at all anymore. It doesn't feel like the house we spent so long choosing together. Now it feels like *my* house.

With *my* furniture;

and pictures *I've* chosen;

and the colors *I* like.

Somehow I don't think I'll be getting that feeling that he's just about to walk in the door anymore. And this makes me feel really good, because sitting in the bath and breathing in the lavender makes me want to let go. I don't want to think about Brett, I don't want to talk about Brett, I don't want to get emotional when I hear about Brett. I just want to let it be, like he's somebody from my past—somebody you might be vaguely interested in catching up with, but wouldn't ever bother to pick up the phone book, look for their number, and give them a call. That's how I want to feel about Brett.

I just don't want to *care*.

And by the time I wash the face mask off, get out of the

bath, don my jammies, and give myself a manicure and pedicure, I *don't* care.

I sit on the couch, all soaked and face-masked and moisturized and so generally *pampered*, that I'm practically purring. And to complete the mood I order in some Vietnamese (prawn and mint rice paper rolls and a large duck soup). I even open up the bottle of red I'd found hiding in the back of the pantry when I cleaned it out. And as I wait for my food, I drink my first glass of wine and delete the article about Brett from the Web site.

Just as I'm pouring my second glass, the food arrives.

Perfect.

In fact, I'm so mellow that when the phone rings and it's my dad I forget about all the nasty things I wanted to say to him before. He's ringing for my birthday, one week after the big event (he always thinks it's a week after it actually is), and for some reason, instead of making me angry, this just makes me laugh. He tells me the story of his latest ex-wife running off with his ex-mistress, then about the problems he had with his business partner who actually ripped *him* off and who (unbelievably) sounds more sketchy than he is. And the way he explains it, everything makes sense. I get to say hello to my mum as well (funnily enough, they're living together again), and we don't fight either. I even feel kind of good that they've gotten back together again like they always do. When I finally get off the phone I surprise myself by looking at it fondly, thinking that my parents are so . . . well, I guess *exasperating* is the word. (This fondness, of course, has nothing to do with the fact that my dad said he'd put a "little something" into my account so I could buy myself a birthday present.)

And then the phone rings again, Michael this time. I'm still so mellow that I apologize for my naughty behavior on the phone the other day quite easily. While I'm talking to him I think about how pleased Dumped2 would be with what's happened in my life in the past two days. Getting closure with Brett, redecorating the house, talking to my dad and, now, making up with Michael.

Before Michael hangs up, he wishes me well for my spot on Mary-Anne tomorrow and says he'll be watching me.

Frigging hell—Mary-Anne!

I'd almost forgotten about that.

The flight from hell

My alarm goes off at 5:45 AM and as soon as I wake up I re-alize I'm coming down with a cold, despite the pamper-ings of last night. That tickle in my throat I'd tried to ignore all day yesterday wasn't the result of the dust I'd sent flying around the house. I think about calling up and canceling the show because all I want to do right now is to lie in bed for three days and get over the cold, but I can't. I've got a plane to catch at seven AM and this is my once-in-a-lifetime chance to meet Heidi Killman. Dumped2 might be brainwashing me into some of her man-loving ways, but no one's going to make me miss meeting my favorite columnist.

As per usual, Chris pulls up in the cab right on the dot. I grab my list that I'd written last night and tick off everything I'm supposed to take. It hadn't taken long to write the list. Usually when I have to catch a plane I'm standing at the door, listening to the cab honk as I tick my items off. But this time I'll be flying there and flying right back—something I've never done before. So all I have to tick off are my handbag and its contents (including spare pantyhose, lipstick, com-pact, hairspray, etc.).

Two minutes later I'm in the cab.

"For a moment I thought you were still in bed," Chris greets me.

"And miss my chance to meet Heidi Killman? Never!"

"Question," Chris turns around in the front seat and looks at me. "Have you got a cold?"

"Yeah, I do actually. Do you?"

Chris holds up a box of tissues. The extra soft ones with eucalyptus in them. The kind you treat yourself to when you've got a cold, even though they're three times the price of a normal box.

"I think my nose is about to fall off. I know who gave it to us too."

"Who?"

"You know that guy we met at the wedding with the nose ring? Gerry, or Gavin or something?"

"Yeah, Gavin."

"Well I saw him sneeze right into his hand before he shook mine, and an hour or so later I saw him in the toilet and he didn't wash his hands. We're probably lucky we didn't catch syphilis."

"Dirty, dirty little boy," I make a face.

We sniff and sneeze all the way to the airport, and I barter my Sudafed against Chris's special eucalyptus tissues. We comfort ourselves with the fact that we get to fly business class.

And it's nice in business class, let me tell you. It's nice to be on the other side of the swishy curtain for a change. For a start you get to check in straight away, no lines. Then you get to board the plane first and they give you a drink before the riffraff arrives (you can even do the royal wave as they file past you to get to economy if you want). The seats are big and roomy and you can recline them without braining the person behind you in the process. You get to eat off *real* plates, with *real* cutlery, and get served *real* wine out of a *real* bottle into a *real* glass.

This is the life.

We toast Mary-Anne and her business-class generosity (or at least her generosity toward me, because I had to pay for Chris).

Chris and I settle in with our champagne and orange juice (strange at breakfast, but what the hell, I'm sure I'll get used to it) and watch the other half file in and stare at us with envy.

310

After the plebeians have been settled, the little curtain has swished closed again and we've taken off, it looks like the entertainment's over. Chris starts reading the book he's had the sense to bring and I busy myself with reading the in-flight magazine.

Fifteen minutes later, Chris puts his book down and starts pushing and pressing his fingers over his face.

"What're you doing?"

"It's my sinuses, I knew this would happen. Can I have another Sudafed?"

I look in my bag. "Well, I don't know. I've only got two left."

"Oh for God's sake, Gemma. Give me the bloody stuff, we can get some more at the airport."

I throw them at Mr. Cranky. "I was only joking."

"Ha, ha," he says, swigging them both down with champagne and orange juice. I open my mouth to tell him this is probably not a good idea, then shut it again, and pick up my magazine. I remember what Heidi Killman said about men and colds and how they like to pretend they're dying.

Right on, sister.

I start reading an article about judges and their rulings on rape, highlighting that Italian judge—the one who said it's impossible to rape a woman wearing jeans because she'd have to help the guy to take them off.

It makes me sick and I think about Courtney, the girl who e-mailed me, and I wonder what she was wearing that day—as if it made a difference with three guys grabbing at her from every direction. How could this judge not understand that it was easy enough to get jeans off a woman who had a gun to her head, a knife to her stomach, or was just too plain petrified to move? By the time I finish the article I'm practically snorting like an enraged bull.

"Read this," I say, flinging the magazine at Chris. "If this doesn't prove that all men are bastards, I don't know what does." But even as the words come out of my mouth I don't

311

really know why I've said this. Maybe it's because of my cold and the fact that I've just noticed Chris has ingested the rest of the Sudafed and there's none left for me now that *my* sinuses hurt. Maybe it's because Chris is cranky and that's usually my job. Maybe it's because I'm just trying to pick a fight. But as I look at Chris, waiting for a reaction, I remember Dumped2 and wonder what she'd say about my comment. Probably something along the lines of "Gemma, just because one man thinks this, doesn't mean they all do."

Chris's reaction is a roll of his eyes. I get even more pissed off. "What?"

"Can't you give it a rest?"

"Give what a rest?"

"What do you reckon? The whole 'all men are bastards thing.' Don't you think it's getting a little old?"

People are looking at us now.

I cross my arms.

"Stop being such a drama queen," Chris says, giving me back the magazine, article unread. "It's one judge, that's all. You know all men don't think like that. And you certainly know I don't."

"So?" I ask a little too loudly, in want of a better argument. I look around me for support from the other women in business class, but all I get back are blank stares.

Chris puts down his book and turns to face me. "Gemma, look me in the eye and tell me every man you know is a bastard."

Dumped2's words keep ringing in my head, but if I want to save face, I have to say it. I look him straight in the eye. "Every man I know is a bastard."

"And you really believe that?"

No comment.

"So what have I ever done to you?"

I think for a minute. "It's not that you've done anything *yet,* it's that you're capable of it. Every man is."

312

"And by that reasoning so is every woman. I can't believe you think like this. In fact, I *don't* believe that you think like this. You're just being stubborn, stubborn and stupid. And you're not really like that, Gemma."

"Well, fiddle-dee-dee."

Chris mumbles something under his breath and I manage to catch the words "Dumped2."

"Aha!" I say, pointing my finger at him. "You've been reading my e-mail again. See, you *are* capable of bastardry."

"I haven't been reading your e-mail, Gemma."

"Oh really, so how do you know about Dumped2 then?"

Chris looks me straight in the eye. "Because I'm Dumped2, Gemma."

For a moment everything stands still and I can't quite take in what he's saying. Chris is Dumped2? The thought of a sex-change operation crosses my mind.

"What?" I ask him, confused.

"I'm Dumped2," Chris repeats. "I'm the one who's been sending the e-mails, the one chatting to you online."

I thump back into reality. Chris is Dumped2. There is no sex-change operation. Chris is Dumped2. There's no woman at all and he's been lying to me, making a fool out of me, for weeks. I can't even look at him I feel so betrayed. For a moment I even think I'm going to be sick.

I struggle furiously to unbuckle my belt, then stand up. And my heart gives a lurch as all the things I've told Dumped2, all those personal things about myself and Brett, come whooshing into my head. I turn and look at him. "I can't believe you let me tell you all those things," I splutter. "You must have had a good laugh, a really good laugh at my expense. Poor Gemma, dumped by her fiancé, let's have a good laugh, ha, ha, ha." I realize I'm babbling now, repeating myself horribly and I turn to see everyone in business class staring at me before I storm off.

Then I storm back because I'm going the wrong way. And

because I can't think of anywhere else to go, I swish open the little curtain.

Now everyone in economy's staring at me too.

So I stalk down to the back of the plane to get away from their stares, but after I walk all the way down to the back, there's nowhere to go but back up the aisle again. I look up there and see Chris. Chris is making his way down here. Quickly, I wrench the door open on the nearest toilet and lock it behind me.

Whew. Safe.

I close the lid and sit down.

Somehow I get the feeling it's going to be a long flight.

With nothing else to distract me, the whole Chris/Dumped2 thing starts replaying in my mind. For a start I can't believe he pretended to be a woman just so he could pry information out of me—information I never would have shared with him otherwise. I didn't even talk about this stuff to *Sarah,* my best friend in the whole world. And then all that bullshit he fed me about the fiancé and getting ditched, just so I'd tell him even more. How could he do that to me? The fact that he was leading this double life, being nice and taking me out for my birthday and to Brett's wedding and everything seems to make the whole situation worse somehow. Like he's taken advantage of me, making me seem like a fool while he has all the control. I'm so angry, I can feel my face turning a nice shade of beet-root that I know will come up just beautifully on television.

I get up and splash some water on my face hoping the redness will go away.

Someone knocks on the door. "Gemma, Gemma are you in there?"

I say nothing, but there is some mumbled talking outside.

"Gemma, I know you're in there. This man says you went in about five minutes ago and you haven't come out."

There is some more mumbling.

"He also says can you hurry up. There're people waiting out here you know."

"Let them wait," I say Marie Antoinette style, they are *economy* after all.

"Gemma, open the door, I want to talk to you."

"Michael was right when he said we've got a lot in common. You're a bastard and I run a site about bastards. It's practically a perfect match."

"Gemma, please open the door."

"I don't think so."

"Fine then, I'll talk to you through the door."

"Fine by me," I sit back down on the toilet lid.

Chris bangs on the door one last time and then there is silence. For a moment I think he's given up and gone back to his seat, but then he starts talking again.

"Gemma, it's true. We do have a lot in common. You were right—I did have someone. I had a fiancée and she left me at the altar for her ex, just like Dumped2 told you."

"Oh, sure," I butt in.

There is a short silence. "I know you'll think what you want to think, but it's true. I never lied to you. Not once."

"Really? So how come I thought you were a woman then?" I ask the door.

"I had to do that, Gemma. You wouldn't have listened to me otherwise—you wouldn't have listened to a man at all. So I had to try and use Dumped2 to get through to you. You were making all the same mistakes I made, and I didn't want you to, not if I could help it."

Chris pauses, waiting for me to say something, but I don't.

"You were pushing everyone around you away, just like I did. When Kerry left me I thought that everyone who looked at me felt sorry for me, and I snapped at them for doing it. Then, slowly but surely, they didn't do it anymore. But not in the way I wanted, they just didn't speak to me anymore, didn't call, didn't ask me out with everyone else. They wanted to help me get through it, but I was too proud to admit that I needed any help. You were doing the same thing with Michael and Sarah. So, believe me, I know what it's like Gemma, I've been there. God, I even took those exact same pills you've got in your bathroom drawer . . . I was just trying to help."

"Trying to help? Trying to teach me some kind of sick lesson, more like it. *And* snooping through my bathroom drawers!"

"Maybe I was trying to teach you a lesson. Call it what you like, but you have to believe I knew what you were going through, what you were feeling. And I wasn't snooping through your bathroom drawers, I saw the pills by accident."

"Go to hell."

"Fine. I just want to say one last thing. I know about the whole Brett thing, Michael told me what's been going on, how you were making him out to be such a bastard when really he wasn't like that at all. But that book Brett gave you, Gemma, that was something pretty special. Maybe you should have a think about how you've been treating the men in your life—Brett, Michael, even your dad. You go around saying all men are bastards because it's an easy label when you're hurting. But I don't think everything's as black and white as you make it out to be, is it?"

I don't grace this with a reply. How can I? Because it's starting to dawn on me that Chris might be half right. Everything that's been going on in my life *isn't* as black and white as I make it out to be. Sarah's lecture, along with Dumped2's argument and Brett's book had already placed the seeds of doubt in my mind. And I'd been pushing these doubts to the back of my mind for weeks, trying to ignore them, hoping they'd go away, but as Chris verbalized them I knew that the things I had been doubting were probably true.

I sit and think about this for a few minutes before I realize everything is silent. I wait for another minute, listening carefully, before I decide Chris has really gone. Still perched on the toilet, I try to digest all the information I've been given. And it's hard—there's too much to think about and random thoughts keep jumping forward in my mind screaming "Analyze me! Analyze me!" I can't seem to think about any of this logically at all. For a start, it's too much to take in that Dumped2 is really Chris and that all those things he said were true, just in reverse. And I know he's right about Brett and the book, which is special to me, really special. But it still hurts, what Brett did to me, he just up and left, walked out the door without so much as a good-bye.

No he didn't, I hear Sarah's voice in my head. *He tried to talk to you, you just didn't want to listen, maybe if you'd have listened to him he wouldn't have left.*

I push the voice to the back of my head and stand up. I've got to control myself and get through this interview, that's the important thing for now. Everything else can wait until later.

I take a look in the mirror. My face isn't so red now and I figure it's OK to go back outside. I'll have to sometime or another, and if I'm lucky I'll be able to find a seat in economy for the rest of the trip. I open the lock on the toilet door, push it open a crack, and poke my head around. There's a long line of people, but I don't see Chris anywhere.

Good.

I open the door fully and step out, trying to ignore the stares and the muttered "about time"s. I straighten my dress and avoid their eyes.

I walk back up the aisle trying to find a spare seat, but don't have much luck. I start to think I'll have no choice but to go back to business, though I didn't see any spare seats in there either.

Standing in the middle of the aisle, I come up with a plan.

I lean over the middle aisle, where a couple of middle-aged women are sitting and try it out. "If one of you ladies will swap with me in business class, I'll give you fifty dollars," I tell them.

They just look at me, like I'm some kind of weirdo.

"All right," I say crossly, "one hundred dollars."

They keep looking at me, one of them pressing the button for the flight attendant quite vigorously now. And I can't believe they're not taking me up on my generous offer. They're crazy. If someone offered me that deal while I was sitting in cattle class I'd have jumped at it.

The flight attendant comes up the aisle. "Is there a problem, ladies?" she asks, smiling her fake smile, and both women look at me. She leans toward me and looks a bit closer. "Aren't you supposed to be in business?"

I give her The Look. She's obviously an evil flight attendant of the sky slut variety.

But The Look doesn't work, because she shoots it right back at me and grabs my elbow, steering me back up the aisle and into business class. "I think this is your seat," she says and waits until I sit down.

I sit down.

And I do the best I can to ignore Chris all the way to the studio.

The studio

We arrive late.

The cab pulls up at the gates, Chris tells them who we are, and they let us in and tell us where to go. There's a guy hovering around the entrance when we pull up, looking at his watch and speaking into a walkie-talkie.

"You're late," he says, but he doesn't wait for any excuses, just walks away, leaving us to hurriedly pay for the cab and catch up with him. We half-run, half-walk down a dozen or so corridors before we stop and the guy opens a door and ushers me inside. "You, here," he says, then looks at Chris, "and you, come with me."

I'm not about to argue, so I step inside the room where I'm greeted by a youngish-looking girl in jeans and a T-shirt who's piling makeup onto none other than Heidi Killman.

"Hey," she says, "I'm Miriam. If you take a seat, I'll get to you in just a sec."

I sit down in shock. Heidi Killman is sitting right over there, in the same room as me. This is so cool. As I watch, I seem to remember Heidi saying in her column once that she never wears makeup because that's giving men what they want, but I figure it's just for the camera so it's OK. I sit and try to think up something witty to say that won't sound like I'm a crazed fan or something.

But I can't think of anything.

And just as I'm remembering some joke about a mermaid granting a man a wish and he wants to be five times smarter and she turns him into a woman, Heidi Killman gets up and leaves the room, ignoring me and not saying good-bye to Miriam the makeup girl.

We both watch her go.

"Do you do her makeup all the time?" I ask Miriam.

"Yeah, all too many times," she answers, leaving me puzzled. "How do you like it?"

"How do I like what?"

"Your makeup, of course. Natural, vamp—I do great Marilyn Monroe or Adolf Hitler look if you're interested."

"Um, natural, thanks," I take the safest option.

Miriam tilts my head back and works her makeup magic. It feels like she's putting on the foundation with a trowel, but I don't argue. The girl obviously knows what she's doing and Heidi Killman looked pretty good when she left the room. While I'm lying back, I check out the pictures on the walls. They're all framed and I begin to recognize the people in them as I look around. There's Mary-Anne with the prime minister, Mary-Anne with assorted famous actors, Mary-Anne with this, that, and the other supermodel. "Did you get to do the supermodels' makeup?" I ask Miriam, thinking it would have been the highlight of a makeup-type person's career.

Miriam snorts. "Not likely."

I get the feeling I shouldn't ask any more questions about the supermodels.

Five minutes later I'm done and Miriam pushes the chair back into place.

"There you go," she says, and I get to look at the finished product.

And I can't believe what I see.

If I thought I needed a PA, I was wrong—what I needed was a makeup artist because Miriam has turned my fluish, red-eyed, red-nosed appearance into something that looks . . .

Well, that looks vaguely human.

Quite a feat, really.

"How did you do that?" I splutter, checking myself out in the mirror.

"It's my job, honey," she says and we both turn as the door opens and the bossy guy comes in again.

"Finished?"

"She's all set to go," Miriam pats me on the shoulders and I get up and follow bossy man out of the room again and up more winding corridors.

"Where're we going?" I dare to ask as we turn into a corridor I think we walked up a minute ago.

"The green room," he grunts, like I'm supposed to know what and where that is.

Eventually he stops and opens a door. "In here," he says and nudges me inside.

Everyone turns as I stand in the doorway and the guy gives me another nudge, making me take a step forward, before he closes the door behind me. The first thing I notice is that, funnily enough, the green room isn't green at all, it's blue, and there are even more framed photos on the wall of Mary-Anne fawning over everyone who's anyone.

Chris is over at the bench running along the far wall, making two coffees. I figure one of them's for me, a kind of peace offering, until he takes it over to the gaggle of women standing near the window and hands it to someone who looks vaguely familiar.

As I take a look at the rest of the group, I realize that all the women look vaguely familiar. The one he's handed the coffee to is that senator. The young one—what's-her-name. The tall one I don't know, but by deduction she must be the editor of the women's magazine, and standing with her back to me is Heidi Killman.

They all seem to be having a great time.

I try to catch Chris's eye, but he's obviously trying to avoid me, because he's flirting with the senator. And I suppress a smirk because I know he's got no hope. If he read any of the women's magazines he'd know she only goes out with the football-types.

So, trying to pretend I'm totally at ease, I saunter over to the coffee machine, make myself a cup, and check out the food situation. There's a kid there, a little boy, maybe nine or ten and he's picking the cherries off the tops of all the muffins.

"Hi," I say to him.

"Hi," he says, holding out his hand. "I'm Buster Killman and I'm eight years old."

Buster Killman. Heidi Killman's son.

"Hi, Buster," I say, shaking his hand and trying with all my might to be serious. "I'm Gemma Barton and I'm twenty-eight years old. You probably think that's ancient, right?"

"No," he says, picking another cherry off a muffin and popping it in his mouth. "My mum's *way* older than that."

I'm interested to hear this because Heidi Killman likes to keep her age a bit of a secret. "Really? How old is she?"

"She's forty-two," Buster says, looking me straight in the eye. "But she says she's twenty-one. She doesn't like me telling people she's forty-two."

I'm sure she doesn't, because there's no way Heidi Killman looks forty-two, and I start to wonder if she's had a bit of a nip and tuck. I remind myself to take a look at her neck when I get a bit closer—it's always the best way to tell. That and the age spots on the back of their hands (you learn these things when your parents live in the Bahamas).

"Does your mum know you're eating all the cherries off the tops of the muffins?" I ask Buster.

"I doubt it," he says, and I can see by the look in his eyes that I've just lost his interest by asking a stupid adult question.

"So it looks like you're skipping school today, hey?" I try to regain my coolness.

"Yeah. I'm supposed to be sick."

"Got a test?"

"How did you know?"

"I was a kid once too. What's your method?"

He gives me the once-over, probably deciding whether he should tell me his trade secret or not. "Sweating. Sweating and stomach cramps."

"A wise choice. Mine was stomach cramps and trips to the loo."

"I tried that once but I ended up at the doctor. He gave me some pill and I couldn't go for *days*."

I shrug. "Hey, it's the risk you take."

Buster nods. "Yeah, I guess."

I finish making my coffee. "Well, I guess I'd better talk to the olds, hey?"

"OK," he says, and goes right on back to picking the cherries off the rest of the muffins.

So much for the stomach cramps. Why is it that all kids pull these stunts and then when they grow up and have their own kids they forget it ever happened?

I make my way over to the group with my coffee and stand a bit behind Chris who's still talking to the senator. He ignores me and I think about going over to talk to Heidi Killman, but she's sitting on one of the couches now, talking to the editor. So I try to look interested in stirring my coffee, like I'm not a loser with no one to talk to, and tell myself there'll be plenty of time to talk to Heidi Killman later.

The door opens and everyone turns to look at who it is. It's Mr. Bossy Man again.

"Five minutes, people," he says.

No one else seems to bat an eyelid, but me, I burn my tongue on my coffee in fright.

The bright lights

Five minutes!

My palms start getting sweaty and I glance over at Heidi Killman who's polishing off a muffin and coffee and laughing along with all the other media-types. As for Chris, he still has the senator bailed up in the corner. But even I have to admit she looks like she's having a good time. And by the way she's leaning in toward him and moving her hands around, it looks like she's telling some kind of a funny story.

Everyone's talking to someone else except me now and I begin to feel a little out of place. Heidi Killman's son has finished eating all the cherries and is sitting on the couch. In a moment of desperation I tell myself I could always go and talk to him again, but he's reading a book now, *The Wind in the Willows*. And even though it's one of my favorites, I know I'll look like a loser if I try to wrestle the book out of his hands and have a meaningful conversation about the benefits of psychoanalyzing Toad.

So, for something to do, I look down and smooth out my dress with my hands and, for good measure, surreptitiously give my shoes a shine on the back of each leg. Suddenly I wish I'd taken a course, something along the lines of "How to Be a Media Slut 101," so I'd know how to act in front of a camera.

At least I forget about all the Dumped2 stuff as I panic about being on TV. I look at Chris, hoping that he'll come over and give me some moral support, but he ignores me. And then the guy comes back and my stomach hits the floor with a thud because this can only mean one thing—it's Time To Go.

He herds us out of the room, leaving Chris and Heidi Killman's son behind, telling them he'll come back for them later and seat them in the audience. I'm desperate to talk to Chris, for him to tell me it'll all be OK, that the interview will be fine, but there's no time. The rest of us file out of the room. In the corridor Mr. Bossy Man sticks his hand on the small of my back and steers me, as if he knows I'm the person most likely to do a runner. We walk down various passageways (probably specially designed so people like me *can't* do a runner) and then we stop. The guy lines us up how he wants us. The editor of the women's magazine, Heidi Killman, then me, and, finally, the senator.

He tells us to wait.

Behind me, the senator touches me on the arm. "You're lucky—your PA's a really nice guy," she says.

In nervousness I say the first thing that comes into my mind. "Yeah, he's mad at me at the moment, but."

And as the words come out of my mouth I could just die. How could I say that. To a senator? And the "but" on the end? I *never* speak like that! I can feel the redness start to creep up my neck and face again.

The senator looks at me for a moment and then smiles her politician smile that I'm sure she uses when kissing the babies with *snotty* noses. "I'm sure he'll get over it."

I turn around, still blushing, and make up some quick rules:

1. I will not say anything more if possible;
2. I will only answer when spoken to;
3. I will think about my reply *before* it comes out of my mouth; and
4. If I can get away with it, I will simply smile and nod rather than reply verbally.

330

In front, Heidi Killman has whipped out a lipstick and a tiny mirror and is re-applying. She sees me watching her and I smile a tiny "I read your column *every* week and I think it's so funny—I'm practically your biggest fan" type of smile. She turns around and smiles back before she opens her mouth. "You little upstart," she hisses under her breath, "you really think you've got it made, don't you? Well, let me tell you, I've seen your site and we've got a phrase for people like you in this business—'one minute wonder.' So don't even think about making any flash moves out there. Just sit down and shut up and we'll get along fine." She gives me the smile again at the end of her sentence and turns back to her lipstick.

I look around in a state of shock, but the editor and the senator don't seem to have heard her. I pause for a moment in disbelief. Heidi Killman—whose column I pore over every Sunday, extracting meaning and wisdom, laughing at men and their foibles and basking in the warm glow of "pass-the-Bolly-sweetie" girly friendship—is nothing more than your common, everyday bitch.

So much for sisterhood.

She glances back at me in her mirror to see if I've taken in everything she's said, but before I have time to search the depths of my mind for a witty rejoinder, the guy tells us we've "gone to break" and it's time to go on stage.

Once again, he herds us around like mindless cattle. The presenter, Mary-Anne Melody, the pinup girl of every retirement village, is already out there and somebody is fixing her hair and patting some powder on her face. The guy sits us down and then, one by one, fixes our mikes to our shirts. As he's fixing mine, he looks up. "Didn't they tell you not to wear stripes?" he asks. And I look down at my brand new, $250 "I'm going on TV" shirt. "No," I say, because they didn't. And both Heidi Killman and the editor look at me as if I should have known better. The senator, who's wearing stripes herself, doesn't seem to care and the guy doesn't say anything to *her* as he's fixing her mike on.

I want to cry.

But there's no way I'm going to do it on national television in front of Heidi Killman, two hundred of the blue rinse set seated in the studio audience, and the rest of the nation, so I take a few deep breaths and try to calm down.

I spot Chris sitting with Buster Killman in the front row. They're talking about something and Chris looks up, spots me, and smiles, giving me the thumbs-up.

It's all I need to calm down.

"Thirty seconds, Mary-Anne," someone behind the cameras says.

And the makeup and hair people disappear and Mary-Anne goes into presenter mode.

"You're the Internet girl," she says to me, looking at her flash cards, "Gemma Barton, right?" I nod. I guess she doesn't need to ask anyone else who they are, because they star right along with her every week in *New Idea*.

"As we told you before, our basic topic for today is 'Men, are they as hopeless as they make themselves out to be?' We'll be having a short introduction to you all first, then talking to Heidi, who I think has a joke for us," she smiles at Heidi conspiratorially like they're old friends. "Then we'll be open for comments from everyone else, all right?" she asks.

As if we could say no.

"Ten seconds, Mary-Anne," the guy calls out.

Now I know how Imogen feels when she pees on the vet's table. It's called stage fright.

The guy keeps counting, "Five, four, three, two, one."

And when he says "one," I know that this is it. Everyone I practically know in the world is looking at me, Sarah, Michael, all the aunts and uncles and second cousins twice removed, Chris in the front row, even my parents will be seeing this on tape. I try to take a few deep breaths without anyone noticing.

Mary-Anne's introducing us now, and apparently I'm "Twenty-eight-year-old Gemma Barton, creator of the infamous 'allmenarebastards.com' Web site that has taken the world by storm."

I smile and say, "Thanks, Mary-Anne," which I feel is a nice touch. And by the time she's gotten through introducing the "senator who needs no introduction," I've had time to look around a little and calm down enough to listen to what's going on around me.

I take another quick glance at Chris, who smiles back again. Buster Killman waves.

He's such a sweetie.

Buster Killman, I mean.

I tune back in to Mary-Anne, who's speaking again. "But before we begin our discussion for today, I think Heidi has a little joke for us. Heidi?"

We all turn to Heidi and watch as she tosses her hair around a bit before she begins.

"Well, a woman gets her test results back from her doctor who breaks the bad news—she needs a brain transplant. He goes on to tell her that there are two brains he can offer her, a woman's brain for $500 and a man's brain for $5,000 . . ." Heidi pauses for effect before she continues.

"So the woman is confused by this. Why would the man's brain cost $5,000 and the woman's only $500? So she asks him 'Doctor, why the big price difference? Why does the woman's brain only cost $500 when the man's brain costs $5,000?' " Heidi pauses again and sets herself up for the punchline . . .

" 'Because,' the doctor says, 'the woman's brain has been used.' "

(Cue: roar from all the oldies in the audience.)

All the women on the panel are laughing now, the editor, the senator, Heidi Killman. Mary-Anne is laughing the hardest of all, wiping the tears from her eyes, but at the same time being oh-so-very-careful not to smudge her makeup.

But I'm not laughing at all, because I'm looking straight at Heidi Killman's son who's staring at his mother as if he doesn't quite get the joke. And instinctively, as I watch his reaction, I place the palm of my hand on my chest. I feel winded.

I take a good hard look at Heidi Killman. Expensive clothes, perfect makeup, high heels—trying to attract men, but loving the power of repelling them at the same time. And I hate her. I hate everything about her. She's beautiful, but ugly. She has an ugly heart. How can she say those things in front of her own son? I ask myself. How will he grow up? What kind of self-esteem will he have?

And then it comes to me.

Everything Dumped2/Chris has said to me is absolutely true. Remember that thing he said about people? *All men aren't bastards,* he'd said. *People are bastards. But just some of them, and only some of the time.* And right now I realize I'm sitting beside one of the worst.

I remember what Chris said to me on the plane.

I can't believe you think like this. In fact, I don't *believe that you think like this. You're just being stubborn, stubborn and stupid. And you're not really like that, Gemma.*

And I have been stubborn and stupid. Listening to what Heidi Killman's said, I'm embarrassed and ashamed that I looked up to her, that I've repeated the things she said in her columns, that I've been asked here today because people think I'm like her.

Chris is right. I'm not like that and I'm not like her. I don't really believe those things.

I don't have an ugly heart.

"What's the matter, Gemma, don't you like the joke?" Mary-Anne drags me back into reality.

Everyone's looking at me now, waiting for my answer.

I turn around to face her properly and take a deep breath because I know I'm going to need it. "No, I don't like the joke," I say, then I look at Heidi. "You should be ashamed, say-

334

ing things like that in front of your son. And in your column. Look at his face. He doesn't quite get the joke now, but you know what? In a few years he will. How can you bring him up telling him things like that? It's emasculating. Do you really think he'll thank you for it when he's older?"

I don't let Heidi get a word in edgeways. I'm on a roll now, and I stand up, ready to let them have it.

"So, no, I don't like your joke. And you know why? Well, let's just substitute woman, black, or Jew for 'man' in that joke and you tell me how it sounds. It doesn't sound so good, does it? No man could stand up and tell that joke the other way around, he'd be shot down!" I pause for breath . . .

"It's a double standard. OK, so many men *are* thoughtless, insensitive creeps. Well, like we've just seen, so are some women! But that doesn't mean to say they *all* are, does it? What kind of society tells women that males are hopeless and emotionally retarded? Well?" I pause again and collect my thoughts for one last bang. This time I turn and look at the whole panel.

"We may all be feminists here, but we seem to have missed the point. We can't become stronger by taking away somebody else's self-esteem, that's just bullying. We have to heighten our *own* self-esteem if we want to get anywhere. We have to stop blaming men for all the problems in the world."

I'm out of breath now, and I stop to take one, but then realize I'm done. Everyone is completely silent and I think quickly about what I'm going to do next. I can't sit back down, so I fling my hands up, turn around, and storm off the stage the way we'd come on. As I go, I sneak a look back at Chris, but he's gone. And I can feel the camera on my back right to the edge of the stage.

When I'm back where we lined up, I stop for a second to consider my options. There's no way I can find the green room—I didn't pay any attention to the way we went. But I try anyway, desperate to get out of this place. I walk back up the

335

corridor and poke my head around the first corner to see if anything looks familiar. It doesn't. But it's a good thing, because there are two security guards coming up the corridor now and I know instinctively that they're coming after me. So I scoot back down near the stage and try to hide behind a couple of those exercise machines that they're always plugging on the show. You know, the ones that go out of date and get replaced by some new contraption every five minutes. Anyway, they've been discarded and are now half-covered with a sheet—perfect for hiding behind. I kneel on the dusty floor and hope that the two guys don't see me, that hopefully I'll be able to sneak out of here without having both my legs broken by Mary-Anne's commandos. I try not to sneeze as they get closer.

And closer.

They're right on top of me now. If I wanted, I could reach out my hand through the various pieces of exercise equipment and touch them. I keep my head down and hope that they don't see me. Thankfully, they don't. After a while they turn around and head back up the corridor. "Maybe she *is* in the green room," I hear one of them say.

Just as I'm about to stand up, I hear footsteps again and duck back down. And just as I'm about to start hyperventilating (I'm starting to believe they really *will* break my legs now), I look through the exercise equipment and realize I know those shoes. And those pants.

It's Chris.

"Psst," I say quietly.

He doesn't hear me.

"Psst," I try again.

He still doesn't hear me.

"Chris, get your arse back here," I try.

It works. His head ducks around to the back of my make shift hideout. "What are you doing back there?" he whispers.

"Hiding," I whisper back.

"I don't blame you," he says. "I think Mary-Anne wants your head on a stick."

"Oh shit. And I thought I'd get away with a couple of broken legs. What happened after I left?"

"They went to an ad break. I don't even know if the whole thing went to air. I think Mary-Anne was petrified you'd start swearing and give all her elderly viewers heart attacks."

I have this sudden vision of numerous elderly people falling to the ground in nursing homes around the country, and it all being my fault.

When I look at Chris again, he's smiling a great big cheesy grin at me. "You were great," he says. "What you said—it was great!"

I realize what a bitch I've been to Chris the past couple weeks. To everyone, really, but especially to Chris. "I've been such a cow. Everyone else has pissed off and you've stayed around. Why?"

He looks me straight in the eye. "Because I know what it's like."

"But the e-mail, the whole Dumped2 thing?"

"Like I said, I knew you wouldn't listen if I told you those things to your face. I knew you'd turn against me too. So I decided it had to come from someone else. Someone you'd listen to . . ." Chris stops and I can see he's trying to suppress a laugh.

"What? What's so funny?"

"You should've seen Mary-Anne's face," he says. "Her eyes almost popped out of her head."

Chris is really trying not to laugh out loud now and I wish I *had* seen Mary-Anne's face as I ranted and raved.

And just when I'm trying to conjure up a picture of the whole scene, I get the surprise of my life.

Chris leans over and kisses me.

I'm so shocked at first, that we kind of miss and I'm about to pull away when I realize I don't really want to, so I lean in too. It's a good kiss, firm and warm and, well, it feels kind of right I guess.

And it hits me that all those months I've been saying "not that I'm looking for anything like that, of course" I've been wrong about that too. Maybe I *am* looking for something like that after all. But with Chris? I don't know. I just don't know.

We both pull back and when I look at Chris I realize his eyes are just as wide as mine are.

"Wow," he says. "I didn't mean to . . . I don't know why . . . I . . ."

"Are you saying that was a mistake?" I ask him.

"Well, I . . ."

So I grab his neck and pull him toward me to check if it was. And this time it's even better and longer and richer than the first kiss.

Not bad at all, really.

We pull back again and look at each other.

"I guess it wasn't a mistake," Chris says.

"I guess not." I don't think it was. Actually, I'm pretty sure it wasn't a mistake at all. And I'd like to do it again, plus more, but we're crouched down behind a pile of discarded exercise equipment. Also, there are various people searching for me who want to kill me, so I tell Chris it's time to get out of here. We make our escape by a back set of stairs that lead to the parking lot. Then we run like crazy.

And, yes, for your information, we do hold hands.

Epilogue

So, you want to know what happens next, eh? Well, I guess I'd better tell you. If you've read this far, you deserve to know.

I had a lot of thinking to do when I got home. Firstly, about the site, because I wasn't sure what I should do with it now I wasn't classified as an A-class full-time Heidi Killman-loving man-hater. I had a couple of options to consider. After the whole TV thing, Mary-Anne Melody called for me to take the site down altogether, as did Heidi Killman and various others of her type.

So, you ask, did I take the site down?

Are you crazy? Did you really think I'd get rid of the site? That's $70,000 a year and counting we're talking here! I don't want to go back to being poor again. I want to eat out like normal people and have a car that goes beep beep when I press the remote so I can look smug in parking lots.

In the end, I went with Chris's suggestion and toned it down a bit. The articles on "Twenty Different Ways to Poison a Man" and "The Girls' Guide to Buying a Used AK47" came down. (I forgot to tell you about those, didn't I? Oops.)

I'm even in the process of setting up a list for men so everyone can have their say.

Really, what I'm trying to do at the moment is get a more balanced view of life (except on Fridays when Sarah and I become unbalanced at Friday Night Cocktails on margaritas). Speaking of Sarah, she's still seeing James the fireman and they seem quite happy together.

Shortly after my television appearance, Imogen and I changed vets. She now has a cat psychiatrist, counseling sessions twice a month, and new medication.

Allison Rushby

She is doing well.

Oh yes. And you'll want to know about the thing with Chris, won't you? Well, we are "together" and we're both really happy. But don't get too excited—there aren't any wedding bells a-pealing yet.

Because we've both agreed to take it slow.

Very slow.

If that's all right with you.